Another of Cheryl Bolen's classic marriage-of-convenience stories

Two staggering coincidences result in the marriage of the reckless young Earl of Finchley and Lady Margaret Ponsby, a shy duke's daughter who's worshipped him from afar. . .

Some of the praise for Cheryl Bolen's writing:

"One of the best authors in the Regency romance field today." – *Huntress Reviews*

"Bolen's writing has a certain elegance that lends itself to the era and creates the perfect atmosphere for her enchanting romances." – *RT Book Reviews*

Lady By Chance (House of Haverstock, Book 1)
Cheryl Bolen has done it again with another sparkling Regency romance. . .Highly recommended – *Happily Ever After*

The Bride Wore Blue (Brides of Bath, Book 1)
Cheryl Bolen returns to the Regency England she knows so well. . .If you love a steamy Regency with a fast pace, be sure to pick up *The Bride Wore Blue*. – *Happily Ever After*

With His Ring (Brides of Bath, Book 2)
"Cheryl Bolen does it again! There is laughter, and the interaction of the characters pulls you right into the book. I look forward to the next in this series." – *RT Book Reviews*

The Bride's Secret (Brides of Bath, Book 3)
*(*originally titled *A Fallen Woman)*
"What we all want from a love story...Don't miss it!"
– *In Print*

To Take This Lord (Brides of Bath, Book 4)
*(*originally titled *An Improper Proposal)*
"Bolen does a wonderful job building simmering sexual tension between her opinionated, outspoken heroine and deliciously tortured, conflicted hero." – *Booklist of the American Library Association*

My Lord Wicked
Winner, International Digital Award for Best Historical Novel of 2011.

With His Lady's Assistance (Regent Mysteries, Book 1)
"A delightful Regency romance with a clever and personable heroine matched with a humble, but intelligent hero. The mystery is nicely done, the romance is enchanting and the secondary characters are enjoyable." – *RT Book Reviews*

Finalist for International Digital Award for Best Historical Novel of 2011.

A Duke Deceived
"*A Duke Deceived* is a gem. If you're a Georgette Heyer fan, if you enjoy the Regency period, if you like a genuinely sensuous love story, pick up this first novel by Cheryl Bolen." – *Happily Ever After*

One Golden Ring
"*One Golden Ring*...has got to be the most PERFECT Regency Romance I've read this year." – *Huntress Reviews*

Holt Medallion winner for Best Historical, 2006

The Counterfeit Countess
Daphne du Maurier award finalist for Best Historical Mystery

"This story is full of romance and suspense. . . No one can resist a novel written by Cheryl Bolen. Her writing talents charm all readers. Highly recommended reading! 5 stars!" – *Huntress Reviews*

"Bolen pens a sparkling tale, and readers will adore her feisty heroine, the arrogant, honorable Warwick and a wonderful cast of supporting characters." – *RT Book Reviews*

Also by Cheryl Bolen

Regency Romance

House of Haverstock Series
    Lady by Chance (Book 1)
    Duchess by Mistake (Book2)
The Brides of Bath Series:
    The Bride Wore Blue (Book 1)
    With His Ring (Book 2)
    The Bride's Secret (Book 3)
    To Take This Lord (Book 4)
    Love in the Library (Book 5)
    A Christmas in Bath (Book 6)
The Regent Mysteries Series:
    With His Lady's Assistance (Book 1)
    A Most Discreet Inquiry (Book 2)
    The Theft Before Christmas (Book 3)
The Earl's Bargain
My Lord Wicked
His Lordship's Vow
A Duke Deceived
One Golden Ring
Counterfeit Countess

Novellas:
Lady Sophia's Rescue
Christmas Brides (3 Regency Novellas)

Romantic Suspense

Texas Heroines in Peril Series:
    Protecting Britannia
    Capitol Offense
    A Cry in the Night

Murder at Veranda House
Falling for Frederick

American Historical Romance
A Summer to Remember (3 American Historical Romances)

World War II Romance
It Had to be You

Inspirational Regency Romance
Marriage of Inconvenience

COUNTESS BY COINCIDENCE

(House of Haverstock, Book 3)

Cheryl Bolen

DEDICATION

For my sister Colleen, who's always there for any of us in her family. I love and appreciate you--even if you did get the name I should have had!

$\mathcal{C}$hapter 1

What a deuced pickle John Beauclerc, the 11th Earl of Finchley, had gotten himself into. The higher he climbed the stairs to his Grandmere's drawing room, the lower he felt. Had he not sworn to that dear lady a mere ten weeks previously that he would curtail his attraction to high-stakes play? Yet here he was like an errant schoolboy, preparing to once again vow that he would change his wicked ways—while begging for a few hundred quid to tide him over to the next quarter.

He needn't tell her he owed every bit of it to Lord Bastingham because of a disastrous turn of bad luck. Nor need he tell her how many tradesmen were dunning him. Nor how he'd been forced to find new positions for his groom and coachman because he lacked funds to continue keeping horses.

Before John reached the landing, he passed the Romney of his late grandfather. His step slowed as his gaze raked over the old fellow. John was certain Grandpapa's eyes had been green, but the paint had darkened over the years to a murky brown. From beneath the elderly man's prim white wig and bushy gray brows, those dark eyes seemed to be glowering at his grandson. A shudder rippled down John's spine, and he looked away.

Good Lord, even the dead must know about John's rakish ways.

A few moments later he threw open the doors to Grandmere's drawing room. Seated upon a sofa, a slant-top portable desk balanced on her lap, she was scribbling on paper, then she looked up at him with a twinkling gaze.

Though she could be an excessively stern matriarch, Grandmere had the looks of an angel. At present, her pink mouth lifted into a smile that accompanied the sparkle in her pale blue eyes. She was small and round and fair and was possessed of fluffy white hair. For as long as he could remember, her cheeks had been pink, but his mother—God rest her soul—had said Grandmere's cheek colour came from French rouge.

He strode to her, bowed, and kissed her hand. "It's good to see you, Grandmere."

Her brows lowered. "Don't pretend you've come just to see your grandmother, John Edward. I know you've been naughty."

He stifled a groan. Ten-year-old boys were naughty. When one was six and twenty, he was . . . well, he supposed *dissolute* described the man he'd become. "I protest. Guilty I may be to the naughtiness, but I am hardly guilty of neglecting my favorite kinsperson."

She frowned. "I am your *only* kinsperson."

"And do I not call on you at least once a week?"

"Your attentions to your grandmother may be the only admirable trait you possess."

So she had heard about the gambling. And perhaps even worse. "Can I help it if I am my father's son?"

A shadow of sorrow swept across her aged

face. "My life's hope was that my grandson would be the man my son could never be."

He sighed. "I am truly sorry to be such a disappointment."

"But not sorry enough to do something to change it."

His countenance brightened. He offered her a broad smile. "I haven't been to Newmarket since the last quarter!" Perhaps he should not have referenced a Newmarket racing meeting. After all, that is where Papa had met his demise when, under the influence of vast consumption of brandy, he was trampled to death when he attempted to mount a horse during the race.

She scowled.

"And," he added brightly, "My valet will verify that the number of mornings in which I awaken snoggered have been greatly reduced." Remembering his father's unfortunate end, John was being somewhat mindful of lessening his own consumption of spirits. Except, of course, when he was with his fellow bloods. One couldn't look like a jessie.

She continued to scowl. "Even your father never used such a word in my presence!"

He effected a contrite look. "Forgive me."

"You might as well sit down."

He would rather not. It made him feel small in the presence of his steely grandmother. He needed all six feet, two inches to gather his courage. "Actually, I cannot stay."

"So you've just come to see that I haven't died in my bed?"

His brow lowered. "I beg that you never speak of such!"

"Then, as I have suspected all along, you're

seeking a loan—a loan you promise to pay back when the new quarter rolls around."

He could not meet her gaze. "You know me too well."

"Sit down, my boy."

He had never been able to refuse her a request (except the request for his reform). He settled awkwardly upon a silken sofa across from her, fully expecting to be subjected to a long lecture on his evil ways. His eyes trained on the Aubusson carpet beneath his feet, he waited. And waited. Grandmere harrumphed but said not a word.

After a moment, he looked up. This stern look upon her face was unexpected.

"I'll not give you a farthing."

His eyes widened. Never before had she actually refused him.

"It has been nearly a decade since you left Oxford, and your habits remain those of a lad getting his first taste of wine, women, and faro!"

Every word she said was true. He still remembered the joy of leaving Oxford behind and re-opening Finchley House on Cavendish Square, of meeting with other like-minded young men at White's for brandy and faro and any other manner of betting, and . . . of the ladies! Could one ever grow tired of such pleasures?

By God, after all those years of awakening to cold stone floors at six in the morning to eat grub and face his lessons, he cherished every moment in the Capital now. He'd never been happier. He rose when he wanted, and not one night of the week was he home and idle. He and Christopher Perry, David Arlington, and Michael Knowles— chums since their Eton days—were always ready for a lark. The four of them loved the ladies, too.

(Not that one would actually refer to the opera dancers and members of the demimonde precisely as *ladies*.) John had not the slightest desire to be shackled to some prim and respectable wife.

His gaze returned to the carpet. "You are—as always, Grandmere—right."

"It's time you settle down."

"Why can I not wait until I reach thirty?"

"At the rate you're going, young man, I'm afraid you won't reach thirty."

Were all women prone to such sweeping statements of gloom? 'Twas another very good reason to avoid parson's mousetrap. "I'm very happy with my life as it is." He glared up at her. "Besides, I've yet to meet the woman to whom I wish to be sha- - -, er, married."

"Of course, you haven't! You have no interest in honorable ladies. Have you even once attended the assemblies at Almack's?"

He grimaced. "Why would I wish to go to that devilishly boring place? They serve nothing stronger than tea!"

She glared at him. Grandmere, who'd always treated him with the most tender of hearts, had never *glared* at him. "My resolve is inflexible. I had hoped one day to settle the entirety of my own personal fortune on my only surviving kin, but I will not do so until you demonstrate more maturity than you have heretofore." She sighed. "It is your good fortune that my Papa did not die and will his money to me whilst your wastrel grandfather and father were alive, for they would have squandered every last penny."

'Twas such pity that the Earls of Finchley did not have a feather to fly with and were dependent on the fortune of John's maternal great grandfather, who'd been the wealthiest brewer in the British Isles. And despite what Grandmere said, John wished to God the old brewer had died whilst his son-in-law *was* alive so the money would be the property of the Earls of Finchley.

"Don't know why it's my good fortune if I can't lay hands on it," he protested like a recalcitrant lad.

"One day, when you find a wife and start your own family, you'll be thankful."

"But I've no desire for a wife and children."

Her eyes narrowed as she regarded him. "Man is not always aware of what he wants. They're creatures highly resistant to change. But I know when you do settle down, you will make a fine husband and a good father. Ever since you were a wee lad, I've seen something in you that was absent in both your father and grandfather."

His brows arched in query. "Pray, what could that be?"

"Honor."

* * *

As much as she loved fashion, Lady Margaret Ponsby was growing tired of the never-ending ritual of dressing and primping and attempting to display oneself to advantage in search of a husband. There were morning calls, and routs, and musicals, and assemblies, and Almack's.

She was now two and twenty and, sadly, she had not taken. Her eldest sister had been happily married for several years. Her next eldest sister was on the verge of plighting her life to the distinguished Parliamentarian, Richard Rothcomb-Smedley. And her youngest sister, Caro, had turned down eleven offers of marriage. (Everyone said she was holding out for a duke.)

It was an acknowledged fact that she and Caro looked almost like twins, but it was Caro and her brilliance and sparkle that captured the hearts of all the men they met.

Not like unfortunate Margaret, who was incapable of holding an intelligent conversation with a gentleman. It wasn't that she was stupid; she was merely excessively shy. Mama had said one of her sisters was the very same. The sole sister who never married.

Her sister-in-law, the Duchess of Aldridge, swept into Margaret's bedchamber, met her gaze with a gentle smile, and softly closed the door behind her. "Before we go to Almack's I wanted to speak to you." She came to sit on the edge of Margaret's tall tester bed. The blonde duchess was already dressed and looked radiant in an ivory frock which perfectly displayed the Aldridge diamonds.

"I don't mean to pry, dearest," Elizabeth began, "but it's time I have the same talk with you that I had with Clair last year."

Margaret gave her a quizzing look. "I did not know- - - oh! Now I understand! It wasn't until you married our brother that Clair began to take an interest in her appearance. Whatever did you say to her to bring about such a transformation?"

"I asked her a question."

Now Margaret looked even more perplexed. "What question?"

"I asked what it was she wanted from life."

"Even though I'm her flesh-and-blood sister, I had previously thought she was happy with spinsterhood."

"She was." A smile softened Elizabeth's pretty face. "But she wanted a home of her own, children of her own, and lastly, a husband to fulfill those desires."

"Methinks her last desire is now first." Whenever Clair was with Mr. Rothcomb-Smedley she . . . well, she'd actually learned how to engage in a flirtation—something they had thought never to see Clair do.

"My dearest sister, I have seen how wonderful you are with the children at Trent Square. I've seen your keen interest in Lydia's devotion to her son. No one is better suited to motherhood than you."

Margaret was powerless not to observe the baby bulge in the duchess's midsection. "I happen to think you'll make a very fine mother." Elizabeth was a natural matriarch. She had single handedly established the rambling Number 7 Trent Square as a home for the destitute widows and children of officers killed in the Peninsula.

"Your brother said the same thing. I do hope to emulate Lydia."

"Oh, me too! It's very sad to me to think most aristocratic mothers give off their children to wet nurses, nurses, and governesses. I want to be like Lady Lydia."

"So I am right. You do want to marry and become a mother."

"More than anything." For some unknown reason, she felt she could reveal more of herself to this woman—a sister by marriage—than to Caro, the sister she'd been closest to throughout her life. "I've often been seized with envy of poor widowed Mrs. Leander."

Elizabeth nodded. "I know you've grown much attached to her baby boy."

Margaret nodded. "I'm so wicked I've lamented

over why I can't have him when she already has four others."

"You'll have one of your own. To attract a husband you shall have to abandon your shyness when you're in the presence of men. They'll mistake your reticence for aloofness. You are, after all, the daughter of a duke, and everyone thinks there's nothing loftier than a duke."

"Would that I had schooled myself better when I was younger. I fear it is now too late to teach an old dog new tricks. I seem incapable of making sparkling conversation—or any conversation— when a man is present."

"Is there not some man whom you admire?"

Margaret thought of the unvarying group of indistinguishable young men who moved in her social circles. Not a one of them had ever elevated her heartbeat in the least. The fact was, she had never met a man who affected her in such a way.

For some peculiar reason, her mind flitted to the old Dowager Finchley's opulent house opposite theirs in Berkeley Square. Why was it Margaret was so fascinated over the woman's rakish grandson? She had never exchanged a single word with him. He eschewed Almack's and other such bastions of respectability. His name was forever being dragged through the newspapers, linked to the most disreputable sort of woman. And the company he kept! His friends were just as profligate as he.

Yet she exercised a fascination over the tall, lanky young earl. She tended to race to her bedchamber window whenever she heard a lone horse trot up to the old dowager's, just in the hopes of feasting her gaze on the man. She had become nearly obsessed over his dark good looks.

It was the same kind of compulsion which had her searching through her brother's newspapers each day, searching for news of the young earl's escapades.

Her gaze met Elizabeth's. "No. I know no man who's ever appealed to me."

"Oh, dear. No one?"

Margaret sadly shook her head. "It appears I am not attracted to respectable men."

Elizabeth gave her a quizzing look. "Surely you cannot mean you are attracted to an *ineligible* man? I would find that difficult to credit, given your . . . well, your meekness!"

"You might as well say it. I'm mousy. Methinks the dullest stone will always be attracted to that which shines the brightest."

"You are not a dull stone." The duchess's gaze went to the window, and she was lost in contemplation for a moment. "Is there a . . . a rake who's captured your attention?"

"There could possibly be, but I've not had the opportunity to make his acquaintance."

"Dear God, you cannot be referring to the Earl of Finchley!"

Margaret's mouth gaped open. "How did you know?"

"I. . . I didn't. But I have observed you standing before this window for long hours."

"Please, do not spare another thought on this ridiculous attraction. It will never come to anything. I've never even spoken to the fellow."

"And I hope you never do! He's completely ineligible." Elizabeth's face softened. "You deserve someone much finer than he."

* * *

John's solicitor, a grave expression on his face,

looked up. "In my five decades of practicing law, I've never been asked to draw up such a document." His thick silver brows drew together. "Does your grandmother know about that advertisement?"

"Not yet, but she's the cause of it. If my grandmother insists upon my marriage, then marriage she will get. She never said I had to be in love with the bride. Nor must we live beneath the same roof."

He smiled to himself as he read over the newspaper advertisement that had drawn more than three dozen responses.

Gentleman of modest means seeks a gently-bred woman to enter into matrimony. The prospective wife will receive the one-time sum of £100 but will hereafter maintain separate abode from the prospective groom and make no further claims upon the husband.

"As irregular as it is, I can assure you the marriage contracts I've drawn up are perfectly legal. I've put in the bride's name of . . ." Mr. Wiggington consulted a letter. "Miss Margaret Ponsby of Windsor."

"I selected her because her name sounded like a name for which my grandmother would approve."

"I've been to Windsor and obtained the lady's signature on the contracts."

John was most pleased with himself.

* * *

No matter what straights John steered himself into, he'd always made it a point to never borrow money from his friends. He had no greater friend than Christopher Perry, who happened to be as wealthy as a nabob. As the only son after five daughters, Christopher Perry's parents had lavished him with affection, attentions, and anything that their fortune could purchase.

John had always known he could depend upon Perry to help him in any financial difficulties, but it was a line he had always preferred not to cross. In his mind, it was as if crossing that line would part him from Perry as effectively as a saw parts a limb from a tree.

An efficient, thoroughly English butler answered the door of the Perry's fine mansion on Piccadilly and, immediately recognizing John, showed him into the library. "I will inform Mr. Perry that your lordship is here."

A moment later, Perry strolled into the chamber. He was a fine-looking fellow who always dressed with impeccable taste. If one looked closely enough at him one might detect a few hints of the Perry family's origins as jewelers of the Jewish faith—a religion long ago abandoned by the family. There was the olive complexion associated with those in Mediterranean countries, and the prominent nose also hooked in the same manner as those whose ancestors had come from Biblical lands.

The Perrys had adopted thoroughly English ways. Perry's late father had even won a seat in the House of Commons.

"I am surprised to find you out and about so early," Perry said, by way of a greeting. "It is but two in the afternoon. Do you not usually sleep until four?"

"I had to see my bloody solicitor today on a matter of importance."

Perry quirked a brow.

"I've decided to get married."

Perry's dark eyes widened. "The hell you say! Who in the bloody hell do you plan to wed? Mind you, if it's Mary Lyle, I'll tie you to that bloody chair and not allow you to leave this house."

He had been moving toward John but upon hearing the announcement altered his path and went to snatch a bottle of port. "This calls for a bloody drink. Join me?"

"Don't mind if I do."

After Perry poured two glasses and handed one to his friend, John said, "It's not Mary Lyle. Haven't seen her in more than a month—not since I had to sell my carriage."

Perry, nodding knowingly, dropped onto a chair near John. "A title can only go so far in impressing the ladies."

Now John raised a brow. "I wouldn't actually call her a lady."

"No, I don't suppose one would." Perry took a long swig of the port. "I know you too bloody well. You can't be marrying because I would know it if there was an interest in that direction." He gave an exaggerated shudder. "Beastly business. Marriage."

John downed half his glass. "You'll get no argument from me on that."

"Then what, pray tell, are you referring to with this talk of marriage?"

John sketched out the details of his plan. "So you see, old boy, I'm going to ask that you be my best man in this bogus marriage. And I shall need you to supply the promised hundred quid to the obliging bride. I'll repay you as soon as my grandmother makes a settlement on the *mature* man she thinks marriage will make me."

"Of course, dear fellow. Anything for a friend."

John got up and shook his hand.

"What if the lady's a real dragon?" Perry's face screwed up as if he'd just sucked rotten lemons.

"I pray I only have to see her once."

Perry stood and showed him to the door.

"Will you meet me at St. George's tomorrow morning?" John asked.

"St. George's Hanover Square?"

John nodded. "And bring the hundred quid to pay my bride."

"What a wretched word. *Bride*. Makes me feel like the morning after imbibing two bottles of brandy."

"It's not a real bride."

"Tell me, Finch, is your grandmother to join us at St. George's in the morning?"

"I invited her but did not tell her what was going to occur."

* * *

The following morning, the unfortunate spinster, Margaret Ponsby, stood in front of St. George's Chapel within the grounds of Windsor Castle. The wedding day she had awaited for six-and-forty years now looked as if it were nothing more than a cruel hoax. Her bridegroom, Mr. Beauclerc, was to have met her here more than an hour ago. At first she thought someone had played a heartless joke upon her, but no one had forced her to respond to the notice in the *Morning Chronicle*. There was also the fact that the solicitor's clerk had gone to considerable trouble to obtain her signature upon the marriage contract.

Chapter 2

Ever since her conversation with Elizabeth, Margaret's mind had been occupied with her sister's sage observations. What she wanted most, she had to admit, was to be wed and to have children. She had, therefore, decided to pray most fervently that she be attracted to *eligible* gentlemen.

She wondered what perverse ancestor had imbued her with this mysterious craving of a most *ineligible* bachelor. Why could she not be like Clair? Clair could speak intelligently upon any subject—and Clair was attracted to a man who was highly respected. In her wildest imagination, Margaret could not imagine Clair ever countenancing an association with a known rake.

Accompanied by her maid, Margaret had silently strolled through Green Park and was now aimlessly walking the streets of Mayfair. She preferred those days when she had purpose, days when she had the opportunity to see the children at Trent Square. What a great feeling of accomplishment she derived from instructing them upon the pianoforte. They were such eager little sponges, and each of them had shown amazing progress.

As they neared Hanover Square, she decided to

go into the church there. She would light a candle and pray that she could be more like Clair, that she could be attracted to an honorable gentleman.

She might light a second candle and beg the Almighty to instill her with the ability to communicate with gentlemen. It was a curse to be so painfully shy.

The church's huge timber door squeaked when she opened it. It was dark and cold inside, but she had the church all to herself. She walked down the center nave, turned to a side altar, where she lighted a candle, then dropped to her knees and began to pray.

Dear Lord, I feel beastly selfish wasting Your Divine time with my insignificant request, especially since I am well aware of the many advantages of my birth. I am profoundly grateful that You saw fit to place me in a loving family. I will continue to minister to the less fortunate whether or not You answer my prayer. My prayer is this: I beseech You to guide me to a noble man. (And it would be lovely if I could shed my eternal shyness.)

The door opened, and she heard men's voices. Because they were the voices of men of Quality, she suspected one of them must be the vicar here. Would he remember her? No doubt he would remember Caro. Everyone always remembered her lively sister. Perhaps he would mistake her for the more popular sister.

Because her nature was to be as unobtrusive as possible, she continued peering at the flickering candle and beseeching her heavenly Father to change her deplorable ways.

To her complete surprise, one pair of footsteps came toward her, and a moment later a gentleman said, "Are you Miss Ponsby?"

Technically, she was, though she had always been addressed as *Lady* Margaret Ponsby. No one ever called her plain *Miss Ponsby*. She was, after all, the daughter of a duke. The vicar should know that. She turned to observe him.

But it was not the vicar. It was Lord Finchley! He peered down at her.

How was it that he knew her name?

Yesterday she had said no man had ever caused her heartbeat to race. That was no longer true.

To save her life, she could not have answered him. Her gaze spun away. All she could do was nod.

Though she wished to drink in his supremely masculine handsomeness, she was too shy to stare at him.

"Miss Margaret Ponsby?"

Averting her gaze, she nodded again. What could possibly account for him knowing her name?

"You've brought someone with you?"

She nodded. Why he wished to know that, she had no idea.

"Good. My friend Perry—Christopher Perry—will be my witness." He turned to speak to his companion. "Be a good man and give the lady the hundred guineas."

Now the other man came toward them. Dear Lord, was he going to give her money? Had they heard about the needs at Trent Square? She was certain she could put the money to good use there.

His lordship must not be nearly so dissolute as he would have people believe.

Christopher Perry handed her a heavy pouch.

She found her voice. "Thank you," she whispered hoarsely as she began to stuff the money into her reticule.

A side door near the sanctuary opened, and she looked up to see the vicar standing there wearing his vestments.

"Will you not accompany me to the altar, Miss Ponsby?" Lord Finchley asked.

Keeping her gaze averted, she stood and did as he bid. It was not in her nature to question a gentleman. She was far too obliging. And shy.

"Where is your companion?" asked he.

"My maid is at the rear of the church." She was rather astonished that she had actually been capable of constructing a complete sentence.

"She will need to sign the marriage certificate," the vicar said.

Marriage! His lordship must be planning on marrying. Today. That would explain why the vicar was dressed as he was.

She suddenly felt very low. Every shred of decency within her knew how utterly unsuitable was Lord Finchley. Nevertheless, the thought of him marrying another woman was rather like contemplating the demise of a loved one. She was seized with envy toward the bride. How shameful to display one of the seven deadly vices in the house of God, but she was powerless to suppress this marked jealousy that infused every pore of her body.

To her astonishment, his lordship offered her his hand. Always complacent and accommodating, she placed her gloved hand in his and rose. He led her to the altar.

Her heartbeat began to roar—a most singular occurrence, to be sure. Where was the bride? Lord Finchley must wish for Margaret to be a witness at the ceremony.

She was truly astonished that he'd known her name. She was, of course, acquainted with his grandmother, but she had never come face-to-face with the grandson. Ever.

Her first thought was that he had her mixed up with Caro. Men always remembered Caro, and there was a strong resemblance between the two sisters. But he had distinctly called her Miss *Margaret* Ponsby.

"Are you ready to begin, your lordship?" the vicar asked.

Lord Finchley nodded.

Were she not so meek, Margaret would have inquired about the bride. Was this marriage to be by a proxy? Perhaps his lordship needed her to stand in for the bride. What a pity it was that she could do nothing more than stand beside him and pray he did not detect the trembling that seized her.

To her further astonishment, Lord Finchley took her hand in his. In her two-and-twenty years, no man had ever before held her hand. The intimacy of such a simple act nearly overpowered her. Never before had improper thoughts visited her whilst in the house of the Lord. Until now.

It was most shameful that this hand-holding had ignited an odd stirring low in her body. Dear God! Added to her sin of envy (for try as she might, she could not suppress her newly acquired supreme jealousy of Lord Finchley's betrothed) was her newly acquired vice of lust! If she remained in the house of God much longer, what other new vices would blemish her? She might never again be permitted in so sacred a place. A long-ago Ponsby ancestor must have cursed her.

Her nerves were in such a state of agitation she paid no heed to the vicar's words. Until Lord Finchley was prompted.

The man she had worshipped from afar turned to her, held both her hands, and gazed into her eyes.

The vicar spoke. "Wilt thou, John Beauclerc, take this woman to be your wedded wife. . ."

Lord Finchley nodded. "I will."

A moment later the vicar addressed her. "Wilt thou, Margaret Ponsby, take John to be your husband?"

Far be it from timid Lady Margaret to rock this boat. Clearly these two men wished for her to answer in the affirmative. Therefore, she nodded.

The balding vicar offered her a soft smile. "Repeat after me. I, Margaret Ponsby. . ."

She swallowed. Her lashes lifted, and she peered into his lordship's eyes. They were black and intense, and she was startlingly aware of the connection between them, the connection anchored by their clasped hands. With prompting from the vicar, she completed the whole long sentence without stumbling. "I, Margaret Ponsby. . . take thee, John Beauclerc, to my wedded husband, to have and to hold from this day forward, for better for worse, for richer for poorer, in sickness and in health, to love, cherish, and to obey, till death us do part, according to God's holy ordinance; and thereto I give thee my troth."

Why she had not been asked to use the name of the absent wife, Margaret did not know. As they stood there in the sanctuary, their hands linked, she allowed herself to imagine what bliss it would be to wed John Beauclerc, the Earl of Finchley.

When the vicar asked his lordship to put the wedding ring upon Margaret's finger, a woman's voice interrupted.

Margaret and Lord Finchley whipped around and saw the dowager countess slowly rising to her feet from the first pew and moving toward them. "I wish for Lady Margaret to have this emerald ring. It has been handed down to each Countess of Finchley for the past two hundred years."

Oh, dear. She really couldn't take the real countess's emeralds. But, of course, Margaret was far too reserved to ever protest.

Lord Finchley's eyes widened. "*Lady* Margaret?"

The dowager presented her grandson with the emerald-encrusted ring. "You've done very well for yourself, John. To think, our new countess is a duke's daughter!"

$\mathcal{C}$hapter 3

John was incapable of speech. Good Lord, was this young woman the sister of his grandmother's Berkeley Square neighbor, the Duke of Aldridge? Isolated memories rushed to his numbed brain. Wasn't the Duke of Aldridge's family name Ponsby? No wonder this Margaret looked vaguely familiar to him. He'd likely seen her entering and leaving Aldridge House dozens of times over the years. But how in the deuce had she ended up here today?

Dread strummed through him. *Windsor.* Oh, dear God, was not the chapel at Windsor Castle also called St. George's? He now had no doubts the *Miss* Margaret Ponsby of *Windsor*—the lady who had responded to his newspaper advertisement—was likely standing at St. George's Chapel right now waiting for her bridegroom—and her one hundred pounds.

How in the devil had *Lady* Margaret Ponsby ended up at St. George's Hanover Square at the precise time he had scheduled his sham wedding? He had told no one save his solicitor, Perry, and—at the last minute—Grandmere. No one else knew of the ceremony, and he was relatively certain none of the parties who did know would have told Lady Margaret.

Even allowing for the preposterous coincidence

of names, why had she consented to go through with the ceremony? He took an instant loathing to the demmed woman. If she thought to snare him in a real marriage, she was delusional.

The sneaking, conniving spinster had even taken the Finchley emerald ring!

He wished like the devil his solicitor were here. He needed advice on how to dissolve this marriage.

He also needed to have a private word with this . . . this usurping woman. Which was not going to be easy, given that his grandmother was fawning over the bogus Finchley bride with the reverence one would accord a bloody queen.

"And where is the duke?" Grandmere asked Lady Margaret.

"He's doing the assizes in Middlesex."

"My late husband hated those days when he had to sit through the assizes." Grandmere lowered her voice. "I do hope your brother's not vexed that you're marrying a . . . a purported rake for I assure you Finchley will prove to be a fine man as well as a fine husband. He needed but the influence of a wife to tame him."

"My brother was not consulted. I'm of age," Lady Margaret said.

Which explained why she did not need her dukely brother's consent to the wedding. In his entire life John had never countenanced the striking of a woman. Until now. He was possessed of an urge to slap this woman whose subterfuge had ensnared him. Of course, he could never raise a hand to a lady.

John's best hope was that the woman's ducal brother would insist on dissolving this marriage of his sister to a notorious rake. He must talk to

Wiggington to see how one went about extricating oneself from such an ecclesiastic mess.

"I shall have a ball to introduce the Earl and Countess of Finchley to Society." Grandmere peered at John. "Will week after next be agreeable to you?"

He shrugged. "Um, it may interfere with . . . our wedding trip." He forced a smile. "So good of you to come today, Grandmama, but I am most anxious to be with my . . . bride."

His grandmother threw her arms around him for a long hug. "I'm so happy you've chosen to wed, and I couldn't be happier with your choice of wife. Lady Margaret will make a wonderful countess." Her voice lowered to a whisper. "Hopefully it will allow her to come out of her shyness, too."

Then his grandmother moved to Lady Margaret and drew that . . . that woman to her breast whilst she uttered sweet words to her.

John took that opportunity to sidle up to Perry and roll his eyes.

"You didn't tell me you were marrying a duke's daughter!"

"There's been a mammoth mix-up. I'll explain it all later."

"Don't see how you can carry on with your abandonment plan now. You know Aldridge has a reputation for threatening duels with men who cross his sisters. Remember the business with Morton? The man still hasn't returned to England. Aldridge has threatened to kill him if he does."

How had John managed to muck up things so thoroughly?

"One good thing, though," Perry whispered.

John eyed his grandmother who was merrily chattering away with that. . . that *Lady* Margaret as if he were not there. "I fail to believe any good thing could result from this."

"You need money, do you not?"

"Indeed I do."

"It's said all the Duke of Aldridge's sisters bring thirty thousand."

John's mouth gaped open. Thirty thousand was an enormous sum. It had never before occurred to him to marry an heiress in order to extricate himself from his financial difficulties. That was because he had never before wanted to be shackled to any woman. Most especially *not* to the younger sister of the powerful Duke of Aldridge.

His grandmother finally took her leave and hobbled down the nave. The vicar had taken his leave, and Margaret's maid sat quietly on the last pew. Which left John, Perry, and the woman to whom he had unfortunately just united himself. He effected introductions between Perry and Lady Margaret.

Perry grinned and looked excessively proud of himself when he said, "I expect instead of calling her Lady Margaret, she'll now be known as Lady Finchley."

The very idea of this . . . this woman being his wife made John ill. His eyes narrowed. "I suppose you're right. Now be a good man and leave me alone with . . . my bride."

Once Perry had left the church, John turned to her. At least she wasn't ugly. If he weren't so out of charity with her, he might even find her pretty. Certainly not a stunner. But she was quietly pretty with her bark-coloured hair and green eyes.

Or were they blue? Perhaps they were a combination of the two. There was nothing to offend in her figure, either, and she dressed with uncommonly good taste, though her soft muslin dress was as quiet as she. Nothing about her would ever demand an attentive gaze. "I beg that you come sit beside me so we can discuss . . . our situation."

They went to the first pew. He had to caution himself not to explode. He was so vexed he wanted to shout at her, but he needed to ensure her cooperation and could not afford to be abrasive with her. "My lady, I'm curious to know why you went through with this . . . marriage. It wasn't as if we'd ever even met. How is it you came here at the very time I thought I was to wed a stranger by the name of Margaret Ponsby?"

Her lashes lowered, and he saw that she trembled. But she did not respond. He recalled his grandmother telling him that Lady Margaret was timid. Was that why she was not answering his question?

After several moments, she looked up at him. "May I ask, my Lord, why you were marrying a stranger?"

It was a fair enough question. "I have no money of my own, and my grandmother—who is most anxious to see me settled—was withholding money until I married."

She was silent a moment before she spoke. "So you were not, indeed are not, planning for this to be a real marriage?"

At least she was not stupid. Terribly quiet, but not stupid. "That is correct."

"I will own, my Lord, I'm still confused by it all. How was it you were planning to marry me?"

Anger rose within him. *I bloody well was not planning to marry the sister of the Duke of Aldridge.* He must control his emotions and speak rationally—even kindly—to this woman. "I had communicated with a Miss Margaret Ponsby of Windsor. We had never met."

Her eyes widened. "She is a distant cousin of mine, my Lord. You are referring to the spinster who's close to fifty years of age?"

He inwardly groaned. "I knew nothing about her. She answered my advert and was willing to go through the ceremony in exchange for a hundred pounds."

"Oh, dear! I thought you—or Mr. Perry—were giving me the money for our home for officers' widows!" She reached into her reticule and handed him back the pouch. "Here. You must give this to Miss Ponsby of Windsor. I believe she is in need of it."

Grumbling to himself, he snatched the pouch. "Now, my lady, I beg of you to tell me why you went through with the ceremony." Though John lacked conceit, he knew that women found him attractive. Had this woman schemed to trap him in matrimony?

Again, she did not answer for a moment. Finally her lashes lifted. "I thought I was to be a stand-in for a proxy bride."

"But I asked if you were - - -" He clamped shut his mouth.

"I was surprised you knew my name."

She obviously knew who he was. He could almost believe that Grandmere had foisted this duke's daughter upon him. Almost. His grandmother was incapable of deceit. Because she was the most honest person he'd ever known, he knew his grandmother would never do anything so underhanded. "Well, it's all become a bloody mess. I'm sorry for getting you involved in my chaotic life. I'll have to see if my solicitor can arrange to dissolve this whole marriage business."

She nodded solemnly.

"I would be obliged if you say nothing about this to anyone."

Her brows lowered as she nodded again.

"I will either come by Berkeley Square to see you, or I'll write you when I know something."

* * *

Wiggington settled back in his chair and regarded John with a grave expression. "The law is very clear on this matter of annulment. Only if you can verify that one of you was mentally unfit before the marriage can an annulment be granted."

John's first thoughts were of the Duke of Aldridge. Fat chance he'd ever allow his sister to be ridiculed for marrying a lunatic.

"And, my Lord, I assure you that you do *not* want to petition the House of Lords to grant you a divorce. The vast expense as well as the public notoriety make that option prohibitive."

First, John did not have the funds to seek a divorce, and secondly, the Duke of Aldridge would never allow his sister to be a participant in so public a scandal. What was he to do? He knew Wiggington must be cursing his client for a fool. Hadn't Wittington told him the marriage contract was the most irregular document he'd ever witnessed?

"Why, my Lord, can you not proceed with your original plan to go your separate ways after the ceremony?"

"Because my original plan did not include marriage to the sister of the Duke of Aldridge! I thought I would be marrying a stranger—a spinster who was happy to accept the one hundred pounds I offered—but as it is, I've married a bloody neighbor of my grandmother." He frowned. "My grandmother is ecstatic over the marriage."

"You are sure you cannot part ways from the duke's sister? If your grandmother is so pleased, she will surely open her purse now for you."

John shook his head. "She will expect me to be in this woman's pocket. Trust me, I know how my grandmother thinks."

"And I suppose being in any woman's pocket is disagreeable to you?"

"Frightfully so."

Wiggington shrugged. "I wish I could help you, but I am powerless to do so."

"I could continue on as if no marriage took place, but what of Lady Margaret? I feel beastly that I've deprived her of the opportunity to wed a man of her choice." Now that he'd had time to think on the situation, he loathed her less. He had also come to understand that her shyness must account for her inability to question either the vicar or him about the wedding ceremony.

"Oh, dear. I hadn't thought of the unfortunate woman's situation."

John stood. "I'm counting on you to consult with lawyers and solicitors to see if you can find something in legal precedent that will allow me to dissolve this disastrous union." He stormed from his solicitor's place of business.

He had a very good mind to get thoroughly foxed with Perry, Arlington, and Knowles. Just being with those three fun-loving friends should lift him from his gloom.

* * *

As her bridegroom had requested, Lady Margaret said nary a word to anyone about the sham marriage, but it still occupied her every thought the remainder of that day and all of the next. It was impossible not to remember the way it had felt standing beside Lord Finchley, their hands clasped, as they pledged their love before God and man. Something unlike anything she had ever experienced had come over her when they stood before that altar. She had allowed herself to believe she really was plighting her life to his. Her heart had soared when she heard him say her name as he recited those wedding vows.

She knew she must be totally without pride to even contemplate how to make her faux marriage a real one though she quite blatantly directed all her thoughts in that very direction. She knew that if she lived to be ninety she would never find a man who could surpass Lord Finchley in sheer, unbridled appeal. To her. Quite frankly, there was no other man she had ever wanted. Just him.

She recalled, too, his grandmother's words when she told Margaret he would make a wonderful husband. Would he? Nothing could please her more than to be his wife.

In the flesh, Lord Finchley was a bit taller than she had thought. And though she had always thought him somewhat thin, in the flesh she realized he emanated a panther-like power, most especially in his muscled thighs that had been sheathed in finely tailored breeches. Though he dressed in fine clothing, his manner and the simple tie of his cravat and the absence of diamond studs and spurs which other men thought necessary bespoke a carelessness that she found attractive.

Her breath grew short when she remembered gazing into the perfection of his youthful face. There was something still of a carefree boy on his face. Perhaps it was the way his mahogany-coloured hair carelessly whisked onto his brow, just above those devilishly flashing black eyes. Margaret suspected the grin he'd directed at his grandmother must have been much the same as he'd shown as a mischievous lad. For Margaret had no doubts he'd been a mischievous lad. And a rakish young man.

It was her lamentable curse to be imbued with so unshakable an attraction to a most appallingly notorious rake.

In her whole life she had never withheld a secret from Caro—other than her secret worship of Lord Finchley.

And now she was not telling Caro about this marriage. She had given Lord Finchley her word not to speak of the marriage to anyone, and in her whole life Margaret had never told a falsehood. (Well, except for the time she had confessed to their governess it was she—rather than Caro, the real culprit—who had tossed the French primers into the fire.)

It was difficult now not to tell Caro about so momentous a deed. But Caro would not understand why it was so momentous, since for her entire life Margaret had withheld even from Caro her adoration of Lord Finchley.

It was even more difficult not to discuss the "marriage" with the duchess. Her brother's wife was the only person who knew of Margaret's profound feelings for his lordship. Even were she not bound by her word to Lord Finchley, she still would not confess to Elizabeth because she knew Elizabeth shared everything with Aldridge, and it scared the wits out of Margaret to contemplate how angered her brother would be to learn she had wed a gambling, womanizing, heavy-drinking rake. Aldridge's threats against Viscount Morton were still spoken of in hushed tones within the family—though none of them knew precisely what Lord Morton had done to Sarah to earn such scorn.

Even on the second night, even though her body ached with fatigue, she was still unable to sleep. It was nearly dawn when a brilliant idea presented itself to her. She bolted up in bed, her heartbeat hammering with excitement.

She thought perhaps she had contrived of a way to give both Lord Finchley and herself exactly what they wanted most.

Now she needed to present her plan to him.

$\mathcal{C}$hapter 4

She hated not going to Trent Square today. Working with the children there was the single most personally gratifying thing Margaret had ever done. But her entire future could depend upon what occurred today between her and Lord Finchley.

To avoid lying to Caro and Elizabeth, she merely lay in her bed that morning well past the hour for beginning her toilette and when Caro inquired, she sighed and said. "It grieves me, but I am utterly unable to go to Trent Square today." Caro, quite naturally, assumed Margaret was not feeling well and imparted a rather long sequence of helpful advice to spur her on to recovery.

As soon as her sisters left Aldridge House, Margaret sprang from her bed, summoned her maid, and instructed her thusly: "Make me look as if I were a great beauty." Secretly, she knew that was impossible, but it was imperative that she appear as pretty as possible.

She had given considerable thought to the selection of a mossy green morning dress. Every time she had ever worn the soft, clinging muslin frock, she had been the recipient of many compliments. In addition to the colour being most becoming on her, she thought it, more than any of her dresses, showed her bosom to advantage.

That is to say that rather than appearing boy-chested, when she wore the mossy green gown, it actually accentuated her womanly *assets*.

Wearing the dress, she sat before her dressing table, watching intently as Annie styled her hair. The girl was so talented Margaret believed her capable of turning a paint brush into a flower. In less than twenty minutes the youthful maid had succeeded in transforming Margaret's hair from a dull, tangled mess into a coiffure worthy of a Grecian goddess.

When Margaret stood and regarded herself in the looking glass, Annie's eyes sparkled. "My lady, I believe we've fulfilled your expectations. You are a true beauty."

Margaret knew she would never be a remarkable beauty like Elizabeth's sister-in-law, the Marchioness of Haverstock, but she was satisfied that she could not look any finer than she did this afternoon.

Much consideration had also gone into the selection of a time to pay a visit at Finchley House. She had some experience with young rakes because her two youngest brothers—now with Wellington—had been terribly wild before Aldridge bought them colours and forced them into the army. They partook of all the actions Lord Finchley was noted for. They avoided Almack's and the prospect of meeting decent young ladies; they wagered more than they could account for; they had a propensity to associate with opera dancers; and they imbibed large quantities of spirits until nearly dawn—and therefore had slept well into the afternoon.

She was reasonably certain that his lordship would be asleep in his bed when she arrived at

Finchley House in Cavendish Square.

She silently left her home and began the short walk to Cavendish Square—via a detour to duck into St. George's to light a candle. She dropped to her knees and prayed that she would not be her typical mute self when she attempted to speak to Lord Finchley.

After leaving Hanover Square, she practiced what she was going to say. First, she schooled herself to try to emulate Caro. Caro had never in her life been at a loss for words. *I must pretend I'm Caro.* Also, she braced herself for the sin she was about to commit.

For Lady Margaret Ponsby, aged two and twenty, was about to tell her second falsehood.

When she turned onto Cavendish Square, her heartbeat began to hammer. She knew precisely which house belonged to the Earl of Finchley. She had been possessed of that knowledge since she was a small girl. Actually, it was one of the more modest of the Cavendish Square mansions.

She approached the shiny black door of Finchley House, and her hand quivered as she rapped upon it. There was not a single cell in her body that was free from quivering. She gave up another silent prayer that her voice would not belie her massive shakiness.

That prayer was *not* answered. When the middle-aged butler swung open the door and drilled her with a haughty stare, her voice shook when she said, "Lady Margaret *Finchley* to see his lordship." She could almost swoon at the thought of being Lady Finchley.

* * *

As Clark opened the draperies in John's bedchamber, John's first instinct was to lash out at his faithful servant. But then he remembered instructing his valet to awaken him at noon. He wasn't precisely sure he could open his eyes yet. Nor was he certain he could lift his throbbing head from the pillow. A pity Perry had gotten that last bottle of brandy last night at White's. Or was that after they'd left White's? Damned if he could remember.

"I anticipated that you might have need of tisane this morning, my Lord," the ever-competent valet said, moving to the earl's bed, carrying a tray with a glass of water on it.

"Be a good man and help me up. I'm not feeling quite the thing today."

While Clark was assisting his master, there was a rap on the door. "Come in," John croaked.

Sanford opened the door but did not enter his master's chamber. His brows lowered, his facial features screwed into a quizzing expression. "Lord Finchley, I'm to tell you that Lady Margaret *Finchley* is awaiting you."

It took John a few seconds to comprehend. When he did realize who this Margaret Finchley was, he leapt from the bed, cursing violently, his headache forgotten in the boiling anger that consumed him.

"It seems my first impression of her as a loathsome, conniving female was right," he mumbled to himself. He had nearly become convinced that she was merely shy and meek. Ha!

"Allow me to shave you, miLord, before you greet the lady," Clark said.

Ignoring his valet, John directed his attention at the waiting butler. "Tell Lady *Finchley* I shall see her in the drawing room momentarily."

Then he directed a menacing look at his valet.

"I'll not shave to face that . . . that clinging female. Help me dress."

Ten minutes later he strolled into his drawing room. The lady stood peering out one of the windows which faced the square. "Oblige me, madam, by telling me what you're doing here—using *my* name!"

She turned around and peered at him, a shattered expression on her face. He was not at all certain she wasn't going to cry. Which made him feel beastly. Though he knew her to be of age, today she resembled a scared child. He had to confess, she was a comely little creature. If he were attracted to virtuous young ladies, she would have appealed to him greatly. As it was, he had no fondness for such creatures.

His voice gentled. "Pray, will you not sit?"

She nodded solemnly and moved to a silken sofa near the fire. He sat on an identical sofa opposite her. Their eyes locked for a moment. Now she reminded him even more of a frightened child—or a cowering pup. "Forgive me for my outburst," said he.

She nodded. Good Lord, she wasn't going to cry, was she? Was she going to say anything?

He waited. And waited. Grandmere must have been right about the lady being excessively shy.

Finally she drew a deep breath and began to speak. He detected a tremor in her voice. "Forgive me, my Lord, for using your name like that."

"I suppose you have the right, but I'd as lief you didn't."

Their gazes locked again. "Because you have no desire to ever be shackled to a woman?" Her voice had become a bit more strident.

"I wouldn't have put it that way to a lady, but,

yes, you have aptly described my feelings on the subject of matrimony."

She nodded. "I am happy to hear that, my Lord. We are in perfect agreement regarding our aversion to marriage."

His brows spiked. "I've never heard of a woman who didn't want to be married."

"That's because the life of a spinster is so completely unattractive. I do not wish to be a spinster. A married woman has so many more avenues open to her—not to mention her own home and a respected place in society."

He'd never thought about it that way. By Jove! She was right. But what about love? "I thought all women dreamed of being in love."

"I've never met the man to whom I would entrust my heart, and I'm heartily sick of the hoards of fortune seekers who constantly pay me court."

So she was a highly sought-after matrimonial prize? Hmmmm.

Before he could respond, she continued. Perhaps she wasn't so shy after all. "In addition to your aversion to being *shackled*, I believe I'm correct in assuming that you might be happy to get your hands on my dowry of thirty thousand." She peered at him from beneath raised brows.

His throat went dry. Not even his grandmother understood him as well as this woman. He cleared his throat. "I will own, such a prospect does have appeal."

She shrugged and favored him with a smile. "Then I propose that we pretend we are a happily wed couple. I hope I do not flatter myself when I say our marriage will make your grandmother excessively happy, and I should love being mistress of this house."

His mouth gaped open, but she continued. She certainly did not strike him as being shy. The lady was practically begging his hand in matrimony! "I would not expect your lordship to ever have to dance attendance upon me. You'll be free to carry on exactly as you always have." She took a deep breath and added, "You can even continue your associations with the sorts of women you're noted for associating with."

"Now see here, Lady Margaret! You're not to speak of such matters."

"Oh, I shan't once I move in."

Move in? He cringed. The very last thing he wanted—except for a wife, which truly was *the* last thing he wanted—was to have a respectable woman living under his roof. She would know what time he came home. She would know when he did *not* come home. She would likely even expect him to be present when she hosted soirees and balls at Finchley House, as his mother had done.

How in the deuce was he supposed to respond to her? He was truly at a loss for words. He continued sitting there, his shocked gaze locked with hers.

"It would be somewhat like having your friend Mr. Christopher Perry living under your roof."

How in the devil did this woman know Perry was his greatest friend? "Madam, I fail to see how you can liken yourself to Mr. Perry—with whom I assure you I have *never* wished to share a domicile."

She sighed. "I mean to be like Mr. Perry is to you. A friend. Nothing more. I propose making a pact that we'll be true and loyal friends to one another. In exchange for giving me your name and the accompanying status of being the matron of Finchley House, your financial difficulties will likely be eradicated when you receive my dowry— and your grandmother's approval. Do you not think she would then bestow much of her fortune upon you?"

She made it sound so harmless. Even appealing. A pity the lady's plan would not work. This duke's spinster sister might understand him, but she certainly did not understand his grandmother. "As long as I continue with what Grandmere refers to as my *debauched* ways, she will never open her purse to me."

Lady Margaret's brows lowered. "May I ask why you thought a sham marriage to *Miss* Margaret Ponsby of Windsor would satisfy your grandmother on that score, then?"

"I was desperate for *temporary* assistance from my grandmother. I knew when she understood the details of such a marriage, she would revert to withholding her money once again."

"Then we must think on not a *temporary* resolution but a permanent one to your difficulties." Her lashes lowered and a pensive look stole across her face.

Her tongue had finally stopped wagging.

For several moments the chamber was so quiet the only sound to be heard was the distant and infrequent clopping of horses on the street below. He was incapable of coming up with any reason (other than money) for acquiescing to this lady's ludicrous proposal, but he could most certainly enumerate a long list of reasons to reject it.

"Your lordship!"

Dread strummed though him as he raised a

quizzing brow and met her excited gaze.

"We can set aside a portion of your new-found funds in which to bribe the newspaper gossip mongers to keep your name *out* of their publications—which I know as fact is a practice exercised by the Prince Regent. That way your grandmother will not know that you've continued your debau . . ." She coughed. ". . . your *former* activities of which she does not approve."

There was some merit to this proposal. He began to think of all the things he could do with the lady's fortune and with an additional settlement from his grandmother. He could get back his carriage and horses. He would be able to reinstate his groom and coachman. He would be able to return to Newmarket for those race meetings which he so thoroughly enjoyed. He could allow himself to play faro at White's again. He could even take a pretty little opera dancer under his protection. Yes, indeed, the situation was looking brighter. He nodded. "That is certainly food for thought."

"And rest assured, my Lord, that I will endeavor to lavish attentions upon your grandmother—of whom I've always been excessively fond—and shall never cease to praise your domesticity to her."

Even the word had the power to make him cringe. Could anything be less appealing than *domesticity*? "How clever you are," he said, no conviction in his voice.

"My Lord?"

"Yes?"

"Did you not tell your grandmother we were to take a wedding trip?"

"I did so as a delaying tactic. She's anxious to

introduce the new Lord and Lady Finchley to Society."

"Since you don't aspire to marrying any ladies of Society, why should it matter to you if Society believes you married to me?"

She had a point there. He did not care a tuppence if every lady of the *ton* believed him wed to her. "I have no objections to telling Society that I married you." What he objected to was marriage. Any marriage in which he was the bridegroom.

"Good. Then you agree it's time we embark on our grand pretense? Shall I break the news to my brother today? Perhaps I can move in later this afternoon."

His stomach went queasy. For many, many reasons. God, but he hadn't thought of her brother. The Duke of Aldridge was widely acknowledged to be extremely protective of his sisters. Would he demand that John be always in his *wife's* pocket?

Just thinking of Lady Margaret as his wife was every bit as disagreeable as the notion of domesticity. He swallowed over his parched throat. "Perhaps you should put your excellent mind on another solution. This whole business about living under the same roof is . . ." *Mortifying*, but he could not tell her that. "Not appealing."

Her face collapsed. He feared she was going to cry. He had never been able to tolerate a crying female, most especially this female, since he knew he was responsible for her distress. If he had not concocted that foolish scheme that led to the wedding ceremony at Hanover Square, she would not be here today. She would not have *lawfully* married him. And she would not be proposing so abhorrent an action as living under the same roof as he!

Dear Lord, she *was* going to cry! She turned her head toward the chimneypiece so he would not be able to see her eyes, but he could not fail to observe the slight shaking of her shoulders that was a tell-tale sign of weeping.

He felt like the lowest sort of degenerate. Here the lady was concerning herself with ways to secure him his fortune, and he was abusing her. "Forgive me, my lady, if I've offended you in any way. I assure you if I *were* in the market for a wife, I could not find a better candidate than you."

She made no response, but he could tell that her sobs were increasing in intensity.

Finally, she slowly removed herself from the sofa, not for a second allowing him a glimpse of her face and its suspected reddened eyes, then she silently moved to the door.

What he devil was he supposed to do? For once he must consider another's feelings over his own. He leapt to his feet and rushed to block the door. She stopped dead in her stride, averting her face from his perusal.

"Forgive me, my lady," he said in a tender voice, "if I've offended you in any way. Can you honestly tell me that you have no objections to being wed to one of London's most notorious rakes?"

She sucked in a deep breath. "I did not object."

He, too, drew in a deep breath and prepared himself to tell a whopping falsehood. "Then, madam, it will give me pleasure to be your husband."

$\mathcal{C}$hapter 5

One would think she had just run uphill. Her heaving breath would not return to normal. All the way back to Berkeley Square she trembled. She was still astonished that her ploy to speak in Caro's matter-of-fact manner had actually worked. Not once when she was with Lord Finchley had she reverted to her customarily mute self. It had, she must own, taken unwavering determination and focus to keep asking herself, *How would Caro act?* and to keep bringing up to his lordship the reasons why the marriage would be beneficial to both of them.

She was even more astonished that he had finally agreed to live—at least to outward appearances—as a married couple. The very notion that she was Lady Finchley, wife of the only man to whom she had ever been attracted, affected her in a most profound way. It was as if she had imbibed an entire bottle of champagne. And more.

But as she neared Aldridge House, knowing she must break the news to her brother, terror gripped her. Though he was stern, her brother had never before elicited in her such fear. He was a kindly brother and a fine man. It was most unfortunate that all of London thought Lord Finchley an incorrigible rake. Aldridge was not going to be happy his sister had plighted her life to such a man. She still recalled Aldridge's violent dislike of Viscount Morton, who had been suitor to their elder sister, Sarah. To this day, Lord Morton had not returned to England.

Even worse than Lord Finchley's reputation was the fact she had hidden the marriage from her brother and from her entire family. How could she ever explain those unimaginable coincidences that had united her with John Beauclerc, the Earl of Finchley? She could not. Everyone must think this marriage was mutually agreeable to both parties. Because of her aversion to lying, that must be conveyed without telling a falsehood.

It was frightfully shameful that she had lied today to Lord Finchley about the many suitors clamoring for her hand in marriage, about her aversion to marriage. Prior to that reprehensible act, she had convinced herself that her goal of being his lordship's wife justified the shabby means of telling falsehoods, though she still felt utterly guilty over her ruse.

When she rounded the corner to Berkeley Square, she was seized with a brilliant idea. Elizabeth could be Margaret's ally in breaking the news to her brother. Elizabeth was acquainted with Margaret's feelings toward Lord Finchley.

At her home, Margaret went straight to the duchess's study, where Elizabeth was sitting at a gilded French escritoire, penning a letter. The lovely blonde looked up at her sister-in-law, favored her with a smile, and set down her pen.

Margaret drew in a breath and collapsed upon the chamber's window seat.

Elizabeth's brows lowered. "What's the matter? You're trembling." Her gaze raked over Margaret's lovely dress. "You shouldn't have gone out after not being well this morning. Shall I call for the apothecary?"

"There's nothing wrong with me. I am perfectly happy but nervous over breaking the news of a certain occurrence to my brother."

"What, may I ask, is this *occurrence*?"

Margaret's voice shook as she said, "I have married the man of my dreams."

An inarticulate shriek emanated from the duchess. "You cannot be serious! Please tell me you have *not* married Lord Finchley!"

"But I have, and I couldn't be happier."

"I most certainly do *not* approve of your actions." The duchess's head shook with an *all-is-lost* finality, then she lowered her voice. "Because I love you, I wanted you married to a good man who will value you and all your good qualities. I do not believe Lord Finchley is that man."

"I've never wanted another."

The duchess did not respond. Silence filled the chamber like a funerary gloom.

Finally, Elizabeth spoke. "Am I correct in guessing that Lord Finchley is in need of your dowry?"

Margaret nodded.

"I am so sorry. I fear you will end up with a broken heart."

"I know he doesn't love me now. I am prepared to wait. Years, if that's what's needed. I hope that one day he *will* value me and the good wife I've been to him. His grandmother told me that underneath his rakish ways, he's a good and noble man. I believe her."

"I will own the dowager countess is a wise woman, but her affection for her only grandchild might colour her perception of Finchley."

"Only time will tell."

"I fear your brother will be angry that he was not consulted. He'll be angry that the deed is already done and angry that you've married a notorious gamester and rake."

"I know."

Elizabeth's gaze lifted to regard Margaret. "I suppose you want me to break the news to Philip?"

Margaret nodded. "You know my feelings toward Lor- - -, my husband. You're the only one I've ever told. I believe you will be able to convey to Aldridge how besotted I am with the man I've married. And . . . remind him that I'm of age."

"Philip will dine with us tonight. I'll see him privately before the meal and convey to him the disappointing intelligence."

Margaret stood. "Thank you."

As she left the duchess's malachite-coloured study, she felt as if the weight of Gibraltar had been removed from her shoulders. Even her trembling subsided. She was relieved that she had not been forced to tell a single falsehood.

Now she had to tell Caro.

* * *

She and Caro had always shared a room. There were but eleven months separating them in age, and they were often mistaken for twins. It was really the oddest phenomenon that it was the younger sister who was the dominant one. Even as toddlers, meek Margaret had always deferred to her baby sister. While Margaret had been slow to speak, Caro was speaking in sentences just after she celebrated her first birthday.

The speaking had never ceased. Margaret was

content to fade into the wallpaper while Caro's lively personality sparkled.

They were exceedingly close to one another and had shared everything. Everything except Margaret's infatuation with Lord Finchley.

She had known Caro would disapprove. Because Caro loved Margaret more than anyone, she wished always to protect her sister against unsuitable men. And everyone considered the wastrel Lord Finchley unsuitable. Even if he was an earl.

Margaret entered their bedchamber. Caro looked up from the chair where she was reading a rather thick book. "I disapprove of your going out after this morning's illness. You might have taken lung fever!"

"I assure you, dearest, I've never been better."

Caro regarded her thoughtfully. "I will own, there's a certain . . . liveliness in your countenance. Where have you been?"

"There's much I have to tell you," Margaret said somberly as she dropped into a chair that was separated from Caro's by a small candle table. She drew a deep breath. "I've been with my husband."

Caro's book slammed shut. Her mouth gaped open. Her eyes widened. For the first time in her entire life, Caro was the mute sister.

After several moments, she said, "You are jesting."

Margaret shook her head. "I secretly married Lord Finchley."

"Not him!" Caro winced as if she'd just been pierced by an arrow.

"I think we will suit very well."

Caro's brows lowered. "You could not have

picked a worse man!"

Margaret straightened her spine and spoke with uncustomary authority. "I will not permit you to malign my husband!"

"Dear God, don't tell me you're in love with the . . . the profligate!"

The elder sister's eyes narrowed. "I will not tolerate abuse of the man I've married."

Tears began to gather in Caro's eyes. She buried her face in her hands and wept.

Margaret understood all the conflicting emotions that must be inflicting turmoil on her beloved sister. Marriage would mean they would be separated from one another. They had never been parted since the day of Caro's birth. There was also the shock of the announcement coming so utterly unexpectedly. And lastly, Caro would join all Margaret's loved ones in fearing that this marriage to a notorious rake would bring Margaret nothing but grief.

How it upset her to see Caro's shoulders heaving with her sobs. She left her chair and came to comfort her sister. "Please don't cry. I cannot convey to you how happy I am to be Lady Finchley."

Caro's reddened, tear-slickened face lifted. "Why him? Of all men. I didn't even know you were acquainted with him."

"I know it's a shock for you. It's wrong of me to have concealed from you my adoration of Lord Finchley, but I knew you would never approve of him, and I never dreamed that anything this . . . this wonderful could come from my fondness for him."

"How could you conceal something like that from me? I've blathered incessantly to you about every man to whom I've ever taken a fancy."

"I knew you would disapprove."

"Indeed I would! You can do so much bet- - "
She was overcome by another sob.

Margaret patted her sister's heaving shoulders.
"Please don't think of my marriage as a bad thing.
It's made me uncommonly happy. And it's not as
if you and I won't see each other every day still.
Finchley House is close, and I will continue going
to Trent Square with you."

"If only you'd confided in me." Sniff. Sniff. "I
could have dissuaded you."

Margaret stiffened. "Exactly why I did *not*
confide in you."

Caro continued crying, and when she finally
gathered her composure, she looked up at
Margaret. "I shall miss you."

"I will own, not living with my dearest sister
will be difficult, but we've always known we would
eventually marry."

"That's true. And you are certainly of age. Have
you told Aldridge?"

"Elizabeth's to tell him today."

"He's going to be angry."

The very thought of her brother's disapproval
sank her even lower.

* * *

Two days after he had agreed to Lady
Margaret's proposal, John found himself
trembling as he walked into the Duke of Aldridge's
library. With every step he took into the darkened
chamber, he cursed himself for ever embarking on
that wretched scheme which had resulted in that
disastrous ceremony at St. George's. *Hanover
Square*. Why or why had he not specified which
St. George's? Why oh why had he ever concocted

such a flimsy scheme in the first place?

He was vaguely aware that the Duke of Aldridge rose as he entered the chamber. A fire blazed in the hearth and a single oil lamp burned upon the desk. Even the walls in this ominous chamber were dark. No doubt they were paneled in walnut or some such wood.

"Will you not sit by the fire, Lord Finchley?" The duke's voice lacked warmth, but at least he wasn't outwardly hostile.

John effected a mock bow, nodded at the duke, then dropped onto a red velvet sofa. Aldridge strode to the fire and stood, his steely gaze boring into John's. Tall and dark and powerful, the Duke of Aldridge projected a most severe countenance.

"I will begin," Aldridge said. "I am aware that my sister is of age and is free to select a mate of her choice, but I will not conceal from you my disapproval of your stealthy wedding. I submit to you that you rushed my sweet-natured sister into such a clandestine affair because you knew I would never approve of you for Margaret's husband."

John was powerless to do anything but nod in agreement with the duke. "Yes, I knew you would do anything in your power to prevent Lady Margaret from uniting herself to the likes of me." John was rather pleased with himself that he'd not told a falsehood. Yet. How in the devil, though, would he speak of this marriage to which he had been so opposed? He could hardly vow to be a devoted husband to the man's sister. That would be an outrageous falsehood. Nor could he proclaim to be in love with Lady Margaret.

"I am aware, Finchley, of the large sums you owe and am convinced you've secured Margaret's hand in order to gain her dowry."

"I will not deny that was a strong enticement, though you must realize Lady Margaret is a fetching creature. What man would not wish to unite himself to her? I must be enormously fortunate to be the man so singularly honored by . . ." He started to say *Lady Margaret*, but for effect said, "my wife." Again, John was satisfied that he had continued on without resorting to telling lies.

"Why so sensible a girl as Margaret wished to wed you is beyond my comprehension," his grace mumbled.

Truth be told, John had wondered the very same thing. John was satisfied that, unlike other young ladies, Lady Margaret really did not aspire to a romantic marriage.

The duke's gaze went to the papers clasped in John's hands. "I see you've brought the papers my man of business delivered to you yesterday. Do you have any questions regarding the marriage contracts or settlement?"

"No, your grace. It's very generous."

"You've signed it?"

John nodded.

Aldridge's eyes narrowed to slits as he stood there, the raging fire at his back, regarding John with open hostility. "I warn you, Finchley, if I learn that you've squandered so generous a dowry on Lady Luck or ladies of the night I will do everything in my power to see that you're ruined."

If the duke's countenance had been stiff moments earlier, it was menacing now. John believed the duke wished him dead. His throat went as dry as burnt toast. "It is a very generous dowry, your grace, and I assure you I do not intend to squander it. It is true, though, that I have many creditors who will be most gleeful at the settling of their accounts."

The duke was speaking to him in much the same way as Grandmere did. John stretched his memory to recall those things his grandmother always stressed when she summoned him for a good set-down. "I believe marriage to your fine sister will bring me a maturity I have heretofore lacked. I need to follow pursuits other than those which have contributed to my reputation as a . . ." He swallowed. "A rake."

"I shall believe that when I see it," Aldridge said, his voice like that of a stern father. He drew a deep breath, his dark gaze never leaving John's. "I have other demands of you, demands that were not put in writing."

Despite the fire, John felt as if ice water were seeping down his spine. "What kind of demands?"

"If I ever learn that you have not treated my sister with respect, I will ruin you. You will not *ever* hold her up to ridicule. No opera dancers. No week-long gaming or drinking binges. If you ever hurt her—physically or emotionally—I will chase you to the ends of the earth and do my best to kill you in a fair fight. Even if it means destroying the man my sister loves."

John felt as if he'd just been slapped in the face. What the devil had he gotten himself into? Had he not wanted the lady's dowry in order to pursue those very things of which the duke wished to deprive him? *Good Lord, no opera dancers*? What gave that sanctimonious duke the right to dictate John's behavior?

The two men glared at each other, their hostility palpable.

After several moments, the duke spoke. "I believe my demands are in harmony with those of your grandmother."

John nodded.

"You are young still. Marriage and fatherhood can make a fine man of you—if you allow it."

Fatherhood? Good Lord, he wasn't planning to bed Lady Margaret! She wasn't his type. Not in the least. She was not possessed of one of those voluptuous bodies he so admired.

After seeing the generous marriage contracts, John had come here today relatively content. But now he felt as if he were entering a prison designed to strip him of every pleasure life had to offer.

He'd never felt lower.

"If you are so greatly opposed to this marriage, your grace, perhaps you would wish to end it." John lifted a hopeful brow.

A thundering expression came over the duke's face. "I will never consent to anything so disagreeable, anything that would subject Margaret to notoriety. Of all my sisters, she is by far the most sensitive."

A bloody sensitive female was the last thing in the world John wanted. "Very well, your grace."

"You're agreeing that you'll be an exemplary husband?"

John's stomach roiled. "I doubt I will ever be as exemplary a husband as Lord Haverstock or you, but your strong marriages will serve to guide me." Again, he was proud that he had managed to answer without telling an outrageous falsehood.

Once more, the chamber went silent, the only sound the hissing of the fire. Then John recalled the duke's words. "*Even if it means destroying the man my sister loves.*" He was not sure which part of that sentence was the more distressing. The part about being destroyed by the powerful duke—or the part about Lady Margaret being in love with him.

Surely she could not be. They were complete strangers. It then occurred to him the lady had told her brother she was in love in order to sway him to placid acceptance of the marriage. John had to hand it to her. She was clever.

A pity he had never admired clever females.

"So," the duke finally said as he stood. "I understand Margaret's things have been sent along to Finchley House?"

John got to his feet, facing Aldridge. "That is so." It still made him ill to think of being forced to share his home with a woman—a woman he had no desire to bed, a woman who was a complete stranger.

"At least she's not going to be off in the provinces like my eldest sister. I shall miss Margaret."

"Your grace's loss is my gain." That wasn't exactly a lie. He *was* gaining a permanent occupant of his home.

"So you've come to collect your bride?"

"Indeed I have."

"I'll have a footman fetch her."

$\mathcal{C}$hapter 6

It was dashed embarrassing that he'd had to accept usage of the Duke of Aldridge's coach in order to bring his bride to Finchley House. Now that he had received her generous dowry, one of his first purchases was going to be a coach for her. He didn't give a tuppence if he had a coach, but he could hardly ask the daughter of a duke to be conveyed around London in a public hack.

He also planned to do his dashed best to get back his coachman and groom. He'd need horses, too, and he had his eye on a stunning gelding to be offered at Tatt's.

He looked across Aldridge's coach at his bride, who sat stiffly on the plush velvet seat. Were husbands and wives expected to sit on the same seat? Even though it wasn't to be a real marriage, he supposed he ought to give the *appearance* of being married. This bloody woman he'd wed was not one bit of help in directing him how to act. She had not uttered a single word since they had entered the carriage.

Because he had no intentions of being properly married to her, the lady's reticent nature should suit him very well. What could a prim maiden have to say that would interest him in any way? Yet even though he should welcome her shyness, it actually made him uncomfortable.

"I say, Lady Margaret, I suppose we should establish the manner in which we are going to address one another. Can't very well have you calling me Lord Finchley, and I don't suppose one addresses one's wife as Lady Margaret."

"What should you like me to call you, my Lord?"

Damn but she sounded timid. More like a school girl than a woman who'd come of age. "My friends all call me Finchley. Or Finch."

The expression on her face remained placid. "And your grandmother? How does she refer to you?"

He shrugged. "She calls me John Edward, to differentiate me from my father, who was John David." He wondered if this new wife he'd taken on was supposed to call him by his Christian name or his title. He'd never given particular notice to married couples and how they interacted with one another—or if they even sat upon the same seat in a carriage.

"Would you object if I called you John Edward? Or John?"

Something inside him melted. His mother had always called him John. He'd not been addressed in such a manner since she had died.

"Of course I wouldn't object. Pray, suit yourself."

"You wouldn't mind if I called you John?"

"Not in the least." He wondered how she would like to be addressed. "Does that mean I should call you Margaret?"

"That would be agreeable."

He wrinkled his nose. "Don't suppose anyone has ever called you Maggie?"

She shook her head. "No."

He favored her with a smile. "Well, we've established that."

"If you'd like," she began, then stopped, apparently too shy to even meet his gaze. "If you'd prefer, *you* could call me Maggie."

The way she said *you* made it sound as if by virtue of that demmed marriage he had been accorded some special intimacy. He now regretted even mentioning the name Maggie. This lady's nature was far too formal for a Maggie. But something told him she wished for her husband to use a name others did not. He supposed it was a spinsterish whim, for he supposed he would always think of her as a spinster.

"I say, Maggie, what were you referring to when you mentioned some home for soldiers' widows?"

Apparently he'd hit upon a subject over which she could express lively interest. She sat up even straighter (were it possible) and her voice changed from docile to interested. "The duchess of Aldridge—before she was even a duchess—established a home for impoverished widows of soldiers who died fighting in the Peninsula. It's located at a large house on Trent Square which is owned by my brother. I am happy to say we now have eight-and-twenty children there—along with their mothers."

"How are you associated with it?"

"I instruct the children upon the pianoforte and perform any other services I can to make myself useful."

His nose wrinkled. "It's very kind of you to put yourself out so much on their behalf."

"Oh, I'm not putting myself out at all. In fact, I enjoy it excessively."

What a most peculiar woman she must be. He

could think of little that would interest him less than instructing children on a musical instrument.

The coach slowed as they reached Finchley House. He'd requested the housekeeper to see that candles were lit in all the public rooms, his bedchamber, and the countess's bedchamber. He had especially requested that the countess's chamber be spruced up.

They departed the carriage, and he offered his crooked arm, then they moved to the front door. A footman swept it open, and he saw that his staff—no doubt exceedingly small when compared to that of her brother's establishment—were lined up in starched finery to greet their new mistress.

He presented Sanford and Mrs. Pimm to . . . Maggie. His wife was gracious but reserved. One would never take her for a duke's daughter. She was completely void of the arrogant manner that normally accompanied one of such exalted rank. In fact, she was meek.

Next, he and the new Lady Finchley walked down the corridor, nodding at each of the servants. Once that duty was dispatched, he led his bride to the drawing room. She nodded but said nothing. Did she find Finchley House shabby? It then occurred to him it had been without a woman's touch for the past seven years. "I say, Lad- -" He paused, then corrected himself. "Maggie, you are free to make changes to the décor. I daresay it could use a woman's touch."

"It's lovely."

She was certainly an agreeable lady. He could have done worse for himself. (And by staying unmarried, he could have done much better.

Except for the dowry.)

He next showed her into the library. Here her expression brightened. She actually strode to a wall of fine leather-bound books, most of them red—and most of them unread—and began to examine some of the titles.

Some minutes later, she faced him. "It's a very fine library you possess. Are you a great reader?"

"If you knew me better, you would not ask such a question."

"What I know of you comes from the newspaper accounts."

He grimaced. "Pray, do not believe half that rot, though I will own that I am an incorrigible rake."

Her soft hazel eyes met his. "Your grandmother would not choose the word *incorrigible*."

She wouldn't. Grandmere, for some unfathomable reason, thought there was something akin to *honor* buried within him. There was no accounting for the prejudice of love. "You must make allowances for an elderly woman," he said flippantly.

The lady politely changed the topic of conversation. "Was your father a great reader?"

He chuckled. "My father was more incorrigible than I."

"But these books . . . they are wonderful. It is a very fine library. Who's responsible for it?"

"It pains me to admit my maternal great grandfather, who was a very wealthy cit, purchased the entire library upon the recommendation of a scholar whose services he procured." John shrugged. "It seems there is nothing that cannot be purchased, providing one's pockets are deep enough."

"Would you object if I spend a great deal of

time here?"

"Do whatever you like. You are, after all, the new mistress of Finchley House. And it's not as if I'll ever be stepping on your toes in this chamber." He moved toward the door. "Should you like to see your bedchamber? Your maid spent the afternoon there sorting all your things that were delivered earlier today."

She smiled brightly at him. "Yes. I'm quite excited."

"I pray you do not expect anything so grand as what I daresay you're accustomed to," he said as they began to mount the stairs to the next floor.

"I have never had a bedchamber of my own before."

He paused, arching a brow. "You shared your chamber with one of your sisters?"

She nodded. "With Caroline. We are less than a year apart."

"I should think you would miss sharing your room with her. It must have been a great deal of fun. Unless you two did not get on."

"Oh, we get along exceedingly well."

"I rather enjoyed sharing a chamber when I first went up to Eton. Being an only child is beastly. I rather like the camaraderie of being around other fellows."

"Like Mr. Perry?"

"Yes, indeed. There were four of us who've been the best of chums since we played cricket together at good old Eton."

"And none of them have married?"

He wrinkled his nose again. "I suppose I'm the first."

"Though it's not really like being married. You'll continue on with your three chums as if you were just down from Oxford."

"Indeed we will," he said rather jollily.

As they passed the door to his bedchamber, he felt uncomfortable. No proper lady had ever before been in this part of his house since he'd succeeded. It seemed awfully odd being there with her. He strode along the wooden-floored corridor until they came to her room, and he swept open the door. "Your chamber, my lady."

Her face brightened as she moved into the room. "It's lovely."

He remained in the doorway. He could not bring himself to step into a chamber that had such intimate associations. After all, this woman, this lady, was almost a complete stranger to him. His gaze whisked around the room. The high, curtained bed dominated every other item within his view. A pity it would never be used for a pleasurable purpose. His gaze went to her. She faced the dressing table, her profile to him, and he observed the smooth lines of her pleasing figure. Yes, a great pity, but there you were. He sighed.

"Did your mother select the draperies and bed curtains?"

Why did she have to bring up the bloody bed curtains? He found himself thinking about lying within the closed bed curtains, ravishing this lady he'd accidentally wed. That would never do! "Yes, I believe she did. She loved turquoise."

"I do too."

Somehow, that surprised him. Turquoise was so vibrant a colour, and she was so . . . mousy. Not that she looked mousy, actually. Her prettiness was undoubtedly above normal. It was just that her temperament was so meek, and she was so quiet. He would have thought she favored insipid colours like gray or pink. "Feel free to change the chamber in any way you'd like."

She shook her head. "There's nothing here I would want to change. Your mother was possessed of unerring taste."

Her comment pleased him inordinately. It validated his own opinion of his lovely mother. "Thank you. She was." He felt closer to Maggie. Not close enough to enter that chamber, not close enough to ever bed her, and certainly not close enough to ever stop wishing this abominable marriage had never occurred. Nevertheless, the two of them shared his good opinion of his sainted mother.

He drew a deep breath as if to clear his mind from any thoughts of her bed. "Well, if you're settled in, I'll be off."

She arched a brow. "You'll be with Perry and the other two gentlemen?"

"I will."

"I would like to know their names. The other two."

"They're David Arlington and Michael Knowles."

"Do you think we could ask them all to dinner so that I could become acquainted with them?"

"Why in the devil should you wish to be acquainted with them?" He wasn't sure any of them knew how to act in the presence of a proper lady.

"As your wife, I'm interested in you as well as in your friends."

How he hated that word. *Wife.* "Very well."

"I shall depend upon you to nail down a date that will be agreeable to all for our dinner."

* * *

His three best friends watched him sheepishly as he strode into White's minutes later. His gaze went from the always-jolly Arlington to Knowles, always the pensive one—who never turned down the opportunity to have fun with his friends. "Perry told you."

Knowles nodded. "We know about your marriage."

"You're losing your touch, old boy," Arlington said. "Your first night with a woman to whom you're properly wed, and you aren't taking your pleasure with her? How flattered we are that you'd rather be with us."

Knowles eyed him with great seriousness. "And Perry says the new Lady Finchley is pretty, too."

John seethed. "Perry should have told you it ain't a proper marriage."

"Perhaps the lady thinks otherwise. You must own, the ladies are always drawn to you," Knowles said.

Perry smiled. "You are, after all, tall, dark, and titled. What more could a lady ask?"

Arlington's brows raised. "A large purse and a large . . . instrument go very well in pleasing a lady."

They all laughed heartily. All except John.

"With the lady's dowry," Perry said, "Finch now has the large purse, but I cannot answer to the second qualification."

Arlington smirked. "I daresay it was lack of those two vastly important resources that prompted Lascivious Mary Lyle to seek *larger* pastures."

They all started laughing. Except for John.

Knowles eyed him. "While we're on the topic of Lascivious Mary, I must warn you, old boy, that just because you're now in funds, you must think twice before taking a mistress. Aldridge obviously doesn't approve of taking mistresses. He doesn't have one. And the duke's beastly protective of his sisters."

"Remember Viscount Morton's fate," Perry cautioned.

Arlington began to howl in laughter. They all turned to him to learn what amused him so. "Finch's love of play, horse racing, drinking, and women is why he needed to marry, and now that he has, it seems those very activities will be denied him."

Knowles solemnly eyed John. "He's right, old boy."

Anger surged through him. "No one tells the Earl of Finchley how he spends his money." His gaze went to Perry. "Shall we play faro?"

"Perhaps, old fellow," Knowles said, "you should give the illusion of having settled down in order to placate your grandmother. Does she not control a rather vast fortune?"

There was merit in what his most serious friend said. If Grandmere thought him settled, he could receive a settlement many time greater than the dowry given him by the Duke of Aldridge. What would it hurt to pretend to domesticity for a few weeks in order to get his hands on what should already have been his?

John swallowed hard. "I have a rather strong urge to drown myself in brandy tonight."

"A jolly good plan," Arlington said.

Perry ordered four bottles.

* * *

Margaret had known that her husband had no intentions of bedding her, but it stung that he found her so undesirable that he would not even step into her bedchamber. Long after he was gone, she refused to douse a single candle. She sat upon a silken settee and surveyed her new room. Though it was smaller than what she was accustomed to, it was as elegant as anything in the ducal home in which she'd been raised.

Knowing that his mother had chosen the selections herself somehow made Margaret feel closer to her, closer to the woman's only child. She wished she could have known her. John obviously had adored his mother. She wondered what he had inherited from her—other than his luxuriously dark hair. She knew his father had been a hopeless rake. Sadly, the son had inherited many of his father's traits.

She had not been much in her husband's company, but she thought perhaps he did not admire the man who'd been his father. What of the grandmother? Margaret's brief interaction with her after the wedding ceremony indicated a closeness between John and her. The old woman quite obviously doted upon her only grandchild. Had she made similar allowances for her wayward son? She seemed to believe that beneath John's wicked ways he was fine and decent.

Margaret preferred to believe that he was.

Even though he had deserted her on what should be their wedding night, nothing he'd done could diminish her binding attraction to him.

When she'd stepped into her new bedchamber and seen the stately bed, her heartbeat had nearly exploded. Her throat went dry. Her insides went all bubbly. How she wished this were a real marriage. How she wished to be crushed into his embrace and carried to that bed. How she wished he would peel every garment from her body and seek the pleasure she craved, the need only he could satisfy.

It was illogical to be so fiercely attracted to him. It was futile to dare hope he would ever be attracted to her. It was idiocy to be so hopelessly in love with him.

$\mathcal{C}$hapter 7

How odd it felt to come to Berkeley Square and not walk up the steps to her old house. Today Margaret meant to visit with John's grandmother. Of course she would not leave the square without visiting Aldridge House—especially with Caro, who had wept when Margaret's things were removed the previous day.

How fun it was to announce to the dowager's butler, "Lady Finchley to see Lady Finchley." It was equally as gratifying when John's grandmother rushed into the saloon and gathered Margaret into her bosom. "Oh, my dear, what a delight it is to see you! Come, we must remove to my own sitting room. It's so much more intimate there."

The much-winded dowager mounted the stairs to the third level, where the chamber to which she brought Margaret was one of the most comfortable rooms Margaret had ever seen. The pastel colours were soothing, and the chintz-covered furnishings were cozy and feminine. The room featured the bric-a-brac which had been collected over the old woman's lifetime. On the wall hung plates with portraits of King George and Queen Charlotte. There was a collection of miniature portraits of various members of the Beauclerc family. The sofa was adorned with needlework pillows, which the dowager must have executed over her long life.

After the two women settled on the sofa, the dowager beamed at Margaret. "And how, my dear, are you enjoying being married?"

"Very much."

"I must tell you, I've never been prouder of John Edward than I was the day I discovered he'd selected you for a wife. I did not even know he was acquainted with you. How long has the . . . romance been blossoming?"

Margaret cautioned herself to respond honestly. She did, after all, abhor lying. "I can only answer for myself." She paused and looked up at her husband's grandmother. "I have always wanted to . . ." How could she express those complex emotions this woman's rakish grandson had always elicited in her? She could hardly say *win his heart* for she had no assurances that day would ever come. "Be the woman fortunate enough to wed John."

"Bless you, my dear. I fear there will be difficult times ahead for you, but I know in my heart that John Edward will settle down, and when he does, he will be a loving, devoted husband—and eventually father."

Margaret's heartbeat hammered. Such a notion thrilled her. "I pray you are right, my lady."

"I won't deny there's a wild streak in all the Earls of Finchley, but John Edward has more redeeming qualities than his forefathers."

"I would be obliged if you'd enlighten me as to those qualities."

The old woman's face softened. "It's the little things. He's always had a soft spot for the women in his life. He was most earnestly solicitous of his gentle mother and of me, too. No son was ever more devoted than John Edward was to his mother. He never left her side when she fell ill with her fatal malady. I am ashamed to say my own son lacked the same compassion which John Edward has in abundance."

"I will own one of the reasons I came to you today was to learn more about John." Margaret loved that she was the only woman in the kingdom who could refer to him by his Christian name.

The elder Lady Finchley smiled. "There are probably those who believe he butters me up in order to secure the fortune left me by my wealthy father, but I know he cares about me. He's incapable of artifice. Even as a little child, he could not tell a lie. I truly believe he'd rather I live a very long life than die and leave him a very wealthy young man."

How Margaret loved learning these things about the man she had married. How fortuitous it was that he detested lying, as did she.

"In order for your marriage to flourish, my dear, you will have to find a way to keep John Edward away from those bosky friends of his." She frowned.

"You refer to Christopher Perry, David Arlington, and Michael Knowles?"

The old woman's eyes narrowed. "I do indeed. You will have a difficult time until those three gentlemen marry and settle down to domesticity."

Margaret shrugged. "I fear that is out of my hands."

"So it is. A pity I cannot manipulate such a change."

"I do feel the same." How jealous she was of

those three men who would spend more time with her husband than she.

There was a knock upon the door, then John strolled into the chamber, a posy of lavender and violets clutched in his hand. His gaze flicked from his plump grandmother to Margaret, and he stopped dead in his stride. His gaze still on his wife, he said, "Had I known you were here, Maggie, I'd have brought you flowers too."

Her heart fluttered. The idea of getting flowers from him was so touching. Even more touching was her husband calling her *Maggie*. It was a name no one else ever called her. Even though there was no intimacy in this marriage, his use of Maggie served her as an endearment, a validation that she alone was his wife. "I am touched by your sentiment."

He turned and presented his grandmother the posy. "I saw these on the street and immediately thought of you, Grandmere. I've neglected you since my marriage."

"As well you should. Your Maggie must come first in your thoughts now." She took the posy and smelled the tiny flowers. "They're lovely, my sweet John Edward, and I thank you." Her contented gaze connected with Margaret's for a silent confirmation of her grandson's thoughtful nature.

Had Margaret herself received the posy she could not have been more pleased. It made her feel more confident over her lifelong obsession over this rogue to know that he did have redeeming qualities.

The dowager patted the sofa beside her and indicated for him to sit between them. "I must compliment you, John Edward," she began. "Your name has not appeared in the newspapers once since the day you had the good sense to marry Lady Margaret Ponsby."

"I wish you wouldn't read those papers," he said. "As I was telling Maggie, you can't believe that rot."

As I was telling Maggie. How she loved hearing him speak like that. It sounded as if theirs were a real marriage, sounded as if they shared intimacies as other married people did.

"Since you wed, I've not seen mention of those rowdy friends of yours in the papers, either," his grandmother said. "Does that mean that you are the leader in frivolity?"

He shook his head. "I'm more a follower than a leader. I would have to say Perry's the instigator. And if you haven't seen mention of me in the papers, it is due in good part to wise counsel I've received from Knowles."

The old woman rolled her eyes. "I have difficulty believing any of those young men of yours wise." She shrugged. "Enough berating of your friends. We must discuss the ball to introduce you and your Maggie to Society. I should like to have it next Friday. Would that be agreeable to you?"

Now he rolled his eyes. "If that's what makes you happy, Grandmere."

"I know you don't fancy balls, but you're no longer a single man who'll be besieged with scheming mamas desiring to unite their daughter to a handsome, titled young man."

"I beg that you not describe me in such a manner."

"You refer to the word *handsome*?" His grandmother's brows arched.

He nodded, shooting a glare at the elder woman.

She spun to face Margaret. "Do you not find him handsome, my dear?"

Colour rose in Margaret's cheeks. She could not tell a lie. "I do."

He eyed her, a softness in his expression, but said nothing.

"Why else, my boy, would you merit so fine a catch as Lady Margaret? Of course she was attracted to your handsomeness. You must own, you had little else to recommend you to so fine a lady. But be assured I am acquainting her with your finer qualities so she won't feel she's made a grave mistake by marrying you." She looked from John to Margaret. "Neither of you will ever regret this marriage."

To keep her husband from being embarrassed, Margaret asked him, "What will you be doing today?"

"I should like to buy a carriage for you." He shrugged. "Should you like to accompany me?"

Her pulse accelerated. "I should love it above all things."

"You two must take my coach, then," the dowager said.

* * *

He felt deuced awkward looking at his prim wife as she sat across from him in his grandmother's carriage. What did one say to a gently bred lady?

How surprised he'd been to find her at Grandmere's. Now that his grandmother was not able to get about as much as she had as a younger woman, he worried about her being lonely and made it a point to visit her often. He was her only living flesh and blood, and she his. No matter how the old woman chided him, he loved her very much.

He thought even more highly of his wife for making a visit to his grandmother one of her first priorities after the acknowledgement of their marriage. "It was good of you to seek out my Grandmere."

"The pleasure was mine."

"Pay no attention to her praises of me. She is vastly partial to her only grandchild."

Maggie chuckled. "You are blessed to have her—and I shall be happy to claim her as my own grandmother."

"Your grandparents are no longer alive?"

"They're all gone. My parents too."

"Ah, something you and I have in common. But you are fortunate to have so many siblings."

"Indeed I am. And with my brother's marriage I've gained another sister of whom I'm exceedingly fond." She looked up at him. "You must now think of Aldridge as your brother."

Why did the duke have to be such a dull stick? He hadn't always been that way. It was said the Duke of Aldridge had been a great scoundrel— before he was snared by Cupid's arrow and fell so blindingly in love with the former Elizabeth Upton, Haverstock's sister.

John could think of no one, except possibly Haverstock, who would be so unfavorable a candidate to be his brother. The two were as serious a pair as he'd ever known. "I cannot deny that I've always wanted a brother."

Silence once again filled the coach. A pity he could think of nothing to say to the woman.

Finally she spoke. "There's something else we

have in common, I've learned."

He raised a brow.

"Your grandmother tells me you do not tell falsehoods."

"It is the same with you?"

She nodded.

He did not know why he had always abhorred lying, but he did know that none of his friends were always truthful. "I daresay not many people can make such a claim."

"I daresay you're right."

More silence.

Finally she broke the icy silence. "Though most falsehoods, I have found, are perfectly innocent. Exaggerations. Unfelt compliments. Lies told in order to avoid punishments, corporal or mental."

"That is true." How odd it was that she—the quiet one—was now carrying the conversation, and he was reduced to making two- and three-word responses.

In the ensuing silence, she peered from the coach window, and he took the opportunity to watch her. If he were attracted to decent women of good birth, she would certainly be a worthy conquest. There was nothing in her appearance to give offense. Had not Perry said she was pretty? Everyone knew Perry was an acknowledged judge of feminine beauty.

She was utterly feminine from the perfection of her nose to the soft pink of her lips to her slender fingers. Though he would not normally notice a lady in possession of such nondescript brown hair, he realized her face was pretty. No one feature dominated. Like her, it was a bland, delicate face. Her slender figure was pleasing, and she dressed with impeccable taste. Knowles would appreciate that.

Quite oddly, he found himself desirous of introducing her to his friends, curious as to what they would think of her. Quite oddly, he wanted them to approve of her.

Of course, she was not really his wife, more like a sister, actually. But, quite oddly, he did not think of her as a sister. Though in a very short time he had come to think of her as an extension of his very limited family. Just minutes ago she had said she wanted to share his grandmother with him. It was a prospect he found comforting.

"So," he said, "when should you like to meet my male friends?"

"I have no plans that are as important or interesting as that."

Interesting? He doubted she would find them interesting. Unless the lady was enamored of shooting. Or fencing. Or race meetings. "I suppose I shall have to invite them to Grandmere's ball."

"For your sake, they will come, though I daresay balls are not to their liking."

How well she understood him. And his friends. "Right you are."

A moment later she asked, "So did you meet with the fellows last night?"

He nodded. "At White's."

"Did you play faro? Aldridge was excessively fond of faro—before he became the serious man he now is."

"I did not play last night. I am attempting to gain my grandmother's approval. She hears of all my evil doings."

"Because they usually get reported in the newspapers."

He nodded. "I suppose I should do as you suggested in our initial meeting and bribe the papers to keep out news of my wicked deeds."

She nodded.

Were she as didactic as his grandmother, she would have said, "It would be better to quit the wicked deeds than to pay to keep them from being reported." Thank God the woman he'd married wasn't some authoritarian harpy. In his wildest dreams he could not imagine Maggie telling him what he should and should not do. He rather liked that about her.

Now that she had asked about his night, he supposed he should ask about hers. He drew in a breath. "What about your night last night? What did you do?"

She shrugged. "Not much. But I assure you I reveled in having the house—my very own house of which I shall be mistress—all to myself. I've never been where I'm not surrounded by siblings." She directed a gentle gaze at him. "Though I would never consider your presence an intrusion."

Her words softened something inside him.

Then they reached the coach maker's on the Strand.

* * *

How she adored being a married woman! Just to ride alone in the coach with him with nary a chaperon in sight was sheer pleasure. She could pretend to herself they were truly a happy married couple.

And now being able to make all the selections for her very own coach was thrilling, definitely something a younger sister three years removed from the schoolroom rarely had the opportunity to do.

The coach maker, recognizing the Finchleys as Quality, extended them all the courtesies due to their rank. When he was called away for a moment, she whispered to her husband. "Pray, have we enough money for that coach he just showed us?"

"Thanks to your dowry, we do. Please, select exactly what you'd like."

Because it was just a family of two—and she was cognizant that it would usually be just a family of one—she did not need the largest, most luxurious of the coaches. Besides, it was not her nature to make a selection that might call attention to herself. She preferred something modest.

When the coach maker returned, Margaret pointed to a coach that was neither cheap nor expensive.

John gave her a quizzing look. "You're sure? It's awfully plain. You can have whatever your heart desires."

"This suits me very well."

"In that case, milady, I can have yours made up and delivered week after next," the coach maker said.

"Can I have the seats covered with pale blue velvet?" she asked.

"Indeed ye can. A very good choice, milady."

When they left the coach maker's, John offered her his arm, and she gloried in the thrill of possession when she linked her arm with his. As happy as it made her, she found herself wondering if this marriage would ever be consummated, found herself wondering if she and John would ever have a child. Would they ever be a real husband and wife?

Once back in his grandmother's coach, he asked, "Is there somewhere I can drop you?"

She nodded. "Back to Berkeley Square. To see my family."

"I suspect your sister Caroline was dreadfully cut up over your . . . marriage?"

She nodded again. "She wept all day yesterday."

He was silent for a moment. "As close as you two are, I expect she knows about the coincidence that brought us together?"

"I've told no one about that."

"Then what did you tell her?"

She shrugged. "Very little. I could not lie."

He groaned. "Then I daresay she cried all day because you've united yourself to one of the most notorious rakes in London."

How could she respond? Margaret knew half of Caro's woes were due to the sisters' separation and the other half due to her worries about Margaret marrying so wicked a man.

Her silence must have pricked at his conscience. "I daresay she thinks I'm a greedy fortune hunter."

She still could not respond.

Moments later, his voice softened. "Would it help if I go meet this sister of yours and play the devoted husband?"

She was powerless to suppress a smile as her gaze met his. "Would you? Now?"

He shrugged. "Anything to keep my reputation from sinking any lower in her eyes—and, of course, if it pleases you, I shall think every moment spent at Aldridge House worthwhile."

If it pleases you. How sweet that sounded. Even sweeter was the prospect of her husband pretending to be devoted to her.

How pathetic she was that pretense must take the place of true affection.

$\mathcal{C}$hapter 8

He wasn't precisely sure how one feigned being the devoted husband, but if it would bring pleasure to the meek little thing he'd married, he would attempt to play the part—and try not to think of the auction at Tattersall's that he'd be missing. He only hoped Perry didn't bid on that gelding John had his eye on. It was just the kind of thing Perry would do. How he loved to lord it over his aristocratic friends, using his hefty purse to take possession of things others desired. Whether he needed them or not.

Perhaps John could breeze into Aldridge House and quickly demonstrate a particular attachment to Maggie, then manage to make Tatt's before the gelding came up for bid.

As they entered Maggie's former home, he drew in a breath and settled a possessive hand at her waist. There was little that was more distasteful to him than marriage, but he was grateful Maggie had extricated him from his financial woes and asked for so little in return. She merely wanted others to respect her position as his countess. With a home and bedchamber of her own. It wasn't much to ask.

She certainly did not deserve for others, especially those who loved her, to think she was nothing more than a dowry. He must show her sister that she was valued for herself, not her fortune.

A most aged butler let them into Aldridge House, and Maggie treated him as if he were some cherished grandfather. Then the newly married pair began to mount the stairs when a young woman who looked remarkably like Maggie came running down the stairs. She threw herself onto Maggie, and the two embraced as if they hadn't seen each other in years.

"I must properly introduce you to my husband." Maggie turned to him and smiled. "This is Caroline."

"She's just as pretty as you." He felt deuced awkward telling her she was pretty, but it was the bloody truth. And it *did* demonstrate his attachment. Which was a very good thing. Couldn't have them all thinking him a bloody fortune hunter. "You two look almost like twins. Which is the elder?"

"I am," Maggie said.

"Though everyone thinks I am. I've been told I have the domineering personality of a firstborn."

Smiling, Maggie nodded to him. "She does."

He took Maggie's hand in his. Just as he had that day at St. George's. Only today it felt different. Of course, she was no longer a stranger. Though he knew so little of her, he hadn't known which was the elder sister.

They went to the drawing room, and he made it a point to sit beside Maggie as they continued holding hands. How was that for showing his devotion! Once Caroline sat opposite them, for effect, he lifted Maggie's hand to his mouth and pressed a soft kiss on top it.

To his amazement, she squeezed his hand.

Now, why had she gone and done that? It wasn't as if her sister could see such an action. He supposed she was merely showing her gratitude that he was willing to pretend to be a caring husband. More than caring, actually. How could he not care for sweet Maggie? But caring for someone was altogether different than wishing to be married to one.

His mission here today was to make Caroline believe that he wished to be married to Maggie.

His glance flicked to the clock on the mantelpiece. One o'clock. The auctions would be starting now. If he was not mistaken, the gelding wasn't to be offered until close to the end. Perhaps there was still time to hurry there. The horse was such a beauty!

"The dowager Lady Finchley is to give a ball for us next week," Maggie informed her sister.

Caroline's gaze went from their clasped hands to his face. It was quite remarkable how much the two sisters resembled, though he thought Maggie prettier.

The sister eyed him, hostility in her demeanor. "I cannot recall ever before seeing you at a ball, my Lord."

"Don't like them."

"But now that you're married," Caroline said, "I hope your interests will be changing."

How in the devil would he answer that? He couldn't very well lie. The fact was, he had no intentions of changing his interests. "I am a different man. As an only child, I've always had only myself to consider. Now I have to consider Maggie's feelings." He was rather proud of the way he had responded.

Lady Caroline's eyes widened, her brows

elevated. A look of sheer mortification emblazoned itself on her face. "*Maggie?* No one has ever called my sister by such a name."

Margaret smiled up at him. "It's a name my dear husband has chosen for me. No one else is to use it."

Dear husband? She was laying in on rather too thickly. How he hated the sound of it. He didn't want to be anybody's husband, much less someone's *dear* husband.

Caroline was uncharacteristically silent. After a long pause, she finally spoke. "I should hope no one else uses that name! I, for one, shall never use it!"

More silence followed. A pity Maggie was such a quiet thing, and a pity he had not the slightest idea how to speak to this sister of hers, who was unable to conceal her dislike of him. "Maggie Mine, you must tell your sister about the new carriage." Good Lord, why had he added that word *mine*? He continued to astonish himself.

He must own, such an endearment should go some distance in convincing the critical Lady Caroline that he wasn't a bloody fortune hunter.

Lady Caroline's hostile gaze went from him to her sister.

"John and I have just come from the coach maker's where we've ordered a new coach for my use."

"Your very own coach! I shall be very jealous."

"It will be at your disposal since I plan to share every day with you as I always have." His wife glanced at the clock, then she turned to him. "Dearest, is there not somewhere else you should be at present?"

How in the devil had she known about

Tattersall's? "I will own, I had planned to go to Tatt's, but your needs and wishes must come first." What had induced him to say that? He certainly had no intentions of lying. Ever. Oddly, he realized he had spoken the truth. He was far from being in love with Maggie, but pleasing her was vastly important to him.

She squeezed his hand. "Then it is my wish that you go to Tattersall's."

He squeezed her hand, stood, then addressed Lady Caroline. "It has been a pleasure to make your acquaintance, and I hope to see you at the ball."

She offered a stiff smile. "I shall be there."

Then he turned back to Maggie, and bent to brush a kiss across her cheek. "Until your new coach is delivered, Grandmere won't object to you using hers. She rarely goes about anymore."

"Thank you."

He strode toward the door.

Maggie called out after him. "John?"

He turned.

"I should love to know if you get the horse you want."

The woman can read my mind. Most frightening.

He hoped to God now that he'd placated her once she wasn't going to demand that he dance attendance upon her. Did she expect him to rush home from Tatt's to share his good—or bad—news with her? He had no intentions of rushing home to her from the auction. He and Knowles would be at Angelo's practicing their fencing later in the afternoon.

Yet as he watched her sitting there with a hopeful look on her sweet face, he couldn't disappoint. Besides, he meant to convince the prickly sister that he was not some lout. "Then see that a place is laid for me at the dinner table tonight."

As he left Maggie's former home, he tried to recall the last time he had actually eaten dinner at Finchley House. It had been years. But what would it hurt? It wasn't as if he planned to spend the night with her. He and the fellows had other plans. Plans that most certainly did not include her.

He walked past Grandmere's carriage that he'd insisted Maggie use. He would walk to Tatt's. As he moved along Piccadilly, he could not free his thoughts of Maggie. How in the devil had she known about his bloody interest in the gelding? He'd not told her. He'd told her damned little about himself. And it wasn't as if she knew the bloods with whom he associated, bloods who could have told her of his interest in the gelding.

It was deuced uncomfortable to think of her intruding on his thoughts.

* * *

Margaret was still tingling inside after her husband left. He'd actually called her Maggie *Mine*! It wasn't a huge declaration. It wasn't the same as being in love with her. But to her it was thrilling. Knowing of his intrinsic honesty, she reveled in the words. *Maggie Mine*. She was his! He knew she was his!

She felt as if he'd just placed the first brick into the foundation upon which their marriage was to be built. There was a lot of work ahead, but she was heartened that they'd made a start.

"I must own," Caro said icily, "your husband wasn't nearly as obnoxious as I'd expected him to be."

Margaret glared at the sister she adored. "I pray you never again use such a word in connection with my husband."

Caro sighed. "I know why you're so beastly in love with fellow. He *is* sinfully handsome."

"I know. I've peered out the window at him for years." Now she could finally be openly honest with her sister. Now that there was nothing Caro could do to prevent the marriage.

"You truly are happy being married to Lord Finchley?"

"I couldn't be happier." Except she could. True happiness could not come until she held John's affections. Would she go to her grave without winning his love?

"Then I must be happy for you. I'm certainly envious of your coach. You make me now regret all those proposals of marriage I've turned down." Caro sighed. "Now that I've lost you, I shall have to accept the next man who offers. Provided he is handsome. And titled."

"Copy cat."

Both sisters laughed.

"Seriously," Margaret said, "It's good that you've not accepted any of the men who've offered for you. You must wait until your dragon-slaying knight comes. I know he will. You must marry for love."

Caro's eyes misted as she regarded her sister. "I believe you really do love Finchley. How could you keep such a strong attachment from me?"

"I knew you would disapprove. Because of his reputation."

Caro nodded. "I don't see when you two could have gotten together. I've spent every day of my life with you."

"All I can say is that the fates brought me together with the man I adored at just the right moment. Now, my dear sister, shall we take the dowager's coach to Madam Duvall's on Conduit Street? I, for one, fancy a stunning new gown for my *bridal* ball."

* * *

When he arrived at Tatt's, his gelding had just come up. Perry was standing in the front row, eying John's horse. John raced through the packed crowd and was winded when he reached Perry's side. "Don't you dare."

The two men's eyes locked. Perry shrugged. "You abuse me. I only meant to assure that that magnificent beast comes into your possession."

"Friends we may be, but you're not above claiming something I want."

"He's right, old chap." It was then that John saw David Arlington standing to Perry's left. "Remember when Finch was prepared to take that Cyprian—what was her name?" He eyed Perry.

Perry glared. "Winnie."

Arlington smirked. "How could I forget? As soon as you knew Finch meant to take her under his protection, you promised her a much heftier allowance."

John shrugged. "You must own that once Perry had installed her in luxurious lodgings, he gave me leave to . . . have her to my heart's content."

"Your heart, old fellow, was not the part of your anatomy directing you to Willing Winnie." Arlington grinned. "Speaking of hearts, how's the marriage going?"

Just then, the auctioneer began praising John's gelding. "Gentlemen, we've saved the best for last. One can look far and wide and never find a horse to match this." John's attention darted to the gelding. What a fine-looking beast it was. Its noble lineage was evident in its perfect symmetry and graceful gait. All eyes were drawn to the rich brown gelding with four white feet.

"Not only has this gelding been bred for speed," the auctioneer said, "but ye'll not find its equal for grace and beauty."

Though he did not want to appear too eager, John was anxious to take possession of such a creature. When the auctioneer picked up the gavel and said, "Who will give me fifty quid?" John's hand was the first to go up. Then he glared at Perry.

Perry shrugged. One competing bidder eliminated.

"Fifty-five," shouted Lord Elsworth.

The two peers continued bidding against one another.

When the price went above eighty guineas, a roar of voices rose from the crowd. It wasn't every day a single horse merited so high a value.

"Eighty-five to Lord Finchley," the auctioneer said.

Then, nodding to the other man, he said "Ninety to Lord Elsworth."

"One hundred," John shouted.

The crowd went deadly silent. All eyes moved to Lord Elsworth, who shook his head. "I'll bloody well never pay a hundred guineas for any beast!"

John, who had managed to lure back his former groom and coachman, entrusted his new horse to his groom. He and his three friends wished to celebrate John's purchase over several bottles of brandy at White's.

Once they gathered around their usual table, Knowles joined them. His brows lowered, and he looked troubled.

"Something the matter?" John asked.

Knowles nodded. "Did none of you see this morning's newspaper?"

Perry shook his head. John shook his head. Arlington said, "Seeing the newspaper and reading it are two entirely different things. I could barely focus my eyes when I left my bed."

"Pray, what was in it?" John asked.

"George Weatherford has died. His name was listed among the casualties in Spain. He was an officer in the 11th Light Dragoons."

John felt as if he'd been kicked in the gut. He was only vaguely aware of the groans and utterances of sympathy from his friends. Everyone had liked George Weatherford.

Weatherford was the same age as he, and they'd known each other since they came up to Eton at age eight or nine. The two had not been close like he always had been with Perry, Arlington, and Knowles, but they shared a mutual respect for one another.

Weatherford was more serious and less affluent than the others, but John admired his intelligence and kindliness. And he was a slap-dash fine cricket player.

Later, when John and his friends had gone up to Oxford, Weatherford's family bought him colours, and he went off to the Peninsula.

It did seem as if John had heard that Weatherford had married. It was just like him to settle into marriage. He'd never been one to enjoy the same things John and his friends enjoyed. How had Grandmere stated it? Wine, women, and faro.

As the only aristocrat in their wing at school, John had always been accorded respect from his fellow students. Weatherford was especially in awe of him.

John set down his glass of brandy and rose to his feet, shaking his head. "I no longer feel like celebrating. 'Tis a bloody, bloody bad piece of news."

He left White's and began to walk to Cavendish Square. To his home.

Not even the prospect of taking ownership of the gelding could lift his spirits on so somber a day.

* * *

He was mildly disappointed that Maggie had not returned. As much as he did not want to share his house with a blasted female, there was something comforting about having someone to talk to when one came home.

Not that he and Maggie had ever really talked. Of the four times they'd been together, only once had she actually spoken much: the day she persuaded him to allow her to pretend this was a real marriage.

He found himself going to the library. What was coming over him? He never wanted to be in a chamber filled with books.

But Maggie did. After all these years, the Finchley library was finally going to be used.

Perhaps the reason he'd come here was because being around these books reminded him of Weatherford. They had helped each other translate an obscure Ovid poem from Latin into English.

John was so unfamiliar with the library he was

not sure where the Romans were shelved, but in a few moments he located two volumes of Ovid in crimson leather, their lettering etched in gold. He sighed, took one of them, and went to the sofa near the fire. For some unexplainable reason, he wanted to find that poem again.

Before five minutes had passed the chamber door burst open. He looked up to see Maggie standing there, a broad smile on her face. "You're home early! I hope you've good news." As soon as she spoke she must have discerned from his expression that he was in low spirits.

Her brows lowered, and she moved to him and spoke in a gentle voice. "I'm so sorry. You didn't get your horse?"

"I got it." His gaze dropped.

"Something's wrong."

He nodded. "An old friend of mine was killed."

She gasped and dropped onto the sofa beside him. "I'm so terribly sorry."

Neither of them spoke for a moment.

"I suppose you didn't feel like celebrating your purchase once you received such terrible news."

How in the devil had she known he and his friends were drinking to his good fortune in winning the gelding? Was she spying on him? He solemnly nodded.

"Can you tell me about your friend?"

It was a moment before he could speak. "His name was George Weatherford. He was an officer in the Peninsula."

"How tragic."

"I met him when I went to Eton."

"So he was a young man. Your age?"

He nodded.

"I hope he didn't leave a widow," she said

solemnly, "But for his sake, I suppose I hope he did find love and happiness before his life was cut short."

Oddly, despite his own aversion to marriage, John found merit in her sentiment. He hoped to God Weatherford had found happiness in marriage. He was just the sort of solid chap who would. "We'd lost touch with each other in recent years, but it seems as if I'd heard he did marry. I pray it was a happy marriage."

"Now," she said brightly, flashing a smile at him. "I wish you would tell me about your horse."

She did know how to lift his spirits. Not that any bloody horse was anywhere near as valued as an old friend. He eyed her. "It's as fine a beast as I've ever seen. A gelding."

"What colour?"

"Dark brown. With four white ankles."

"Oh, he sounds beautiful."

"Not exactly a he."

Colour stole into her cheeks. Neither of them spoke for a moment.

"I wanted to thank you for your extreme kindness to me in front of Caro."

"You don't have to thank me. I was only doing what any husband ought to do." Not that he wanted to be a husband. "Did I succeed in lessening your sister's loathing of me?"

"My sister doesn't dislike you. She merely worries about me."

"With good cause. Am I not the most profligate rake in all of London?" He cocked a smile.

"You said I couldn't believe that rot one reads in the newspapers."

He smiled. This wife of his did have a way of lifting his low spirits.

$\mathcal{C}$hapter 9

Margaret, Caroline, their sister Clair, and the duchess all descended upon Number 7 Trent Square the following day. Carter, the house's steward who'd formerly been a footman at Aldridge House, let them in. Seconds later, the youthful, widowed Mrs. Hudson, who had taken it upon herself to be the home's resident matriarch, happily greeted them. "Should you like me to send the children to the music room now, Lady Margaret, or do you fancy a cuddle with Mikey first?"

Did everyone at Trent Square know how completely besotted Margaret was over the adorable little toddler?

"My sister is no longer Lady Margaret," Caro snapped. "She's now Lady Finchley." From her tone, Caro sounded as if she were still unhappy over Margaret's unexpected marriage.

Mrs. Hudson whirled at Margaret and smiled. "Felicitations on your nuptials, my lady. That's very exciting."

Margaret smiled. "Yes, it is awfully, and yes, you may summon the children. I do hope Louisa has recovered from her fever."

Mrs. Hudson managed a smile. "She's not recovered yet, but at least the fever is past. Last night was the first night she hasn't been burning with fever."

"Oh, you poor dear," Margaret said. Louisa was Mrs. Hudson's only child, and Margaret knew how worried the mother had been about her. "I suspect you've not slept much this week."

"You sound exactly like Carter. He offered to stay up with Louisa the night before last so I could finally get some sleep, but I knew I wouldn't be able to close my eyes for worrying about my little one—even though he promised that if there were any change or if Louisa called for me, he would knock loudly upon my chamber door."

Whether Mrs. Hudson knew it or not, the house's handsome steward Abraham Carter was in love with her, and he also adored her little girl in the same way a father would. Margaret thought too that whether she knew it or not, Mrs. Hudson was falling in love with him. Poor Mrs. Hudson had known her share of pain. She deserved happiness. Now if only the two could get together.

Abraham, too, deserved happiness. It was devilishly difficult for Margaret to think of her family's former footman as anything other than Abraham. She was ever so proud of how hard he had worked to "better" himself, of how much all the children at Trent Square loved him, of how efficiently he kept Number 7 moving. She could not remember when a servant had ever commanded such respect.

But then she realized that to these widows and their children, Abraham Carter was *not* a servant. He was like an engaging uncle, a caring father, and a jack-of-all-trades all rolled into one and put on this earth to keep their lives running smoothly.

"I fear several of the other children have caught Louisa's malady," Mrs. Hudson continued. "Only

Peter and Sarah will come to you today."

Margaret's brows lowered. "The poor dears. Should you like me to send for an apothecary?"

The widow shook her head. "I don't think that will be necessary at this time, but many thanks for your kind offer." Mrs. Hudson then faced Clair and smiled. "I was so impressed to see you named in the newspapers, Lady Clair, and with such a famous person! The right honorable Richard Rothcomb-Smedley."

Clair looked inordinately pleased. "He's a wonderful man, to be sure."

"Is it true he will be Chancellor of the Exchequer before he's thirty?"

Clair shrugged. "We certainly hope so. He's worked very hard."

A pity he'd not yet offered for Clair, Margaret thought. They were not only perfectly suited for one another, they also held each other with the greatest affection.

Perhaps after learning about the thirty thousand Lord Finchley received upon marrying a Ponsby sister, Mr. Rothcomb-Smedley would beg for Clair's hand. As a younger son, he could certainly use Clair's fortune.

Mrs. Hudson regarded Margaret from beneath lowered brows. "I believe I've read about your Lord Finchley in the papers, too, but I cannot remember in what context. Is he also in Parliament?"

To Margaret's consternation, her sisters began to laugh. Her eyes narrowed as she glared at them, then addressed the widow. "No, my husband is not yet in Parliament, and he's told me not to believe the wicked things that are printed about him in the newspapers, and I beg that none of you will, either." She stalked to the stairways and began mounting them.

"Oh, I almost forgot to tell you our own wondrous news," Mrs. Hudson said.

Margaret turned back around.

"Mrs. Nye will be leaving us."

"I fail to see what's wondrous about that," Caro snapped.

"She's to remarry. It seems one of the gentlemen in the village where she was raised was always smitten with her, and once he learned of her widowhood, he began calling on her. They're to marry after the banns have been posted, then he'll be taking her to her new home."

"I'm very happy for her," the duchess said. "And that will mean there will be room for one more family."

"We're all very happy for her. We understand her Mr. Miller has a bit of property and a solid old manor house."

"That is good news indeed," Margaret said. "It's my hope that all of you can find such happiness as Mrs. Nye."

Mrs. Hudson's brows lowered. "I should feel a traitor to my dear Harry."

Margaret stepped back and settled a reassuring hand upon the widow's shoulder. "From what I've learned of your late husband, I'm sure he would want you to find love again, to be happy. You and Louisa."

Surely Mrs. Hudson's loyalty to her dead husband was not the obstacle that was keeping her from finding happiness with Abraham. What a serious impediment it was to any budding romance with Abraham. She turned back and climbed the stairs.

* * *

"Now that you're in funds, old boy," Perry said, "What do you say to playing whist for twenty quid a rubber?"

John smiled. "It's been a while since I've been able to do that."

He and his three closest friends were sitting at their usual table at White's. Knowles' brows lowered, and he set a hand on John's arm. "Do you not think the Duke of Aldridge will learn of it? If I were you, I'd be more cautious. The duke's a man whose wrath you don't want."

"Don't listen to him," Perry said.

"It's not as if I'm going to lose the whole thirty thousand. What will it hurt to lose a few quid here and there? Besides," he said, flashing a smile to his most serious friend, "I could win."

Arlington regarded him with a quizzing expression. "You *have* paid back Lord Bastingham?"

John swallowed. He hated to think of the sizeable chunk of Maggie's dowry that had gone to repay Bastingham for former losses. He nodded gravely.

Perry called for pasteboards.

"Perhaps we should start a bit lower than twenty quid a rubber," John suggested.

Arlington chuckled. "I see marriage is already having a maturing effect upon Finch."

"Marriage has nothing to do with it," John spit out. "I just prefer not to alienate the Duke of Aldridge. I have reason to believe he despises me already."

"No one could ever despise you," Knowles said, his voice surprisingly gentle. "I remember how poor old Weatherford idolized you. He used to say you were the most down-to-earth, kindly aristocrat he'd ever known. He thought of you as a true friend."

"And I, him," John said over the huge lump in his throat.

"Enough maudlin talk," Perry snapped. "How about ten quid a rubber?"

Arlington shrugged. "How about five? It's a long way till quarter day."

"By the way," John said, "I shall expect to see each of you at my grandmother's ball Friday."

Perry rolled his eyes and frowned. "I'll be there."

"I wouldn't miss it," Knowles said. "I'm anxious to see this wife of yours."

"Me, too," Arlington chimed. "I have to see for myself. How could Finch have ended up with a lady of fortune *and* beauty? The woman obviously doesn't read the newspapers."

"Is she as tolerable looking as Perry says she is?" Knowles asked John.

John would be pleased if they found her comely. "I expect she's prettier." He was still puzzled at how such a fine lady would consider plighting her life to his. One with her attributes could have anyone she wanted.

* * *

The night of the ball arrived.

One night and one night only was Margaret assured of spending the evening with her husband, and she meant to make the best of it. As soon as John's grandmother had announced the ball, she and Caro had gone to the dressmaker's, where Margaret commissioned the loveliest gown she had ever possessed.

Madame Duvall had called it a bridal dress,

which Margaret thought most appropriate. A striped French gauze fell gently over a white satin slip, and the bottom of the frock featured deep flounces of Brussels lace wreathed with pale pink satin roses. Margaret thought the bodice particularly flattering. As was the custom, it was very low—but not so low as to lose respectability—and it was embroidered with more of the pink flowers and elegant leaves. Her shoulders would be completely exposed, but she'd been told her shoulders were most graceful. She enjoyed the good fortune of possessing extremely pale skin that was free of blemishes, so she thought perhaps her flatterers had been right. Just off her shoulders the delicate fabric puffed over her upper arms like a pair of clouds.

Caro had been exceedingly jealous. "It is quite the prettiest dress I have ever beheld. There's nothing for it but I shall have to marry and commission a so-called *bridal* dress every bit as beautiful."

"A very poor reason to marry," Margaret had said with disdain.

Now Caro was back at Aldridge House getting ready for the ball, and Margaret and her maid had spent hours on her toilette. She had slipped into white satin slippers and long white gloves made of French kid. She smiled as she unfurled the beautiful hand-painted fan Elizabeth had given her as a wedding gift. Dear, thoughtful Elizabeth. It was the only wedding gift she had received, she lamented. She hated that her family was so opposed to John.

Perhaps tonight he could sway their opinions in a more positive direction.

Even more important, perhaps she could sway

his attentions in a more desirable direction.

"Oh, my dear Annie," she said to her maid, "I do believe my hair has never looked so lovely."

"Thank you, my lady. I tried to make it look exactly like the lady in Akermann's."

Margaret's gaze went to a torn sheet from last August's Akermann's that featured a beautifully coiffed lady of fashion. For some time she had been saving that picture, wanting to have her hair styled in the very same fashion, but she had been waiting for an important event.

Nothing could be more important than tonight.

Then she eyed her reflection in the looking glass, comparing it to the Akermann's image. Annie was a true gem. She had pinned up Margaret's hair in the exact same fashion, and it was most becoming with its irregular curls in the Eastern style and bound with a strand of tiny pink flowers made of silk.

She chose simple pearls for her necklace and earrings.

Will he even notice me? She stood and peered into her looking glass. If he did not admire her tonight, the man was hopeless. Though normally modest, tonight Margaret thought herself exceedingly handsome. She found herself wondering, what did his opera dancers have that she did not.

Well . . . it did not bear contemplation. She had told him he was free to cavort with women of that sort, but she had not countenanced how painful to her it would be if he did so.

She heard heavy footsteps in the corridor outside her bedchamber, then a solid knock. Whoever could it be? "Yes?" she asked.

"It's Finchley, er, I mean John Edward, or

John."

Her heartbeat pounded. Her palms went wet. Her throat dried. "Come in," she managed in a shaky voice.

Already dressed for the evening's festivities and sinfully handsome in jet black, he strolled into her chamber, a velvet box in his hands. He was looking down at the box rather than at her. "I've brought you some of the Finchley jewels Grandmere sent over this afternoon." Then he looked up at her.

He stopped in his stride as if he'd suddenly become rooted to the floral carpet, and he gawked at her with widened eyes.

She felt the slow, lingering sweep of his gaze and could not have felt more mortified had she been standing there stripped of every article of her clothing. Why was he so silent? Would he see how terribly she trembled?

She was powerless to keep her own gaze from perusing him. Though there was still something of the carefree youth about him, tonight he exuded a manliness with his imposing height and his lantern jaw that was ever so lightly shadowed with dark stubble. He would have made a splendid dark knight of yore.

He seemed so imposing. Especially here in this feminine bedchamber. Her heartbeat thundered at the very notion that he was actually standing in her bedchamber.

Another barrier destroyed, another brick laid.

Finally he spoke again. "By Jove, Maggie, you look awfully fetching tonight."

And she felt the air swish from where it had been trapped in her lungs.

$\mathcal{C}$hapter 10

She looked like Maggie, yet she didn't. The elegant woman standing there rendered him nearly speechless. When he'd strolled into her bedchamber, he'd been much more interested in seeing her reaction to the jewels than in seeing her. He hadn't a thought in his head about how she might appear.

He'd known she was possessed of tolerable good looks and excellent taste in clothing, but he'd not considered how much different one looked in a pastel morning frock than one looked in an exquisite ball gown. He was completely unprepared to gawk upon those creamy ivory shoulders, but that is exactly what he found himself doing. And he was powerless to stop from gazing at the heavenly swell of breasts that dipped into the fragile silk of her stunning dress.

He had become startlingly aware of her as a woman. And it made him feel deuced uncomfortable to be in the lady's bedchamber.

Though he'd been incapable of speech, his slow perusal of her detected a slight trembling. Was she nervous? Their eyes connected. He'd never seen so vulnerable an expression as hers at that moment. It suddenly occurred to him she needed to be told how beautiful she looked. How could she possibly doubt it? Only a blind person could fail to see her exceptional loveliness tonight. So he'd blurted out how lovely she looked. He'd never spoken more true words, yet they made him feel awkward.

"Thank you," she shyly responded.

All thoughts of his own temporary discomfort vanished with his concern for her. "I say, Maggie, you'll be the absolute belle of the ball."

"It *is* our ball. I wanted a special gown just for it."

"I've never seen anything prettier." *Than you.* Of course, he had to own, his experience with ball dress was limited, owing to his long-standing absence from such activities. "Now, shall we see if these Finchley jewels will do it justice? Will you allow me to remove the pearls?"

"Please do." Her gaze whisked to the velvet box.

"Permit me to show you the diamonds first." He opened the box.

She gushed her enthusiasm. After many declarations on their loveliness, she said, "How honored I shall be to wear something so exquisite."

"Grandmere says these are the best of the lot, and she was hoping you'd wear them tonight."

Her eyes widened. "I'm incredibly honored." She did not sound one bit like the haughty daughter of a duke.

He unfastened the pearl necklace as she removed the earrings. "It's I who am honored," he said. "I shall be escorting the most beautiful woman at the ball." He suddenly realized he meant every word. In fact, he was greatly looking forward to introducing the lovely lady to Arlington and Knowles. And even if Perry had seen her before, John knew Perry would be dazzled by the way she looked tonight. He rather fancied moving about Grandmere's ballroom with so lovely a creature on his arm.

He fastened the magnificent diamond necklace at her elegant neck and stood back to observe.

Thank God that vulnerable look of a frightened child had been replaced by one of happiness. Was it the diamonds or his flattery that was responsible for the transformation?

"They're beautiful," she said in almost a reverent whisper.

He found himself clasping her by her elegant shoulders and peering into her eyes. "Not nearly as beautiful as you."

Their eyes briefly locked. Neither said another word. He was self conscious over his praise of her. In his six-and-twenty years he had never uttered those words to another woman. He'd certainly never thought to utter them to a duke's daughter! But, as always, he was guided by honesty.

He offered his arm. "Come, Lady Finchley. My grandmother has sent her carriage. She wanted us to arrive shortly before the guests."

* * *

It was the most wonderful ball ever! How proud she was to stand at the base of the dowager's broad staircase with the elderly lady at one side and John at the other as the three of them greeted their guests. How proud she was that all the *ton* knew he was her husband. How proud she was that her husband—at least in her eyes—was the most handsome man at the ball. *Their ball.*

She could not deny that John's lavish praise of her looks greatly contributed to her happiness. Knowing that he did not lie made his compliments even more treasured. She was thankful, too, that so many of the Aldridge and Haverstock family members came, including the Marchioness of Haverstock, whose babe was expected any day.

"How happy I am that you came," she said to Lady Haverstock. Margaret was far too shy to comment on the lady's impending confinement, even though she wished to tell her how much prospective . motherhood complemented her already legendary beauty. Lady Haverstock's huge dark eyes sparkled, and the happiness she exuded extended to all around her.

The Marquess could not conceal his delight with his wife. Settling a gentle arm about his marchioness's shoulders, he murmured as they walked away. "Come, my dearest, we must find a place for you to sit down."

Next up was Margaret's sister-in-law. The duchess and her spouse often accompanied her brother—Haverstock—along with his spouse. The small bump beneath the duchess's softly draped gown would not be discernible to those who had no knowledge the Aldridges were to be parents. As always, the Duchess of Aldridge was gracious, especially to John. "Welcome into the family, Lord Finchley. You are a most fortunate man to have secured Margaret's hand."

"Indeed I am," he responded.

Margaret's chest tightened when her grim-faced brother moved toward them. *Please let him be civil to John.* She held her breath as Aldridge came face to face with them. How mortified she would be if her brother spoke rudely to her spouse. "My dear Margaret, I have known you for your entire life, and you've never been more beautiful. Marriage must agree with you." He then flicked a glance at John. "Good evening, Finchley."

"Good evening, your grace."

The Duke and Duchess of Aldridge gave one last nod, then moved along and began to climb the stairs to the ballroom.

And Margaret almost swooned with relief. Though her brother had not been particularly amiable to John, he had said nothing to give offense.

Next was the duchess's sister, Lady Lydia Morgan, with her husband, whom everyone called Morgie. Since Lady Lydia disliked such functions and had an aversion to leaving her baby son, Margaret considered it an honor to receive them.

Morgie spoke first. "I say, you two are a most handsome couple." His gaze perused John. "Don't think I've ever seen you dressed for a ball before, Finchley."

Lady Lydia stepped up. "That's because, my dear husband, Lord Finchley has the same aversion to balls that I do. Do you not, my Lord?"

John cracked a smile. "That is true, but one must attend one's own ball." He eyed his wife. "And you must own it would be worth any sacrifice to be accompanied by such a lovely lady."

Margaret could feel the blush stealing into her cheeks.

Mr. Morgan nodded.

His wife spoke. "Lady Margaret—er, Lady Finchley—has always been lovely, but I do believe she's more beautiful than ever tonight. I daresay, being newly married and madly in love accounts for how agreeable you two look."

Margaret was too embarrassed to even steal a glance at John. "Thank you," was all she could say.

"You do dance, do you not, Finchley?" Morgie asked.

John shrugged. "Not in many, many years."

Morgie nodded. "Love to dance, meself. Lydia don't. I say, if you should need me to stand in and do the husbandly duty thing with Lady Finch- - - " A mortified look came over Morgie's face. "Pray, Lady Finchley, put your hand over your ears and do not ever listen to a thing I say."

Once again this night, Margaret felt the heat rise into her cheeks.

"Ah, but Mr. Morgan," John said, smoothly covering the awkward moment, "You must admit that dancing with one as lovely as Lady Finchley will be worth any embarrassment my dancing should cause."

"Oh, yes. Right you are," Morgie said, "Not that I believe your dancing would draw censure."

After the Morgans began to climb the stairs, John glanced at the open doorway, drew her hand into his, and murmured. "It appears that my three best friends have arrived."

Even though she had confidence in her appearance, she stiffened as if frozen with fear, when she realized she would soon be put on display to her husband's greatest friends. She did gather enough presence of mind to smile as the trio came forward.

Mr. Perry was the first to greet them. "Ah, Lady Finchley, allow me to say that your beauty robs me of breath."

She continued to favor him with a smile. "Thank you."

Next, John presented Michael Knowles to her. Like Mr. Perry, he was dressed impeccably. Both men were fine looking, and both were in possession of nearly black hair. Mr. Knowles was perhaps an inch or two shorter than Mr. Perry, but his slenderness made him appear the same height. "It is a pleasure to make your acquaintance, my lady, though I must say in the fifteen years I've known Lord Finchley, I've never been more envious."

She did not know how to respond. Was he jealous that John had married a duke's daughter, or was he jealous that John's wife was so lovely? The last thing she wanted to do was to come off as conceited. A humble, "Thank you," was her response. "I've been most anxious to meet John's dear friends."

David Arlington nudged Mr. Knowles toward the stairs so he could face Margaret. He was as tall as Knowles but a great deal more muscular. Like the others, he was possessed of agreeable looks. "I would say your loveliness robs me of breath, my lady, but Perry has already said that. I'd tell you how jealous I am of Finch, but Knowles beat me to that, too. Therefore, allow me to say that it is an honor to be invited here tonight to make your acquaintance." He then took her hand and actually pressed his lips to the glove. Their eyes locked for just a second before he moved on.

Her heart beat erratically. She was uncommonly embarrassed over the intimacy of Mr. Arlington kissing her hand. She was accustomed to men brushing the air over her hand with mock kisses, but never before had the kisses been the real thing. Even her husband had never taken such liberties!

As there was a brief lull in the guests, her

thoughts stayed on John's friends. How curious that all four of them were possessed of brown eyes. Though all of them were handsome, the other three could not compare to John.

* * *

"You, my dear grandson, will be expected to lead your wife onto the dance floor for a waltz the first dance of the night."

John's stomach dropped in the same way it did when he lost five-hundred quid to Lord Bastingham with one turn of a pasteboard. How mortified he would be to humiliate himself in front of the one-hundred-and-fifty people Grandmere had invited here tonight.

Even worse, what if he stepped upon Maggie's dainty feet? At two and twenty, she would have been dancing at balls and assemblies for at least three years. No doubt, she was a graceful, accomplished dancer and had danced with dozens—if not hundreds—of men who were very light on their feet. Would his inferior dancing embarrass her? What if his ineptitude repulsed her? He already had so many other vices to prejudice one against him.

He turned to her and drew a breath. "Be forewarned that my dancing begs improvement. I just pray I don't tread upon your feet."

She smiled up at him, a much warmer, more spontaneous smile that she'd directed at that damned Arlington when he'd made a cake of himself smushing his lips to her hand. "Don't spare it a thought. I assure you my feet have been trod upon many a time, and I shan't mind if you do."

He recalled what she'd said that first day she'd come to him to propose they act like a man and wife. She'd said, "*We'll be true and loyal friends to one another.*" At this moment, he realized they *had* become true and loyal friends. She did not cast judgment on him. She accepted him for who and what he was.

He took her hand and lightly pressed a kiss to the back of it—something he had never done before. "You're too kind, my dearest." The *my dearest* he threw in for his grandmother's sake, as she still stood beside them, staring affectionately at them as if they were the king and queen. "I daresay no one will be watching my steps when my wife's loveliness will draw everyone's attention."

A few minutes later the orchestra struck up a waltz, and he turned to Maggie. "It will be my honor to dance with you."

He was exceedingly nervous as they moved onto the dance floor, all eyes on them. When they reached the center of the wooden dancing surface, he settled one hand at her waist, then clasped her hand with his other. As they came closer, he was pleasantly suffused with her sweet rose scent. "I know you'll make me look as if I know what I'm doing," he said as they began to dance.

At first he was self-conscious over his moves, over the way he held her, over the possibility he might make a complete ass of himself. He could not help but be struck immediately over how gracefully she moved. She danced so smoothly and with such practiced ease, he did not have to concentrate on what he was doing. It was not long before she made him forget his nervousness by engaging him in conversation. "I am so happy to no longer be a spinster, to have to stand up with every eligible man who asks."

He recalled her telling him of how heartily sick she was of being courted by fortune hunters. Even though he had happily accepted her generous dowry, she at least knew he had not courted her for her fortune. Which in an odd way made him feel absolved of at least one misdeed. Of course, he hadn't courted her at all.

Yet now here they were. *Married.*

The word still rankled him. But she did not. "It's a great loss to all the unmarried men in the *ton* that it was my good fortune to wed you."

"You will embarrass me, my Lord, with your flattery." While other coy misses might pretend to be embarrassed at flattery, Maggie was sincere.

He could not discuss unmarried men and not think of his friends. He was pleased that the three of them saw Maggie as she looked tonight, pleased that they praised her. But that damned Arlington had carried it too far! John would have to speak to him.

It occurred to him that because his friends knew his and Maggie's was not a regular marriage, those friends might get it in their heads that Maggie was available for their . . . their attentions! The very thought made him angry. Yes, indeed, he would have to speak to Arlington.

She looked up at him with shimmering eyes, light from three huge chandeliers illuminating her face. "I am happy to be Lady Finchley."

He was happy that she was happy. But he was not happy that she was Lady Finchley. He had never wanted a wife. *Never.* Would the day ever come when he was comfortable with the notion that he was a married man?

He had to own that if one must be married, one could not find a sweeter mate than Maggie. He squeezed her hand. "Given all my faults, that is very good of you to say."

"Oh, but you've told me not to believe the scandalous things that are written about you in the newspapers."

"Daresay that's excellent advice."

A moment later she said, "Your friends could not have been nicer to me."

A bit too nice. "You have bedazzled them."

She giggled. "I've never been accused of bedazzling a man before."

"That's because it's the kind of praise whispered behind one's back. Few admirers would admit to the bedazzler that they were bedazzled."

"I rather like the notion of being a bedazzler."

"Well, Lady Bedazzler, I suppose you'll have to stand up with each of them tonight. I should warn you. There's not a skilled dancer in the lot."

"You put too much importance upon dancing skill. I know of no lady who's swayed by something as shallow as that." She shrugged, sighing, as she looked up at him. "May I suggest you stand up with Caro?"

He stiffened. "I suppose good breeding would prevent her from turning me down, though I know your sister wishes me to Coventry."

"That's not true." She peered up at him with a mock pout. "It's your mission to *bedazzle* my sister."

"A pity your brother cannot be bedazzled!"

"Did you not hear him say that marriage must wonderfully agree with me? It was Aldridge's stiff way of welcoming you."

"Would that it were- - -" His step abruptly halted. By God, he'd crushed her foot beneath his. She winced but said nary a word. He peered down at her with concern. "Have I hurt you?"

She shook her head.

She was probably being polite. "Are you certain?"

"I've had much fatter men than you accidentally tread on me and have yet to suffer a broken bone."

"I shall have to call them out."

His comment caused them both to laugh.

The sweet tones from the violins were fading away. The dance would soon be ended. "I must tell you what an uncommonly good dancer you are," he said.

She giggled. "You, my Lord, would not know if one was *uncommonly* good at dancing or not, given that dancing has never been a skill you exercise."

She had him there. "Perhaps I shall poll my friends—after they dance with you—to see how they would rate your dancing abilities."

"I beg that you don't."

They stopped when the music trailed off. He was vaguely aware that he would much rather remain dancing with Maggie than have to move about the chamber speaking to all these boring people, most of whom were married. He offered her his arm and patted her hand when she settled it upon his sleeve.

Even before they had cleared the ballroom floor, Arlington approached Maggie. "I shall be prostrate if you do not do me the goodness of standing up with me, my lady."

Her gaze went from the worshipful Arlington to John.

"Since it is NOT to be a waltz," John said, glaring at his friend. "I will allow you to dance with my wife."

Arlington regarded John from beneath an arched brow, his lips curved into a smirk. "Are you saying I'm not to waltz with Lady Finchley?"

"That's exactly what I'm saying."

Arlington started to chuckle, then offered his arm to Maggie.

John sighed. Now was as good a time as any to do his duty to that abrasive Lady Caroline. He strode to where she was standing with the Duke of Aldridge, who at present was smothering his attentions on his duchess. What a different man he appeared in his wife's presence! All his rigidness melted when he was solicitously hovering over his adored wife.

John was having a devil of a time remembering how all these people were related. Duchess Elizabeth Aldridge was a younger sister to Lord Haverstock. Now John had finally gotten that straight. Lady Lydia Morgan was another of Haverstock's sisters, which would make Morgie a brother-in-law to the duchess. After a moment's thought, John determined that Maggie was not related to Morgie by blood. Nor was she related to the Marquess of Haverstock, not that Maggie put much store in blood relation. She had stressed that she was almost as close to the duchess as she was to her birth sisters.

A pity he wasn't about to dance with the duchess. She was much nicer to him than Maggie's sister. Perhaps he should attempt to take his wife's advice and try to bedazzle Caro. But how did one go about trying to bedazzle someone?

Chapter 11

There was little opportunity for him to speak with Lady Caroline (which he thought a very good thing, given her aversion to him). The dance for which he claimed her was a set where they mostly stood about in longways. That much he could handle quite well. But when it came time for their turn to gracefully move down the pair of facing rows of fellow dancers, he became nervous again after he drew Maggie's sister's hand into his. It was as if he'd been seized with amnesia. He could not remember a single step. That's what came from lack of practice.

In fairness to his partner, he had to admit Lady Caroline took his incompetence in good stride and helped him along, acting as if his dancing was perfection. He gave her a sideways glance. She still looked much like Maggie, but she wasn't nearly so pretty tonight as her elder sister. He had not exaggerated when he'd told his wife she would be the loveliest woman in attendance.

After the set was finished, as he was restoring Lady Caroline to her companions, she asked, "Have you met our other sister, Clair?"

"Do not tell me there's another who strongly resembles the two of you!"

She shook her head. "No, Clair looks nothing like Margaret and me. Except for her hair colour and size. And she's nothing like us in temperament, either. She is disinterested in fashion and rather thinks like a man. Likes philosophy and political economy, whatever that is. She's exceedingly intelligent." She glanced at their family circle gathered in one corner. "Clair's just arrived with her . . . suitor, Haverstock's cousin, Richard Rothcomb-Smedley."

"I didn't know Rothcomb-Smedley was related to my wife."

"Only by marriage. He's the duchess's first cousin."

Would he ever learn all these connections? He was pleased to see Maggie there, standing beside the duchess. They both stood next to an armchair where the Marchioness of Haverstock was seated. He had to own that even though her stomach was huge with the babe that was expected any day, Lady Haverstock was a remarkably beautiful woman. But as his gaze scanned the three women, he realized they were all pretty, all considerably above average.

As highly as he prized his friends, he was glad to see that Arlington was not there ogling over his wife.

Maggie stepped forward to greet him, her gaze moving from him to her sister and back to him. "Oh, dearest, you must meet our other sister."

"Lady Caroline's been telling me about her." His gaze moved to his left, and he nodded at the up-and-coming Parliamentarian, Richard Rothcomb-Smedley, whom he had known since Oxford and continued to see regularly at White's.

"Then you already know Mr. Rothcomb-Smedley?"

"Yes. I did not know he was contemplating

marriage."

Maggie frowned. "That's because he's not. There is no understanding between him and my sister. Come, I'll introduce you."

When Lady Clair turned to face him, he was surprised. From the back she looked like Maggie and Lady Caroline, but from the front she was altogether different. Her face was heavily freckled, and as they had drawn closer, he saw that her shoulders were not the smooth ivory of Maggie's, either, but were dotted with freckles. At first he thought it was a pity she was not as pretty as her sisters, but after he was introduced to her and heard her speak, he realized she was pretty in her own way. Not as pretty as Maggie, but pretty nevertheless.

Most cognizant of doing his duty, he claimed Clair for the next set, and Maggie stood up with Perry. The next set he begged to stand up with the duchess, and Knowles claimed Maggie. When that dance was over he practically sighed. He was relatively sure he had stood up with all the ladies who mattered to Maggie while she'd no doubt charmed his friends. As their eyes met when he left the dance floor, she smiled. He thanked the duchess, then went to Maggie and drew her slender hand into his. "I have a feeling my friends will be ready to leave now. Shall we go speak to them before they go?"

She looked up at him with shimmering eyes. "I should love that."

They found the three men in the drawing room where Grandmere had seen to it that several tables had been set up for those who would rather play than dance. The trio was not playing but standing about talking when he and Maggie strode into the chamber. The fellows looked up and offered broad smiles.

"I appreciate that you've come tonight," John told them.

"I cannot say it was a pleasure," Perry said almost under his breath to John. Then Perry faced Maggie and flashed a bright smile. "Dancing with the divine Lady Finchley was undoubtedly the highlight of the evening's festivities. Tell me, my lady, have you a sister who looks remarkably like you?"

"Indeed I do."

"Her name's Lady Caroline," John said.

"I should like to stand up with her."

Perry had never before shown the slightest interest in respectable ladies. John was perplexed. He could not determine if such attention was good or bad. He did not want his friends to change. He did not want them to ever marry and grow serious and forget about drinking one another under the brandy table or arguing over ladybirds of unquestionably scandalous repute or laughing themselves silly over memories of good times they'd had this last decade. He wanted all four of them to stay exactly as they were when they'd first come down from Oxford and tasted the life of wine, women, and faro unfettered for the first time in their lives.

John did not want to contemplate becoming a responsible citizen, dutiful husband, or . . . heaven forbid, an exemplary father. And he didn't wish for his friends to, either.

He still woke up every morning (or, in many cases, afternoon) blissfully happy with his life. Until he married, that is. Now he woke up regretting the imprisonment of marriage, an imprisonment that did not originate with Maggie, who was sweetly compliant.

"Allow me to introduce you to her," Maggie said to Perry.

Before John knew it, his wife and Perry swept from the chamber and began climbing the stairs to the ballroom.

He faced Arlington and glared. "Do. Not. Ever. Smush your lips on my wife's hand again."

His characteristic smirk was back on Arlington's face. "My, but you've changed your tune. You're acting like a jealous husband—when you've insisted all along that your marriage is not a *real* marriage."

"Any court in the land would uphold the legality of our marriage." *Our* marriage. It seemed strange that he and Maggie were now a single unit. *Our.* How odd it felt—especially for an only child—to be sharing his life with another.

His dark eyes flashing with mirth, Arlington started laughing almost in guffaws.

John glared. "I fail to see what's so blasted funny."

"You are. Despite your claims that this so-called marriage will not change you in any way, you *have* changed."

John's gaze flicked to Knowles.

"He's right, old fellow. Whether you realize it or not, you've changed."

"There's no point in arguing the fact with the two of you." But I'll show them! Every day he would demonstrate how little control Maggie exerted over him.

Knowles' face grew solemn. "You'll be better off, Finch, if you'll just accept the fact you are a married man."

Arlington's eyes flashed devilishly. "A most fortunate married man, to be sure. I, too, may have to find this sister who looks so remarkably like your countess. And the duke settles thirty thousand on his sisters?" He went to turn back to the door, but John caught his arm.

"Feel free to dance with Lady Caroline, but I give you warning, she's turned down eleven matrimonial offers. Grandmere says it's believed she's saving herself for a duke."

"Too high for my touch," Knowles uttered.

A frown tugging at his normally merry face, Arlington concurred.

* * *

It was nearly dawn when she and John rode back to their house in his grandmother's luxurious coach. She had never in her life drunk so much champagne. It seemed every time she turned around someone was lifting a glass to toast the newlyweds. She felt magnificently bubbly, yet a bit unstable. Had she not had John's arm to lean on, she doubted she could have walked to the carriage without falling on her face.

Seconds after the coach door slammed, the horses spurted forward. She was eying her husband on the seat opposite hers, then he appeared to be sideways. *Oh, dear.* She had leaned over so far she was almost in a reclining position.

"I say, Maggie, are you feeling all right?"

She giggled. "I feel wonderful. I feel as if I could fly—round and round in this spinning carriage."

"You've had too much to drink." His voice sounded older, more mature. Then he moved to her side of the coach and helped restore her to an erect position. He kept his arm around her. "I'm not trying to take advantage of a lady who's not completely in control of her faculties, nor am I trying to take liberties. I am merely placing my arm around you because I fear you may fall off the seat and injure yourself."

She could almost swoon. Even if she'd not had a single drop of champagne, she would still have felt like swooning from being held so close to him. Hand-holding was child's play next to this. It wasn't just the blissful feel of his arm encircling her, it was also the feel of his body brushing against hers. His very solidness, his scent of sandalwood, his undeniable virility nearly overpowered her.

She looked up at him adoringly. "If I fell and broke into pieces, I wouldn't even feel it because I'm so happy. This was the best night of my life."

* * *

What a wretched life she must have had. Were it not for his fellow bloods coming to the ball, it would have been one of the most exceedingly dull nights of his six-and-twenty years. "I fail to understand what about this evening could produce such feelings of felicity. Was it not much the same as any other ball?"

"Not at all! This was *our* ball."

There went that word again. She said it as if it were bloody sacred. *Ours.* He told himself he needed to become accustomed to being one half of their *ours.* "Oh, I see. You really were the belle of this ball."

"Just as you said I would be." Her head flopped onto his shoulder.

Good Lord, was she dicked? "Maggie, are you awake?"

"Of course I'm awake. I don't want this night to come to an end."

"Then you may need to close your eyes against the rising sun."

She pouted. "I could have waltzed with you all night."

"Even though your feet were not exempt from my mauling?"

"Don't say that. You're my partner. I am incapable of criticizing you. One doesn't do that to one's friends."

"So you are loyal to me."

"Just as I promised. Are you loyal to me?" Her arm came around him as if to steady herself against the sharp turn the coach made, but once they were on a straight street again, her arm stayed.

At this moment he became startlingly aware of Maggie as a woman. A desirable woman. Even earlier that night in her bedchamber he hadn't thought of her as a man thinks of a woman. Then she had been an elegant object of beauty, not unlike a cold marble statue of a Roman goddess. But there was nothing cold about this warm, womanly body joined so closely to his. And there was nothing respectful about the sheer animal lust that pulsed through him.

As if she could read his very thoughts, she lifted her head to face him, her lids lowering seductively, just as her voice did. "It would be the perfect night if you'd kiss me."

Heaven help him, he was powerless to resist.

$\mathcal{C}$hapter 12

His lips lowered to brush against hers with great tenderness. He'd thought to just barely kiss her—to satisfy her. After all, he was being charged with making this her perfect night. Until a moment ago, kissing this lady had never crossed his mind. He had planned to take her dowry, allow her to share his house, and go about his merry way as he always had. Kissing had never been part of their pact. No bonds would ever connect him to this woman who had accidentally married him as a result of almost inconceivable coincidences.

Yet here he was holding her in his arms. Here he was kissing her.

And not wanting to stop. Something in the purity of her sweet, breathless kiss stirred him in a way no courtesan ever had. The passion of the kiss deepened. Was it from him? Or her? His heart pounded fiercely when he realized it was from both of them.

He found that he, too, was short of breath.

To his astonishment, her mouth opened beneath the pressure of his, and she eagerly sucked at his tongue.

Good Lord! He would have sworn that Maggie had never before kissed a man, but she kissed with great abandonment. How had she learned that?

It's the champagne. She was foxed. All her inhibitions had been destroyed. In that instant he realized he could take her to his bed and make love with her, and the lady would not protest in the least.

Until the next day.

Taking her to his bed was exactly what he wanted at this moment. He wanted it like he'd never wanted anything. He wanted her so compulsively it was as if fire singed through his veins. His loins ached with the need to slake this hunger.

Something in the outer recesses of his mind even told him "*Do it. She is, after all, your wife.*"

He did not want a wife. He must not allow her to believe otherwise.

Also, the small sliver of honor he possessed would not allow him to take advantage of an innocent lady who'd had too much champagne.

He stiffened and gathered the strength—no easy task—to pull away.

She pouted. "I enjoyed that excessively. Could we please do it again?"

"I vowed I would not take liberties with a lady under the influence of strong spirits."

Her eyes narrowed as she looked up at him. "You're saying cham-paying is strong spirits?"

"See, you can't even pronounce it correctly."

The coach pulled up in front of Finchley House. Thank heaven. 'Twas bloody difficult to maintain control when she was so enticing. After the coachman opened the door and offered his mistress a hand, she went careening from the carriage—to the coachman's mortification.

John leapt from the carriage and managed to

break her fall. He swung her up into his arms and eyed the servant. "I believe I shall carry Lady Finchley tonight. If you'll just get the door for me."

He carried Maggie into the house, up the stairs, and into her bedchamber. Once again, he fleetingly felt as if he did not belong there. Her maid had left a candle burning beside the bed, and it had almost gone out. He brought her to the bed, and when he went to place her in it, he realized she had fallen into a deep sleep. She truly was dicked.

After he covered her, he stood there staring down at this woman he'd married. He shouldn't be there. Yet he felt compelled to watch her. How pretty she was in repose.

The memory of the searing kiss sent his heartbeat scurrying. Despite all his reasons why he couldn't make love to her, he still wanted to.

Perhaps he, too, had imbibed too much drink.

* * *

When she awakened the following morning she was mildly disappointed that she was fully clothed. She had not drunk so much champagne that she did not remember the exultation of being kissed—and kissed with great passion—by her husband. How she wished that passion had culminated in the union she craved.

She allowed herself to lie there for several moments as she leisurely recalled the events of the most perfect night of her life. How joyful she'd been when John's arm came around her during the carriage ride home, but that joy was eclipsed by the profound pleasure of his kiss. Her first.

Minutes later as she went to rise from her bed, her head felt as if it had been whacked by a hammer. She fell back and rang for her maid.

"I beg that you bring me tisane," she told Annie when she arrived seconds later. "I've got the bad head."

"Then your ladyship won't be going to Trent Square this afternoon?"

Oddly, she thought of Mikey and could not deny herself so satisfying a cuddle. Mikey was so precious. "No, I shall manage."

After she was dressed she asked her maid, "Do you know if his lordship has risen?"

"Yes, Sanford just took the post to his bedchamber."

Margaret nodded and dismissed her maid. She took the velvet box which held last night's diamonds, drew in a fortifying breath, and went to the bedchamber door she knew connected to John's.

When she entered his chamber, he was fully dressed and sitting before a small secretary desk, his hand gripping a single piece of paper. His eyes were moist, and an incredibly sad look marked his face.

"Is something the matter?" she asked.

Her comment jarred him, and he looked up.

Seeing his face so ravaged was like a thwack to her heart.

"I've just received a letter from Weatherford."

Her brows lowered. "Your friend who died in the Peninsula?"

He nodded.

"He must have written to you shortly before he was killed."

His glance fell to the letter. "Yes, it's dated in February."

"I thought you hadn't communicated with him

in years."

"I hadn't." His voice grew even more solemn. "Somehow he knew he was going to die, and he asked if I'd look after his family."

"So he *had* married?"

"Yes, and he's got . . . he fathered a lad." He handed her the letter.

My Dear Finch,

I am cognizant that it has been a long time since I've been in communication with you, but that does not mean you've been absent from my thoughts. I hope I do not flatter myself that our separation was governed by divergent circumstances more than from a lack of affection on either of our parts.

I write to you now because I am gripped by a conviction that my mortality will soon be ended, courtesy of the bloody French. I'm vastly worried about my wife, Sally, and our young son. Since I did not learn Sally was breeding until I was already in the Peninsula, I was unable to speak to a solicitor about a guardian for the child. I had hoped to ask if you would perform that service. Alas, it is likely too late. I pray this letter will serve to persuade you to undertake such a commission in the event that I meet my end here in Spain.

I have never known a finer man than you, and I would be honored to have you guiding the all-important decisions in my son's life. I hope, for example, you can use your influence to secure a seat for him at Eton.

There are many other things I want for my lad, but I fear I shall not live to see them.

I beg that you look out for Sally and the boy. At the same time I pray that you will never have to.

With deep affection and gratitude,

George Weatherford

Margaret was wiping away tears when she restored the letter to her husband's desk. "So very heart wrenching."

His head had been in his hands, then he looked up, eyes red and moist and a puzzled look on his face. "I feel . . . I feel strangely honored. Sad and unhappy and in mourning for my lost friend, but honored nonetheless."

"It *is* an honor. Because despite your own feelings on the subject of your conduct, you are an honorable man." After all, he had *not* taken advantage of her last night. More's the pity.

"You've been listening too much to my grandmother."

She put hands to hips and gave him a mock glare. "I live with you, my Lord. Give me credit for knowing something about you."

He looked back at the letter, brows lowered. "He did not give me his wife's direction. I'll write to his parents for it."

"Better yet, I'll run along to Whitehall. My brother knows everyone at the War Office. He will be able to get Mrs. Weatherford's direction for us this very afternoon."

Her husband stood. "I'll come with you."

* * *

In his grandmother's carriage he watched Maggie. "How are you feeling today? Do you have a bad head?"

She frowned. "Indeed I do. I shall never again drink so much champagne."

He chuckled. "Since your . . . ah, overconsumption occurred at your bridal ball, I daresay such an occurrence will never be repeated."

Sitting there in the coach with her—albeit on opposite sides—made him recall the intimacies they had shared there the night before. His breath hitched at the profound memory of The Kiss. His gaze trickled over her. Thank God she was not dressed as provocatively today. No bare shoulders. No bosom smushed beneath the bodice of the lovely gown. No diamonds clasped about her kissably elegant neck.

Today her eyes were the same shade of blue as her simple frock of an exceedingly soft-looking muslin that covered her arms and came rather high in the neck. Her hands were sheathed in white gloves and folded in her lap. Nothing provocative looking about her today.

He was grateful she'd not mentioned The Kiss. Did she even remember it? Many a time in his life—far too many, actually—he'd drunk so much that he could not remember on the following morning what had occurred on the previous night. He rather hoped that's how foxed she'd been the night before. He did not want her to remember how captivated he'd been by her kiss. Was he embarrassed over the way her kiss had ignited something in him? Or was he embarrassed because he had crossed the line between friends and lovers, a line he'd sworn never to cross? He might even fear that if she did remember, she would be angry with him. For crossing that line.

Had she not made it clear to him that she wanted no part of a *real* marriage? But she *had* asked him to kiss her last night. Even if she had been inebriated.

He had come to regret kissing her. He regretted the way he had desired her so acutely.

He vowed not to ever kiss her like that again.

When they reached Whitehall, he grew nervous. He disliked facing her stiff brother. Would the haughty duke ever accept him as a brother-in-law? John knew the answer to that question. If he comported himself as a dull stick who was ecstatic over domesticity, the Duke of Aldridge would then approve of him.

John would just as soon fall on his own sword.

The duke, as he was on the previous night, was amiable with his sister and abrupt with John.

But John must give the fellow credit. An exceedingly privileged duke he might be, but the man showed great compassion for Weatherford's situation. Aldridge personally rushed to the war office in the adjacent building and returned ten minutes later with the address for Weatherford's widow. "She's in the Capital!" the duke said.

John eyed the piece of paper. *Twenty-six Foster's Croft Lane.* It was not a street he knew. He was familiar with every street in Mayfair and Westminster, but then he'd not really expected Weatherford's wife to be living where the upper classes did. How in the deuce did the duke know Foster's Croft Lane? "I would be obliged, your grace, if you could direct us there."

"Actually, it's not very far from here. Keep going down the Strand, past all the print shops. I believe Foster's Croft Lane is primarily used for mews, but some lodgings are located there. At least that's what the young clerk at the War Office told me a few minutes ago."

So that's how a mighty duke—who only saw London streets from the window of his fine coach-and-four—knew about an insignificant lane where those of the lesser classes resided.

Margaret took the paper from John's hand and eyed it before facing her brother. "We're very grateful to you, Aldridge." Then she linked her arm in John's, and he too thanked her brother before they descended the stairs and went to their waiting coach.

"See," she told him after the coach began to move along the slow progression of conveyances on the Strand, "my brother was harmless."

"Your brother was exceedingly helpful. I'm indebted to him."

Were they walking, they could have arrived at Foster's Croft Lane much more quickly. Their coach moved at a snail's pace. This was likely London's busiest street, if the hackneys and potato carts and ale drays and coal wagons and stage coaches were any indication. It was certainly the nosiest, what with those hawking chestnuts and flowers along the pavement, hackney drivers addressing counterparts in the opposite direction, donkeys braying, children playing.

He peered from his coach window as a huge slab of marble passed by in the opposite lanes, seven horses pulling its lengthy cart. No wonder that lane was moving even slower than his.

He directed his thoughts at George Weatherford's widow. *Sally.* What could he say to her? He was happy Maggie was with him. Even though she was quiet, his wife would know what to say.

The coachman had quickly nodded when John had given him the direction, saying he knew right where it was. Nearly half an hour later they turned off the Strand just a handful of blocks from where they'd met with Aldridge. There was a quick fork in the road, and to the right was a dark alley where a crude sign had been hammered to the upper story: *Foster's Croft.*

They passed eight or nine mews before they came to a skinny building with two windows across each of its four floors. The building was a style that had been prevalent more than a century earlier. The numbers two and six were affixed to the faded black door. "This is it," he said.

* * *

Margaret was reminded of the lodgings where she and Elizabeth had located some of their widows when Number 7 Trent Square first opened. Some of the neighborhoods she and Elizabeth had gone to in search of the needy widows were so bad that Aldridge had insisted an armed footman—dear Abraham—accompany them for protection.

She and John left the coach, climbed the steps, and he rapped at the door. A thin, gray-haired man who was missing one of his front teeth opened the door and eyed them curiously. He was, no doubt, not accustomed to having those of The Quality come to his lodgings.

"I am looking for Mrs. Weatherford," John said.

"She be on the top floor."

Margaret and John began to trudge up the steep wooden staircase that was in almost total darkness. How wretched it would be to have to live in a dismal place like this.

At the top of the stairs there was but a single door. John knocked on it.

Seconds later the door opened.

There stood a woman with her young son. She looked to be the same age as Margaret; her son who shielded himself in his mother's skirts, three or four.

"Mrs. Weatherford?" John asked.

She smiled at him. "Yes."

Even though this woman had lost her husband, even though this woman was probably poor, even though this woman was forced to live in a dreary building on a dreary street that blocked the sunlight, Margaret envied her glorious beauty and her adorable son.

$\mathcal{C}$hapter 13

Even her black widow's garb could not quiet the radiance of her luxurious cinnamon-coloured hair or those sparkling emerald eyes set in an uncommonly fair face. The beautiful woman looked almost as if she'd stepped off the canvas of one of Titian's colorful Renaissance paintings.

If being the possessor of such stunning beauty were not enough, Mrs. Weatherford also was blessed with a precious son. Margaret—who was decidedly fond of little boys—did not know which she envied the most.

Then the full force of the woman's grievous loss slammed into Margaret, making her excessively ashamed of her jealousy.

"I am John Beau- -"

The widow cut him off. "Beauclerc, the Earl of Finchley." Her voice was cultured.

John raised a brow. "We've met before?"

Mrs. Weatherford shook her head. "No, it's just that George spoke of you so often—and with high praise." She widened the opening of the door. "Won't you please come in?" Then her glance alighted on Margaret. "You've married, my Lord?"

"Indeed I have. Allow me to present you to my wife."

The women sketched barely discernible curtsies to one another.

"My rooms are not what your lordship is accustomed to, but they're clean." She lifted up her son, who must be frightened of strangers.

Margaret smiled. It had been the same with Mikey at first, but now they were devoted to each other. As she thought of her special bond with Mikey she thought of the babe Elizabeth was carrying and hoped for a nephew of her very own. It did not look as if she were ever going to have her own child.

Their steps clapped along the sagging wooden floors as Mrs. Weatherford directed them to a shabby, sparsely furnished drawing room. Because it was at the front of the house, it featured two tall, slender windows, but because the street those windows faced was so exceedingly narrow, most of the sun was blocked by the buildings opposite.

Lord and Lady Finchley sat upon the faded velvet sofa, and Mrs. Weatherford sat in an arm chair near the fire, her son on her lap. Despite that is was a cool day, there was no fire. No doubt, an economy measure, Margaret mused.

It was a very good thing they'd come. "What is your lad's name?" Margaret asked.

"He's also a George. Named after his father."

"I never knew a finer man," John said solemnly.

The widow smiled. "I quite agree."

Margaret wanted to know more about the boy, but did not want to interrupt. After all, John had come here today out of respect for the father. He and the widow would quite naturally wish to discuss the fallen soldier.

But it seemed as if neither the widow nor John knew quite how to proceed.

To fill in the silence, Margaret asked, "Pray, how old is little George?"

"I'm not wittle!" the boy protested. "I'm free."

A year older than Mikey. Mikey still wasn't speaking in sentences.

His mother hugged him closer, smiling as she rolled her eyes. "He may be three, but he'll always be my b-a-b-y."

She obviously spelled it out because George did not want to be called a baby. They all laughed.

A moment later, John drew a deep breath. "You've been in London long, madam?"

"Not long enough to have any friends here. When George was attached to the Horse Guards, I wanted to be near him. This place was close—and affordable!"

"Why do you stay here now?" John asked, his voice gentle.

"I've nowhere else. I'm an orphan, and it is not possible to move in with George's mother—his father died last year, you know—since his sister and her family moved in to help out."

Poor John. He was at a loss for words. Having lived a privileged life, he likely did not understand the hardships others faced. As a duke's daughter, Margaret had also been totally shielded from the deprivations so many had to endure. Before Elizabeth opened her eyes. Margaret had joined Elizabeth in rescuing the widows who, with their children, had been sleeping as many as twenty to a single room. Now at Trent Square, each fatherless family had its own chamber, and the duchess and her sisters-in-law provided for all their needs.

"Without your husband's support," Margaret said, "are you even able to afford these lodgings?"

John whirled to face his wife, his brows lowered. Though he said not a word, she knew he must think her question ill mannered. After all, one was not permitted to inquire about others' incomes or particulars pertaining to others' income.

The woman flicked her head away from their view, as if in humiliation. When she spoke, her words splintered painfully. "Not actually."

"Then I'm very happy I've come today," John said. "Your husband asked that I look out for you and the lad."

Mrs. Weatherford began to sob. Her slender shoulders shook, and her young son looked terrified. "Mama! Are you hurt?"

She gathered the boy to her bosom and held him close, running her elegant fingers through his mop of dark brown tresses. "I am just happy, love, knowing how much Papa loved us."

It was all Margaret could do not to burst into tears.

"Indeed he did," John said solemnly.

"Of course, my husband is prepared to assist you in any way needed, but allow me to tell you about what I think is a lovely place for officers' widows."

Mrs. Weatherford dabbed her tears upon her sleeve and turned back to face the Finchleys. Even with now-reddened eyes, she was beautiful. "There's a place for officers' widows? Here in London?"

"There is *a* single place. My brother, the Duke of Aldridge, and his wife established it solely to give officers' widows a decent place to live. The women all have much in common, and they get along exceedingly well. They live rather as one big, happy family."

"I cannot tell you how much I've longed to be with other women who might understand my loss, other women who've also lost husbands in the Peninsula. And . . ." She faltered. "I would be most grateful not to have to worry about how I should pay my rent."

"We've currently eight-and-twenty children there. George would have playmates." Margaret thought of Mikey and pictured him and George running about with one another.

Mrs. Weatherford smiled at her. "That would be lovely."

"As it happens, we will have an opening within the week."

The widow arched a brow.

"One of our widows—a mother of four—will remarry and have a fine home of her own in the village where she was raised. We're all very happy for her. It's my own personal wish that each of our widows can find happiness with a new husband and homes of their own. I look at Number 7 Trent Square as a transitional place for them as they adjust to life without their husbands."

Mrs. Weatherford's eyelids lowered, as did her voice. "I cannot imagine ever loving someone as I loved George."

Silence filled the chamber like a dreary fog.

Finally, John spoke. "No one will ever take George Weatherford's place, not in your heart, nor in mine. But I know George would want you to find happiness again. He'd want you to remarry."

The widow held up a palm. "I beg that we speak no more on that topic."

More silence.

"If you'd like, before you make a decision, we can take you and George to Trent Square so you can judge for yourself if it is suitable," Margaret said.

The widow's face brightened. "Today?"

Margaret looked at John.

He nodded. "If you'd like."

Mrs. Weatherford sighed. "I should be grateful for the change of environment such a journey would provide."

Within a few moments the four of them were driving to Bloomsbury. Little George was fascinated by the carriage ride. No doubt, it was his first.

This would be John's first visit to Number 7 Trent Square. With a smile on her face, Margaret recalled the duchess telling her about the first time she took Aldridge there—before they married and before any of the widows had moved in—and he stole a kiss from her. It was their first kiss. Judging from their present devotion to one another, it must have been a most potent kiss.

Which made Margaret think of the kiss John had given her last night. Their first. The very memory sent her heartbeat roaring, sent a tingling sensation low in her torso. She longed to be kissed like that again.

She longed for even more . . .

* * *

If someone had told John on the previous day that he would be assisting a widow instead of joining his friends at the race meeting this afternoon, he would have been incredulous. Quite oddly, though, as they traversed the city he realized he was not lamenting having selected duty over pleasure. This must be a first.

Less than half an hour after leaving Foster's Croft Lane, they turned onto Trent Square. That bloody Duke of Aldridge owned the whole damned square. John's eye went to the shiny brass 7 upon a freshly painted black door.

The house was the largest in the square. They were all rather modest whilst retaining a solid respectability. Probably populated by solicitors and clever merchants. Were he an army officer with a family, this is just the type of neighborhood he should want his family to reside in.

At the door they were greeted by a fine-looking man whom Margaret introduced as their house steward, Carter. John had never heard of a bloody house steward. But then he'd never heard of a house like Number 7 Trent Square, either.

After bestowing a bright smile upon Carter, John's wife explained that the steward had been a footman at Aldridge House, and that she sometimes slipped and referred to him as Abraham.

The man must have demonstrated great competency to have been so elevated.

Whilst they stood in the entry corridor, a youthful woman rushed to greet Margaret.

Margaret turned to him. "Darling, I should like to present to you Mrs. Hudson. She was our first tenant."

The pretty woman, who was about the same age as Margaret, curtsied.

He was taken back for a moment at being called *darling*. It was a bloody difficult concept to stamp upon his brain. He was Maggie's husband. To others, he was her *darling*. "Was it your husband who served with the duchess's younger brother?" he asked Mrs. Hudson.

The lady nodded.

Then Maggie introduced the widows to one another. "How long since you lost Mr. Weatherford?" Mrs. Hudson asked her in a somber voice.

Mrs. Weatherford's eyes moistened. "He died in February but I only learned of it last month."

Mrs. Hudson clasped the other widow's hand. "I know how you're feeling right now. Won't you allow me to show you our home?"

Those two—along with little George who clung to his mother—started to climb the stairs. Another little lad who was even smaller than George came running up to Maggie, holding up his arms for her to lift him.

Like the luminosity of a fireworks display, his wife's face brightened when she beheld the little fellow, and she swung him up into her arms and began to plant kisses on his face—much to the lad's pleasure.

He'd never seen Maggie like this before. One would think she was the boy's mother. A sadness came over him at the thought that she would never experience motherhood, owing to their sterile marriage. Maggie was clearly a born nurturer.

She turned to face him, smiling broadly. "My Lord Finchley, I should like to present Mikey to you, and I must tell you that he owns my heart."

"I shall be jealous." Why in the devil had he said that? Especially after the . . . intimacy of the previous night. In Grandmere's carriage. The memory still had the power to accelerate his pulse.

Until last night, until seeing her now with

Mikey, he had not realized how affectionate was this woman he'd married.

He eyed the little fellow. "And how old are you, Mikey?"

Maggie giggled. "Age is not a concept Mikey's yet grasped. He's not quite two."

John's brows lowered. "He seemed rather near little George's age." He did not think he could ever mention Weatherford's son without prefacing his name with the diminutive. The boy's appearance so closely resembled his father's that upon viewing the lad, John's memory had immediately flashed back to his first year at Eton. He pictured George Weatherford as he'd looked as a lad of eight or nine.

If only he could suppress such melancholy thoughts. It was not fair that it was he who was here in this house with Weatherford's son, that Weatherford would never see the boy, that John would never again set eyes on Weatherford.

"They are separated in age by a little over a year. Would it not be wonderful if they became friends—like you and Captain Weatherford?"

Before he could respond, the Duchess of Aldridge swept into the house. They exchanged greetings all around, then the duchess asked him, "Is this your first visit to Number 7 Trent Square, my Lord?"

"Indeed it is."

"You're a most dutiful husband, to be sure. Aldridge hasn't been here since we initially toured the house—before there were any inhabitants." Her face softened and she murmured. "I do have fond memories of that visit. It was the first time my dear husband ever kissed me—we weren't yet married."

He seemed to recall some sort of minor scandal that compelled Aldridge to wed the former Lady Elizabeth Upton, but dashed if he could remember what it was. Had they had a tupple here that day?

The duchess then faced Maggie and the little fellow. "I see Mikey's getting his requisite cuddle from Lady Finchley."

Maggie smiled every bit as exuberantly as she had last night when she'd told him it was the happiest night of her life. "He's learned my new name. He no longer calls me Wady Margaret. I'm now Wady Finchley."

The small lad, his tiny fingers sifting through Maggie's hair, appeared as content as a calf chewing his cud.

Once again, John's thoughts turned to The Kiss. Maggie's kiss. He thought too of the stiff Duke of Aldridge stealing a kiss from his future wife. And John found himself wanting to sweep his wife into his arms and carry her to one of the bedchambers. . .

Chapter 14

Three days later John and his wife were assisting Mrs. Weatherford in her move. Maggie's new coach had arrived, and she was offering its use to take the widow and her possessions to Trent Square.

"Are you sure?" he asked. "What if the lad—or the woman's possessions—scratch it up?"

"I care not. People are far more valued than possessions." She looked up at him. "Do you mind?"

He shrugged. "Not really."

To his astonishment, Maggie had meekly asked that he sit beside her in the new coach as they went toward the Strand. He could not disappoint.

Why in the deuce was it that every time he was with Maggie now he kept remembering the intensity of that one kiss? He had rather astonished himself the last time they were at Trent Square when he'd been seized by the desire to ravish this sweet woman he'd wed.

As much of a libertine as he was, he would never countenance such bawdy behavior.

At least, not with a lady, and not with respectable widows as witnesses to his depravity.

"Did you not think Mrs. Weatherford possessed of uncommon beauty?" Maggie asked.

He shrugged. "I hadn't thought of her

appearance one way or another. I daresay I was too shocked by the lad's strong resemblance to his father."

Her hand settled on his. "Oh, dearest, that must have been difficult for you."

"It was, actually. Wished to God Weatherford was still alive."

"I know."

As their coach turned onto Foster's Croft Lane, he pictured his friend's widow. He supposed she would be considered lovely. No wonder George had married so young. John found himself wondering if the woman would marry again.

He also wondered who would be a father figure to the lad.

Then he knew the answer. *It must be I.* He must step into his friend's empty shoes and try to treat the lad as he knew Weatherford would have.

When they reached Mrs. Weatherford's lodgings, he was thankful his friend's widow was not going to have to live in such a dreary place anymore. Trent Square was a bright, solid home in a respectable neighborhood.

Sadly, the Weatherfords had pitifully few possessions to carry to Trent Square. This one trip should do it. All their clothes had been stuffed into a shabby valise, and Mrs. Weatherford carried a few books in her arms.

"What of the furnishings?" he asked.

The widow shook her head. "They aren't ours." As she took a seat opposite them, he noticed that little George no longer sat upon his mother's lap. Now the lad was comfortable in their presence. The little boy caught Maggie's attention. "My lady, could you swing me into the air like you do with Mikey?"

"If you'd like, pet."

Maggie was in her element when surrounded by children. *A natural mother.* What a pity!

"Ay, but Georgie," John found himself saying, "I'm much taller than Lady Finchley, and I could swing you higher in the air." Now that he'd called the lad by that name, he thought he should prefer *Georgie*. It would be impossible—because it was far too painful—for him to ever call the lad by the same name as he'd once addressed his father.

The lad's face brightened even more. "When?"

"As soon as we reach your new home, if you'd like."

"Oh, yes! I'd like it very much."

Georgie was unusually excited. "At my new home, there's a park acwoss the stweet! And Mama says I can run with the other lads. That they'll be like my bwothers! I have always wanted a bwother."

Now that the boy had shed his shyness, he was proving to be a most determined talker.

The park across the street, John realized, was the plot of land in the center of the square. "Right! You'll have great fun there." Was the lad old enough to begin to learn about cricket? Would George's son be as competent at the sport as his father had been?

John would have to see to it that the lad got the opportunity. In fact, he thought of something he was going to have made for the boy. A smile crossed his face.

"Have you any regrets, Mrs. Weatherford? About moving?" Maggie asked.

"None whatsoever. Mrs. Hudson was uncommonly welcoming. In fact, all the widows were." Her lashes lowered, her voice softened.

"You see, we share a bond that others cannot understand. Also, I must own that I've been exceedingly lonely since the day George left England. My son has been a great comfort, but one needs other adults with whom to converse." Then Mrs. Weatherford smiled upon him. "How fortunate I am, my Lord, to have you looking out for my welfare."

"It's what George wanted." Surprisingly, fulfilling his old friend's wishes oddly pleased John. He was still puzzled that he bore no acrimony that his last visit to Foster's Croft Lane prevented him from attending the most controversial race meeting of the year. His friends could not stop talking about it—Perry rubbing it in that he'd won a great deal of money, and the others protesting that their horse should have been declared winner. "There wasn't an eyelash separating the two!" Knowles kept repeating.

John regretted not seeing it. He regretted that he had not gotten the opportunity to wager on Perry's horse. Winning money was always invigorating. But oddly, he did not regret spending time with the widow and her young son.

"Mama says I'm to ask his lawdship if I might call him Uncle Finchley."

The little boy's words plucked at John's heartstrings. "I should be honored, but I think you should address me as your papa did. Your papa always called me Finch. You can call me Uncle Finch. "

"I declare, your lordship," Mrs. Weatherford said, "I almost said your name was Finch the day you showed up at my door! It's how George always referred to you."

"Ah, but I'll not permit you to refer to me as

Uncle Finch," he said to her, a devilish gleam in his dark eyes.

They all laughed.

When they reached Trent Square and departed the coach, his wife addressed him. "You have fulfilled your duty, my dear husband. Now, pray, go spend time with your friends. I know Trent Square can hold no allure for you."

There she went—reading his bloody mind again! He had just been wondering if he could still catch up with the bloods at White's before their customary game of whist started. "As soon as I swing Georgie into the air, I believe I will take my leave. I'll send your coach back after it deposits me in St. James."

He reached down and lifted Georgie up and up until he was over John's head and twirled the squealing lad around like a windmill.

Georgie did not want him to stop, but John finally managed to set him down. "Now you need to follow your mama. The other lads will be wanting to play with you."

Maggie stood at John's side, her eyes shimmering with delight as she peered up at him. Keenly aware of her rose scent, he bent toward her and pressed his lips to her cheek. Why had he done that? Was he feeling guilty about leaving her? Feeling guilty that he had no intentions of seeing her that night? Or was it because she looked so very innocent—in a mature, maternal, almost saintly way? He realized he'd been unable to suppress the vision of her displays of affection to the little mite named Mikey. While John was touched by her affectionate nature, he was also swamped with feelings of guilt. Because of him, she would be deprived of the opportunity to have a happy home and family.

* * *

Mikey had stood on his tip-toes to watch from the window of the morning room as Lord Finchley tossed Georgie into the air. When Margaret entered Number 7 moments later, he rushed to the door, arms over his head. "Me!"

She lifted the little fellow into her arms and hugged him close for a moment before whipping his little body into the air and twirling around as he squealed. She felt as if every care in the world could be forgotten in a child's hug, in a child's infectious laughter.

Though she was cognizant of the many good fortunes in her life, on this day she'd become melancholy. There was no getting around it. These poor widows' lives were far more enriched than hers. They had known what it was to be loved. They had children. Margaret knew that despite the strong affection Mikey felt for her, he would always love his own mother best. Mrs. Leander was incredibly blessed. Mrs. Weatherford was blessed. All those women who shared Number 7 Trent Square were blessed.

Though Margaret might be rich in material wealth, she was poor in most other ways. She did not even possess her own husband's love.

She looked up from swinging Mikey around to see his mother standing there, an apron tied around her and a gleam in her eye as she regarded her youngest child. "Don't be bothering her ladyship, love. Come to Mama."

As he happily climbed into his mother's arms, a little piece of Margaret's heart flaked away. "He's no bother. You know how fond I am of him."

"Aye." Mrs. Leander looked at the door, which

Abraham was in the process of opening. "It's the duchess. She and I are going to be interviewing prospective cooks today."

Margaret had not heard that Number 7 was going to be engaging a cook. "It's well past time. Cooking for nearly three dozen people is far too much work for you," she told Mrs. Leander.

"I've had help, but I will own, it's been exhausting." Mrs. Leander kissed the top of Mikey's curly head. "And I haven't had much time for my own children."

As the duchess swept into the house, divesting herself of her pale blue pelisse and handing it to Abraham, they greeted her. "My sister is absolutely right, Mrs. Leander," Elizabeth said. "You've done too much for too long."

"You did get me the scullery maid the second month we were here."

"Even with her help—and the other widows taking turns assisting you—it's too much," the duchess said. "It was remiss of me not to relieve you of all this cooking months ago. You're an officer's wife, and I daresay if your husband were alive he'd not approve of you taking on such duties." Elizabeth gave her a quizzing glance. "Tell me true, madam, did you not have your own cook when your husband was alive?"

Mrs. Leander shyly nodded. "That I did. But I've always liked cooking. My mother prepared our food herself, and I have enjoyed working in the kitchen for as long as I can remember."

"Then you'll just have to train the new cook on how to prepare food exactly the way you like it," Elizabeth said.

"Yes, you must see that your recipes are followed or we may have a mutiny on our hands,"

Margaret said with a laugh. "If there's one thing all the residents of Number 7 agree upon, it's the excellence of your cooking."

Mikey scooted down from his mother's arms until he was placed on the floor. " He moved to Margaret, his little brows lifted in query as he looked up at her. "Boy?"

Mrs. Leander's eyes narrowed. "What do you want, love?"

"I think he's looking for the lad who's just moved in today," Margaret said. "Georgie. I believe he's the closest to Mikey in age—or at least the closest *male* to him in age!"

Mrs. Leander laughed while shaking her head. "All my lads want to associate only with other boys, yet I do believe my girls would rather associate with lads than with other little girls!"

Margaret understood that only too well. Her husband would much rather be with his male friends than be with her—or with any females. Respectable females, that is.

As happy as she was that Mrs. Leander would be freed of her never-ending kitchen chores, Margaret was saddened, knowing the woman would now have more time with her youngest child. That would certainly diminish Margaret's opportunity to spoil him as his mother had formerly not been able to do.

"Would you like to see Mrs. Weatherford's new chambers?" Mrs. Hudson asked Margaret after the duchess and Mrs. Leander moved into the drawing room.

"Indeed I would."

The two women began to mount the stairs. "I cannot tell you how happy I am for Mrs. Nye," Margaret said. "The woman positively glowed when I said farewell to her yesterday."

"I'm happy for her, too. She has truly fallen in love with the man she's marrying."

Margaret's voice softened. "You know it's what Mr. Hudson would have wanted for you. How old are you?"

"Two-and-twenty."

A year older than Abraham Carter, if Margaret's memory served her correctly. "The time with your husband was but a short interlude in what I feel is going to be a long life. You cannot spend the rest of your days dwelling on your lost love. Not when you're pretty. And the object of another man's devotion. A breathing, living man."

Mrs. Hudson stopped climbing the stairs as if her feet were nailed to the tread, and she turned to face Margaret. "Pray, my lady, to whom could you be referring?"

"I think you know."

"Carter?" Mrs. Hudson whispered.

Margaret nodded. "You must be the only one who's not aware of his adoration of you."

Mrs. Hudson shook off the comment. "It's only that he's grateful to me because I taught him how to read and write."

"If you think that, you cannot possess the intelligence I credited you with."

Mrs. Hudson resumed the stair climbing.

It had been difficult for someone as reticent as Margaret to bring up so personal a matter, but after seeing how happy Mrs. Nye was on the previous day, Margaret was determined to see that Mrs. Hudson also had another chance at a loving marriage. The young mother obviously needed a push.

On the top floor, they found Mrs. Weatherford

and Georgie's chamber at the end of the corridor. The beautiful widow whirled around to face Margaret, a smile brightening her face. "I am very happy with my chamber, and already George is begging to play with the other lads. I owe you and his lordship a great deal, my lady."

"Your happiness is our reward. I hope you will enjoy your time at Number 7 Trent Square. I think your son has already demonstrated his preference in lodgings."

"Indeed he has!"

Footsteps on the wooden corridor came closer and soon Mrs. Leander, carrying Mikey, stood in the open doorway to Mrs. Weatherford's chamber. "The first applicant's not due for ten minutes, so I wanted to come and welcome Mrs. Weatherford to Number 7." She eyed the newcomer. "You must tell me if there's anything you need." She set down Mikey. "My little laddie wants to play with your young fellow."

Margaret's melancholy was vanishing over her satisfaction that John's dead friend's widow was happily ensconced at Number 7 and that Mikey had a playmate, both owing to her.

When she turned away to go to the music room, Mikey did not even notice her departure. She was pleased that he had a lad to play with. Sooner or later, he would have found other interests in things little boys liked to do. One couldn't keep a child on one's lap forever.

But it saddened her nevertheless.

Each and every widow residing here was far richer than she. Would Margaret ever know the love of her husband? Ever have a child of her own?

* * *

When he reached White's, he was pleased to find his three best friends sitting at their regular table—two bottles of brandy reposing there also. He took the fourth seat.

Arlington looked up first, quirking a brow. "Ah, here comes Lady Finchley's peckee."

John frowned as he sat down. "What's that supposed to mean?"

"I believe he's intimating that you're henpecked, old fellow," Knowles said.

"Which makes me believe that somehow the bride has coaxed our dear Finch into her bed." Christopher Perry gave his old friend a patronizing look. "And I believed you when you said you had no intentions of making the union a real marriage."

Since they'd been lads, the four of them had shared everything. They'd even passed around Cyprians as if they were a bowl of Brussels sprouts. But for reasons John was incapable of understanding, he did not want his three best friends to be privy to the intimate—or lack of intimate—details of his and Maggie's marriage.

He knew the fellows' code of honor would prevent them from *gallantry* with their friend's wife, but if they believed he and Maggie were not on intimate terms, what was to prevent one of these fellows from trying to make a conquest of sweet Maggie?

He could never condone that.

He glared at Arlington. Why was the fellow so obsessed over the details of John's marriage? "Henceforth," John said in a commanding voice whilst his gaze scanned the three friends, "There will be no discussions of my wife, no questions to be asked regarding . . . bedchamber activities. Is that understood?"

"But, my dear friend," Arlington said, gleaming, "Your so-called bedchamber activities can be conducted anywhere."

Perry snorted. "Like standing up behind the stage curtains at Drury Lane."

"That was you—not I!" John protested.

Smiling, Knowles nodded. "Or on top the coachman's box between St. Albans and Oxford."

John had to admit they'd all had a go at that *sport* on the night to which Knowles was referring. At least, that's what John had been told the following morning. An overabundance of spirits had been involved.

"Then there's the fountain at Tolford Abbey . . ." Perry eyed him with mirth.

Not amused, John held up a flattened palm. "Enough!" It embarrassed him to think of Maggie ever learning what unorthodox activities had been performed in the fountain at his country home.

Another case of too much strong spirits.

"Then prove it to us. Tomorrow night," Perry said, "That you're our same old, fun-loving friend. Act like you did before you got shackled."

John's brows lowered. "What do you propose?"

"You're in the blunt now. Get yourself a lady-bird."

"And Perry's got just the one!" Arlington nodded. "The new buxom little redheaded dancer at the opera. If I weren't under an agreement with Mrs. Flannagan, I'd take her myself."

"It's too soon after his marriage," Knowles protested. "The Duke of Aldridge would not approve."

John nodded enthusiastically. "He's right. I can ill afford to behave in a manner that would increase the duke's hostility toward me."

Perry's face was screwed up in thought. "Finch, did you not mention that now you've got funds, you can afford to bribe the gossip writers to keep your scandals out of the newspapers?"

"He most certainly did," Arlington asserted.

Perry faced John, smiling. "There you have it! Come with us tomorrow night, and I'll introduce you to the gloriously top-heavy Loosey Lucy."

"And," Knowles added, "That's L-o-o-s-e-y."

"An apt description for the affectionate lady." Perry grinned.

John could not have his friends thinking him henpecked. It was an affront to the agreeable woman he'd married. "Very well. Tomorrow night."

$\mathcal{C}$hapter 15

Seeing Barrow's white hair when he swept open the door of her former home was as welcoming as a warm hug. She had seen the beloved old fellow every day of her life. Until she married. "Hello, Barrow."

His bushy white brows scrunched together. "Did you not move away, my lady?"

"You know very well I did, but I must visit my sisters. Are they here?" She was one of the few who understood—along with the footmen whom he supervised—that to be heard by Barrow, one must greatly elevate one's voice.

"Yes, Lady Clair and Lady Caroline are both in, but Lady Clair will be departing soon. Mr. Rotten-Smelly will be collecting her."

She tried not to burst out laughing at the butler's mispronunciation of Clair's suitor's name. She turned to scurry up the stairs. "Thank you, Barrow."

Both sisters were in Margaret's old bedchamber that she had shared with Caro. Clair was seated in front of Caro's dressing table, peering into the looking glass. "Can you not make my hair look like yours?" she said to Caro. "You've received eleven proposals of marriage, and I've not received a single one."

They turned when Margaret entered.

"But, my dear Clair," Margaret said, "You've never wanted but one proposal—and speaking of Mr. Rothcomb-Smedley, why is Barrow now under the delusion the poor man's name is Rotten-Smelly?"

Both sisters giggled. "That's because Aldridge took it upon himself to try to correct Barrow's mispronunciation of Rotten for Rothcomb," Caro explained, "and the poor old hard-of-hearing butler thought he'd got the Smedley part wrong. Barrow immediately changed the name to Rotten-Smelly, informing Aldridge he was a dutiful servant who intended to abide the master's wishes—even if he did not agree with them."

"And," Clair added, "Aldridge didn't have the heart to attempt to correct him a second time."

Margaret's gaze locked onto the image of her two sisters in the looking glass. Sadly, there was nothing Clair could do to be as pretty as Caro. The singular deviation in their appearance was their skin. Where Caroline's had the colour and luminosity of fresh cream, Clair's was dotted with freckles. Margaret did not find freckles at all offensive, but the comparison to Caro's completely unblemished skin was not to Clair's advantage.

"What does Mr. Rothcomb-Smedley think of dear Barrow's moniker?" Margaret asked.

"He's been very polite when poor Barrow addresses him as such, but when others playfully call him *Rotten-Smelly*, he gets rather miffed," Clair said.

Caro shrugged. "As long as it doesn't come out in the newspapers, it makes for great fun."

The very mention of newspapers reminded Margaret of that odious newspaper man and his vile practices. "If the press did get a hold of that name and start using it—particularly in the political caricatures—it could be disastrous to Mr. Rothcomb-Smedley's Parliamentary aspirations."

"That has also occurred to me," Clair said, her voice troubled.

Caro adopted a unconcerned air. "I daresay it's too late now. That cat has been out of the bag a good long while. I believe if someone were going to pass that name on to the press, it would have occurred by now. And it's not as if we can erase memories of those who've already heard it."

"Caro does have a point." Margaret began to circle her seated sister. "Pray, dearest, what's all this fuss about copying Caro's hair in order to wrangle a marriage proposal?"

Clair pouted. "I'm desperate. It's been nearly a year now since Mr. Rothcomb-Smedley became my suitor. We are infinitely compatible with one another. We never tire of each other's companionship. Everyone in the *ton* has been expecting an announcement of our nuptials for several months. The only explanation must be that I'm not pretty enough."

"Nonsense!" Margaret said. "I have on more than one occasion heard Mr. Rothcomb-Smedley praise your beauty. Besides, you truly are pretty."

"I am aware that I'm not as lovely as you two."

"I have no doubts," Caro said authoritatively (but then, Caro said everything authoritatively), "that Mr. Rothcomb-Smedley admires you vastly. I have no doubts that a marriage between you two would be spectacularly successful. I do have doubts, though, about Mr. Rothcomb-Smedley's desire to be *shackled.* I believe he's likely petrified at the prospect of being tied down in marriage."

Just like John. "Many men are."

"Then perhaps we need a scheme to make the man realize how much he wants to marry Clair," Caro announced.

"That sounds devious." Margaret's eyes narrowed as she regarded Caroline.

"That's because you're so beastly honest!"

"There's nothing beastly about being honest," Margaret defended. Though, she must own, she was hardly one to exemplify honesty, not with all the secrets she was harboring about her own marriage.

"You are absolutely sure that you desire to wed Mr. Rothcomb-Smedley?" Margaret asked.

Clair nodded. "I've never wanted anything more."

"That does it!" Caro flung down the comb she'd been using on Clair's hair. "I know exactly what is needed to coax a declaration."

Through their reflections in the looking glass Margaret saw Clair's eyes widen as she regarded Caro with skepticism.

"We must make him jealous."

Margaret and Clair both gawked at Caroline. "How does one do that?" Margaret asked.

Caro puckered her lips in thought. "I believe I have a plan, but first, Clair, before I can bring my plan to fruition, you must give me your word you will feign encouragement of another man's interest."

"I cannot possibly pledge to any such ridiculous scheme! Nothing could be more calculated to drive away Mr. Rothcomb-Smedley."

"She's right!" Margaret concurred. "Mr. Rothcomb-Smedley's a very proud man. If he thought for a moment Clair preferred another man over him, he'd bow out."

"Allow me to rethink this." Caro began to pace the carpet. After several moments, she turned around and eyed Clair, smiling brightly. "Then I propose you continue those things you do exclusively with Mr. Rothcomb-Smedley, things like your afternoons riding in the park, but at the more public functions, another man will give the impression to all that he's prostrate with love of you. He will need to be handsome. And rich. Otherwise Mr. Rothcomb-Smedley could never consider him a threat to his secure position in your affections. He will be so charming in public, and you will appear so flattered over his attentions, that Mr. Rothcomb-Smedley will hasten to secure your affections for himself."

Clair's jaw dropped. Margaret's eyes widened. Both stared at Caroline as if she'd started speaking in extinct tongues. "Where, may I ask," Clair demanded, "will you find such a *faux* suitor?"

Caro favored her sisters with a smug smile. "Actually, I met the man at the Finchley ball."

It was a moment before Margaret remembered she was Lady Finchley, and her sister was referring to *their* ball. On the night of The Kiss. Even before Caro told her who this man would be, Margaret knew. *Christopher Perry.* He was handsome. He was exceedingly wealthy. But he had scarcely noticed Clair. All his attentions had been on Caro.

"Pray tell, who?" Clair squinted at her sister.

"Mr. Christopher Perry."

"I've never heard of him."

"That, my dear sister," Margaret said to Clair, "is because he's not in Parliament, and you are only interested in matters of government."

"He's a great friend of Lord Finchley. He's called on me once or twice. I'm persuaded that, as a favor to me, he would pretend to be infatuated with you. Shall I ask him?"

Margaret knew that Mr. Perry's interest in Caro on the night of the ball had been decidedly keen, but she'd not heard that he'd actually called on her sister since that night. How very novel! John and his friends had heretofore never been attracted to well-born ladies. "Would you tell Mr. Perry the truth?" Margaret asked.

"I don't know yet how much I will tell him. I'm not sure if I know him well enough to trust his confidentiality."

"Men are supposed to be better at keeping confidences than women," Margaret said.

There was a knock at Caroline's chamber door. "A caller for you, Lady Caroline," Barrow said. "Mr. Christopher Wren."

All sisters exchanged amused glances, then burst into giggles. No doubt, by the time poor old Barrow had hobbled up two flights of stairs he'd gotten Mr. Christopher Perry's name mixed up with London's most famed architect, who'd been dead for many years.

Caro turned to Margaret. "Won't you accompany me?"

It took no persuasion since Margaret was always happy to have the opportunity to visit with her husband's life-long friends.

Mr. Christopher Perry was pacing the drawing room when the two ladies entered. His gaze leapt from Margaret to settle upon Caro, and he effected a bow, first to Margaret before resting his admiring gaze upon her sister. "How remarkably you two beautiful ladies resemble one another."

"I declare, Mr. Perry, you shall make us blush," Caro said. "Pray, won't you take a seat?"

He waited until the ladies sat, then he lowered himself into the nearest chair.

"I'm surprised to see you here," Margaret said. "I assumed you were with my husband." Then she clapped a hand to her mouth. "I beg that you not think me a prying wife."

He shook his head. "Finch says you're one in million. If a man has to be shack- -" He coughed. "What I'm trying to impart is that Finch is most gratified that he's wed a woman of your good nature and understanding."

It did not escape Margaret's notice that Mr. Perry had failed to address her husband's whereabouts. Her heart sank. Was he with his ladybird? Had he been with his ladybird on all these afternoons she'd thought he was at White's or race meetings, or boxing mills with his friends?

"You have perfectly described my dearest sister," Caroline concurred. Then she batted her lashes at her caller. "It's such a remarkable coincidence that you've come just as my sisters and I were discussing you."

He strutted like the cock of the walk. "How honored I am, my lady. Permit me to ask in what manner I was being discussed."

"Our older sister, Clair, is in need of an exceedingly handsome man of means."

"I should think every unmarried woman in the Capital would aim for the same."

The sisters laughed. That was too true.

"How clever you are, Mr. Perry," Caro praised. "Actually, our sister's affections are already engaged, but the man she wishes to marry has failed to see how advantageous their union would be."

"How is it that I came to be discussed. I don't believe I've ever met your other sister, and I don't mean to be unkind, but I don't believe I'd like to offer for her, either."

"Oh, you haven't met her, and you needn't offer for her," Caro said. "I was just telling her that you're just the man to sweep in, pretend to woo her, and make Mr. Rothcomb-Smedley so jealous he'll be down on bended knee begging for her hand."

Mr. Perry's brows squeezed together. "Shouldn't like to alienate Rothcomb-Smedley. Finch says he's a young man who'll be ruling Britain before he's thirty."

"It's just that you are the only man in the kingdom possessed of so many attributes—manly attributes—that would make Mr. Rothcomb-Smedley jealous." Caro had adopted her sultry, flirty voice that never failed to reap results from her gentlemen callers. "I assure you, I've thought long and hard to select the perfect man, and no other man, save you, Mr. Perry, will do." More eyelash batting.

How could two sisters who looked so very much alike be so very different? Caro had most certainly *not* given the matter long consideration! And look at how completely flirtatious she was! No wonder she'd received eleven proposals of marriage. Caroline could manipulate men as easily as winding a clock. And, unlike Margaret, she had absolutely no compunction about stretching the truth to suit her needs.

What man could refuse after being flattered like that? Mr. Perry looked rather like a strutting peacock.

"Very good of you to say that, my lady, though I fear you've excessively exaggerated my attributes," he said.

Caroline's lashes lowered with great solemnity. "Not at all, Mr. Perry. You possess all those attributes. I was hoping, for my sake, you'd . . . come to Almack's next week."

"For your sake, Lady Caroline, I would be honored." He tossed a glance at Margaret. "Provided Finch will come."

"I cannot speak for my husband. You must ask him yourself." She knew her husband would not refuse Mr. Perry. Refusing his wife was another matter altogether.

Caroline's face brightened. "I shall depend upon seeing you Wednesday night."

* * *

He'd sat at White's for nearly an hour before it struck him he was doing the same things he'd been doing nearly every day for the past seven years. Today, his friends' companionship felt flat. Especially when there was something else he wished to be doing.

"Wagers are being laid in the betting books on when Lord Styne lays Lady Baltimore," Arlington announced. "Perhaps we should throw you and Lady Finchley into the speculation."

"When will Lord Finchley's heir be born?" Knowles added.

John sprang to his feet, his hands coiled into fists, his eyes cold as agate. "If you value your life, I'd advise against that," he threatened Arlington. "I've a commission I'd meant to undertake this afternoon."

"You're not going to spar with me at Angelo's this afternoon?" Perry asked.

"I daresay Angelo will be grateful to be relieved of my presence one day out of three." Did his friends never tire of doing the same activities day in and day out?

"I will see you tomorrow night?" Perry asked. "In my box."

"Certainly."

As he left the slender building on St. James, John realized he'd not told his friends what his commission was. Nor did he mean to. They would not understand.

He mounted his gelding and began to weave his way through the busy streets of London, past Mayfair, past Westminster, along Charing Cross and into the old City. It had been a very long time since he'd come to this establishment, but he thought he could recall where it was. And if the proprietor had not deceased, John was sure he'd be able to recognize the man's shop by its distinctive sign.

In just over twenty minutes, as he meandered down a darkened alley, John spotted the sign swaying in the day's mild wind. It was shaped like a cricket bat.

He dismounted and went into the shop.

From the back room came ambling an aged man with only wisps of fine white hair above his ears preventing him from total baldness. Instantly sizing up John as a Gentleman of Quality, he bowed and greeted him. "What brings such a fine gent to Frederick O'Toole's establishment on this fine day?"

"I wish for you to construct a cricket bat for a very small lad."

"How tall does the boy be?"

John thought on it a moment. "He's three—if that gives you some idea. I'd say he stands about this tall." John held his hand three feet parallel to the ground.

"Ay, it does. I know just the size to make it for the little laddie. I can do it whilst you wait, if ye'd like."

"I'd like that very much." John found himself eagerly looking forward to returning to Trent Square and playing with Georgie.

$\mathcal{C}$hapter 16

As her maid was putting the finishing touches on Margaret's hair the following day, there was a tap at her chamber door. "Yes?"

"It's Finchley, er, John."

"You may come in."

He did not come in. He eased the door open and stood at the threshold, peering at her. "Will you be going to Trent Square today?"

"I used to go every day, but now just twice a week. That's when I instruct at the pianoforte." She noticed that his face fell, and she quickly amended her reply. "However, it always gives me great pleasure to go there. Should you like to go see your ward today?"

A smile tugged at his mouth. "I should. I've gotten something for Georgie."

She was relieved it was the lad—and not the lad's beautiful mother—whom her husband wished to see. "What?"

"I had a miniature cricket bat made for him. The carver assured me it was the perfect size for a lad of three." Her husband conveyed far more excitement over a three-shilling bat than he had over a gelding that had cost a hundred guineas.

It pleased her that he'd thought of the little fatherless lad instead of pursuing his hedonistic activities. Then she realized he must have been at the carvers the preceding afternoon when she'd feared he was with a ladybird.

How shameful that her mind had lowered in so prurient a direction. She stood, not sparing a glance into the mirror. "I'm ready now, if you are."

He nodded but waited until she had crossed her bedchamber's threshold before offering her his arm. That he had not stepped into her chamber rather deflated her. It seemed every time she thought they had taken a step forward in this marriage, he would push them back to the starting gate.

He made up for the regression by sitting beside her in the coach. Like a truly married couple, she thought with contentment. She hoped there would be a great deal of traffic between Cavendish Square and Trent Square this afternoon in order to prolong this trip. She was close enough to smell his sandalwood, to see the little beads of water still on his freshly styled dark hair, to observe the rise and fall of his manly chest. Her gaze trailed to his long legs stretched across the carriage, and her heartbeat accelerated.

She thought of his body stretched out beside hers. On her bed. Bare. She thought of her body stretched beside him. Bare. Her throat went dry. She tingled low in her torso. She grew more winded with each passing second. She experienced a gush of molten heat at her core. She was almost desperate to assuage this ache for him.

But she would never be able to mount the obstacle of her pride. Never would meek, timid Margaret be able to confess to John either her love or her desire for him.

Why can I not be more like shameless Caro?

She tried to force her mind anywhere but within this cozy coach. "Did you know that Christopher Perry has been calling on my sister Caroline?"

He whirled at her, brows hiked. "You must be mistaken. Could you have perhaps heard incorrectly? Percy, perhaps? We know a Christopher Percy."

"Why do you say I'm mistaken? What makes you believe your friend would not be attracted to my sister?"

"It's rather delicate. Don't like to speak of such in front of a maiden."

"Pray, do not think of me as a maiden! I am a married woman."

"So you are. But being wedded is not at all the same as being wedded *and* bedded."

She wanted to beg him to bed her. She wanted to scream it from the bell tower at Westminster Abbey. "Nevertheless," she said firmly, "I wish to be considered a married woman." Margaret never exerted herself, never spoke in so commanding a tone. He looked oddly at her. "Of course, my lady. I shall abide by your wishes."

"Then, pray, continue telling me why you believe Christopher Perry would not be interested in calling upon my sister."

"Because he doesn't like respectable ladies. In the past eight years he has never paid a morning call upon a well-bred maiden. That's why." He folded his arms across his chest.

"Then I daresay it will surprise you to learn that I was present yesterday afternoon when he called on my sister at Aldridge House for the third time."

His eyes widened. "I'm slap-dashed astonished,

to be sure!" He solemnly thought on the subject for a moment. "I believe I know what he's up to."

"Why does he have to be up to something in order to call upon my sister?"

"Because what he's doing is diametrically contrary to anything he's ever before done!"

"And so was your marriage!"

"So it was," he mused. "I believe my dearest friend means to imitate me."

"What do you mean?"

"There has never been a time in our lives when my friend did not covet everything that I possessed. Never mind that he possesses ten times my wealth."

It took her a moment to understand. Was Christopher Perry as adverse to marriage as his best friend had been? Would he merely wish to add Caroline to his conquests? "So you're saying that because you've married me, he's wishing to possess the woman who is almost my twin?"

"Exactly."

She was stunned by her use of the word *possess*. A month earlier, Margaret would never have used the word *possess* in connection with a man's relationship to a woman. She not only used it now, she used it in its most carnal sense. Physically, Margaret might still be considered an innocent, but her thoughts were those of one fully aware of her womanhood.

"Are you saying your friend might not have honorable intentions toward my sister?"

"I'm so stunned over his actions I don't know what to think, though he would *not* dishonor a noble lady. I'm sure of that."

"Oh, he comports himself as a gentleman."

"I'm just jolly well shocked that he wants to be

with your sister. She's not his sort, if you know what I mean."

"John?"

"Yes?"

"Do you think that since you are now married, Mr. Perry wishes to marry?"

"Ten minutes ago, I'd have wagered everything I possess that he wouldn't. But ten minutes ago I didn't think he'd ever consider calling upon your sister. Now, it wouldn't surprise me if he didn't want to copy me. Even by marrying into the Duke of Aldridge's family. It's just the sort of aristocratic toadying he'd be interested in!"

"Dearest?"

His brows scrunched. "Yes?"

"Mr. Perry does know the truth about . . . about our lack of intimacy, does he not?"

"He knows."

A pity. A pity there was no intimacy. A pity his friends knew she was nothing more than a spinster masquerading as a married woman. "Could you please ask him to keep my sister from learning the truth about you and me?"

"I can't believe as close as you two are that you've not told her the truth."

"My sister is accustomed to me obeying her. If she thought the marriage occurred because you were my secret love, she would not stand in my way."

A moment later, she continued. "Mr. Perry told my sister he'd come to Almack's next week—if you will accompany him."

He mumbled beneath his breath. "He's merely currying her favor. He knows bloody well I'll not step foot into Almack's."

She eyed him thoughtfully.

A devilish look flashed across his face. "Or will I? I believe I'll force his hand! I jolly well *will* go to Almack's Wednesday night! It will be worth it just to see Perry there."

The announcement that her husband would accompany her to Almack's made her almost as happy as his sitting beside her in the carriage. "I should love that, John." Her gaze connected with the oiled piece of wood that had been fashioned into a cricket bat for her husband's ward. How thoughtful that had been.

"Do you think Georgie's old enough to play cricket?"

He shrugged. "I started when I was just a wee bit older than he."

"Living where he's lived his entire life, I wonder if he's ever seen a game of cricket."

"Surely his mother has taken the lad to the park to see the men in white. What lad wouldn't love watching a cricket match?"

"I suppose all little boys are attracted to those kinds of pursuits."

"Not just boys. I have a female cousin who used to be uncommonly talented at cricket when she played with us. Did you never play with your brothers at Glenmont Hall?"

"My brothers were far too competitive over their play to allow us to join. Besides I would be hopeless. I know not the first thing about the game."

"Then I can instruct you as I instruct Georgie."

She shook her head. "As much as I wish to share my husband's activities, I must decline. My lack of skill is matched only by my lack of interest."

"A girl through and through."

* * *

He wished like the devil he hadn't sat beside her like this. It was impossible to do so and not remember the passion of that one kiss they'd shared. He had vowed not to allow that to be repeated. Yet, here he sat, acutely aware of her desirability.

He'd intentionally done this to himself in order to please her. She liked it when he acted like a husband, and he'd decided that husbands *did* ride beside their wives in carriages. She'd not precisely asked him to sit at her side, but he was coming to read her as one reads a familiar poem. She had been unable to conceal her pleasure the last time he'd ridden on the same seat as she.

In the same way as he was coming to know her, she instinctively knew him. Better than Perry. Better than Grandmere. Better than anyone ever had. From the very beginning, she revealed an astonishing understanding of him. His aversion to marriage, his desire to be with his fellow bloods, even his plan to bid on the gelding at Tattersall's—all these things she knew without ever being told. How in the deuce was she so successful at reading his mind?

She knew too that he could not be pushed or cajoled to her purposes. Nothing could have destroyed this precarious marriage more. Gentle, sweet Maggie was the ideal wife.

A pity he did not want a wife.

"You realize, do you not," she said, "that every single lad at Number 7 will be clamoring to play cricket with you and Georgie."

He hadn't thought of that. Nothing would make him feel lower than to disappoint those other young lads, lads who had no father to play with them. He thwacked his forehead. "I hadn't thought of that. Would you object if I have the coachman turn back?"

"Why?"

"Somewhere in our house all of my old cricket gear is packed away, and I mean to find it. By Jove! I'll have all the boys playing in the center of Trent Square!"

"A splendid idea!"

He tapped the roof of the coach and subsequently told the coachman to return to Finchley House. Once there, he quickly found the items in the attic—the first place he looked. Then he and Maggie climbed back into the coach.

"Do you know, my dear," she said to him, "I would not presume to tell you what to do, but do you not think it a good idea to show them a game of cricket first? Give them something to emulate."

"You mean at a place like Hyde Park?"

"I do. I've been thinking about such ever since you mentioned that Mrs. Weatherford might have already taken her son to the park to watch the men in white."

"I think that's an excellent plan, but Trent Square's not close to Hyde Park."

She frowned. "And some of the lads are far too little to walk that distance."

"I'll plan a future outing for the lads on a day I'm certain a cricket match will be held at the park. How many lads are there?"

"I've never counted. We had a total of eight-and-twenty children before Mrs. Nye wed, but her four children are now gone, replaced by a single boy, for a net loss of three."

"So you've got five-and-twenty children of both sexes."

She began counting on her fingers as she named them. "Of course my Mikey's too little, but he'd best not get a glimpse of the lads playing, or he'll have a fit to get in the middle of the action."

My Mikey. That troubled him. She was far too fixated on a lad who already had his own mother. It would have been different were the lad an orphan, and Margaret could claim him. "Why do you call him *My* Mikey?"

"It's shameful of me, I know. He was just a babe when I first came to Number 7, and his mother was so busy with the cooking and with trying to keep up with five children of her own, and worrying about him falling down all those stairs, that I delighted in taking the responsibility for Mikey when I was there. I've always adored babies. And Mikey has become very special to me."

She needed a child of her own. *But it will not be mine.*

He felt as if he were shirking his responsibilities, but he had no intentions of settling into marriage like Haverstock and Aldridge had. Those two—or so he'd been told—used to really know how to have a merry time of it.

He did not know what to say to her. He didn't want her to get hurt. Mikey could never be hers as long as his own mother drew breath. "Should you like me to find a little orphan boy for you to adopt?" he asked, his voice grave.

A wistful look passed over her face, then she shook her head. "Don't worry about me. I know Mikey already has a mother. A very fine mother of whom he's exceedingly fond."

He could not bear to think of Maggie ever

hurting. "Mikey loves you very much. One has only to see you two together to understand that."

"We are special to each other."

He wished he could assure her she'd have children of her own one day, but he could not lie.

As a gloomy silence filled the coach, he kept thinking about her addressing him as her *my dear*. He should be mortified if his friends heard it, but coming from Maggie, he thought it sweet.

When they reached Number 7 Trent Square, he met privately with Mrs. Weatherford and Georgie in order to present the lad with his special gift. The boy had no idea what it was to be used for.

"Oh, my Lord," his mother said, "I know my son will come to love the game as his father once did. It is impossible for me to adequately convey to you the depths of my gratitude."

"You have nothing for which to thank me. I'm doing what I believe George would want me to do. Besides, it brings me great satisfaction."

"Not to mention," Maggie added, "my husband enjoys playing cricket."

Maggie then helped him gather up lads who were interested in playing, and to his surprise, their mothers rushed to thank him. One plump mother said, "Oh, my late husband was ever so fond of cricket. He'll be smiling down from heaven at our boys. It's so kind of your lordship."

"Indeed it is," Mrs. Weatherford said, her voice a husky purr, her eyes flashing with approval. "Would you permit me to come and watch?"

He shrugged. "If you'd like."

He counted ten lads, including Georgie, who was the smallest.

"I'm just happy Mikey is down for his nap because he would want to barge into the game, and I daresay he's far too small," Margaret said.

Mrs. Weatherford shook her lovely head. "I do question if my George is old enough, but we'll soon see. I am certain he will enjoy it."

Before they set off, Lady Caroline arrived with the duchess and Lady Clair, and Maggie chose to stay with them.

* * *

The duchess and Mrs. Leander were continuing their interviews with prospective cooks. "Will you look in on my little lamb and get him when he awakens?" Mrs. Leander asked Margaret.

"You know it will be my pleasure."

As those two women strode toward the kitchen, Mrs. Leander was commenting to Elizabeth about how attached Margaret was to Mikey.

Clair turned to Abraham, and even though he'd been footman in her house far longer than he'd been steward at Number 7, Clair remembered to refer to him by his surname. "Carter, it has been determined that one of your new duties will be to keep the household ledgers, and I'm going to show you how to do that. Mrs. Hudson tells us you have an aptitude for sums."

"'Tis kind of her to say," the handsome young man said.

"Oblige me by coming to the dinner room. We can sit at the table there," Clair said. "Unless you have pressing duties now?"

"Nothing that can't be put off until later, my lady."

As they walked along the corridor toward the dinner room, Clair said, "Pray, do not get discouraged if you don't learn everything in a day. This will take some time. Perhaps weeks."

When it was just the two look-alike sisters

standing in the entry hall, Caroline turned to Margaret. "Did Finchley agree to come to Almack's on Wednesday?"

If Margaret wasn't convinced Caro wished to marry a duke, she would have thought her sister was romantically interested in Mr. Perry. Then she realized that Caro's scheme to have Mr. Perry make Mr. Rothcomb-Smedley jealous accounted for her interest in the gentlemen coming to Almack's.

Margaret hated subterfuge of any kind. Yet her whole life was now one big lie. "My husband has said he will go on Wednesday."

A smile lifted Caro's face. "That's wonderful!"

Margaret looked askance at her sister. "Are you happy that you'll be able to launch your deviant trap for Mr. Rothcomb-Smedley, or are you happy because you're smitten with Mr. Perry?"

"Both, actually."

Margaret was so surprised over Caro's admission she could not speak for a moment. "But what of your plan to hold out for a duke? Or least a marquess?"

"I thought a duke or marquess would have to be an improvement upon those eleven men who've offered for me in these past three years. But I'd not met Mr. Perry. I'd not seen your handsome earl, either. Those two—excluding their wretched reputations—put all the others to the pale. Do you not agree?"

"I cannot speak to Mr. Perry's attributes. I can only speak for my John, for how he affects me. He does put all the others to the pale." Margaret would never have believed that Caro would be attracted to a man without title or ancestral lands. Of course, Mr. Perry's late father had *purchased* a very fine ancestral estate, but that wasn't the same thing at all. "You know Mr. Perry does not come from an aristocratic family?"

Caro's eyes flashed mischievously. "Yes, but I daresay he's one of the wealthiest men in the kingdom, is he not?"

"I am told he is."

"And he is most handsome."

Margaret was astonished. Caro had never before admitted to being attracted to a man. Never.

"It seems, my dear sister, I owe you an apology," Caro said, "for hastily judging your husband without even being acquainted with him. Now that I'm attracted to his friend—and I daresay there's little difference between the two men's so-called profligate backgrounds—I can easily understand your attraction."

"I am so happy that you understand."

Changing the topic, Caro said, "Tell me about this beautiful Mrs. Weatherford."

Margaret filled her in the widow's connection with John.

"Does it not bother you the way she cannot remove her gaze from your husband?"

Margaret had thought perhaps her jealousy saw something flirtatious in the widow's demeanor where nothing existed. But if Caro, too, saw it, the widow must really be attracted to John.

"It does bother me. She's far too lovely."

"And he's acting like a father to her boy. I wouldn't trust her not to throw herself at Finchley."

Even Margaret's jealous thoughts had not traveled in the direction Caro's did. Her heart sank. What if there were a single kernel of truth in Caro's accusations? Margaret knew there was nothing whatsoever between her husband and Mrs. Weatherford at present. But what did the future hold? What woman could fail to be attracted to so handsome a man? What woman from the middle class would not want to unite herself with a peer of the realm, especially when that peer was possessed of dark good looks? It would be quite natural for Mrs. Weatherford to hope for a liaison with her protector earl.

Though Margaret's fears sharpened, she was determined to fight against such destructive thought. "Watch what you're saying. You are accusing the poor widow of the most vile conduct without any provocation. I beg that you not be so critical of her."

"You're too good."

Margaret shook her head.

"You need to be out there right now," Caro said. "Don't allow that woman to get her tentacles into your husband."

How Margaret longed to be there watching John with the boys, watching to see if the Widow Weatherford hungrily eyed Lord Finchley. Were his wife there, neither of them would ever act upon a mutual attraction.

"I cannot. I have to be here when Mikey awakens," she said solemnly.

"I'll watch out for your Mikey."

Margaret shook her head. "He only goes to me and to his mother. He'd be frightened to awaken and find another standing over his bed." She started up the stairs, steeped in melancholy.

* * *

At the theatre that night, instead of ogling the

comely bits of muslin on the stage, John found himself peering into the boxes opposite, peering into every box in the whole blasted theatre. What if Aldridge were here? Or Haverstock? They would be sure to be watching him, waiting for him to take a misstep. How bloody difficult it was to appease both Maggie's fearsome brother and John's oldest friend. Aldridge forbid him to take up with a doxie; Perry encouraged it.

What was a fellow to do?

Since they were lads, John had always allowed Perry to dictate to him. Perhaps because John had never been around other children until he came to Eton. Perhaps because, as the only son among several doting sisters, Perry was accustomed to ordering his siblings about. Whatever the cause, the mold had been set. A peer he might be, but John was subservient to Perry's whims.

When the final curtain was drawn, Perry would take him backstage to introduce him to Loosey Lucy. Perry had taken the lease on a nearby house where he had already installed the fair dancer for the mutual enjoyment of his friend and him.

But what if someone saw John mingling with the juicy little piece of crumpet? What if Aldridge had spies? The very thought launched a fresh search throughout the darkened theatre, trying to discern if anyone were paying particular notice to the box where he was sitting with Perry, Arlington, and Knowles. Unfortunately, when only men occupied a box, it was understood they were there to further their dalliances with the tarts who tread the boards. When the box holders were accompanied by respectable women, it was understood they were there to see the performance.

Wherever he looked, all eyes were upon the stage and its bevy of beauties. No one appeared to be watching him.

He'd never been plagued like this before his cursed marriage. He'd not spent a single moment in the presence of a doxie since he married. Oddly, he'd not for a single moment desired the presence of a doxie since he married.

Why in the devil had he consented to come here tonight? He'd thought of several excuses to explain to Perry why he couldn't, but he hated to let down the fellow. Perry was so slap-dash excited over this new dancer. And under no circumstances did John want Perry to accuse him of settling into domesticity.

That, John vowed to fight at all costs. *Can't have the bloods thinking I'm some old family man.*

It had briefly occurred to him to tell his friend that a man whose vital itches were being scratched at home had no need to go elsewhere, but decided against that, too. Not that he objected to his friends believing he and Maggie had joined together as other marital partners did. His objection was to speaking to anyone of his personal life with her. She did not deserve to have her sexual activities—or lack of—bandied about in clubs.

He grew nervous as the production neared its end and the entire cast assembled on the stage, all their voices raised in song. He'd only been married a month, but already it was as if he'd forgotten how to flirt with a loose woman.

After the play, the men sat there while the theatre emptied. A few gentlemen of their acquaintance popped in to greet them—and to make lascivious comments about the dancers. John could hardly make eye contact with the visitors because he kept scanning the theatre for Aldridge or someone Aldridge may have asked to spy on his wastrel brother-in-law.

When they finally went backstage, he was still nervous, still fearing that he'd been seen.

He and Perry and a handful of other men (thankfully none who appeared to be spying on him) waited outside the dancers' dressing room. Loosey Lucy was the third to depart. Up close and beneath the light of the wall sconce, he saw that some kind of white substance covered her face—he suspected to cover her freckles. Her cheeks were heavily rouged. She looked first at Perry and curtsied, then turned to curtsy to him, batting her eyelashes, then returned her gaze to Perry. "Do this be your Lord?"

Perry's dark eyes flashed with mirth as he nodded. "Lord Finchley, allow me to present to you Mrs. Lucy Dankworth."

John knew the marital title was nothing more than a fictional prop to lend these types of women respectability. He nodded and attempted to force a smile. After being with Maggie these past several weeks, it was impossible not to compare the woman who stood before him with the woman he'd married. With Maggie, he found nothing that could fail to please. She imbued many of the same fine qualities his mother had exemplified. Virtue. Loveliness. Modesty.

With Loosey Lucy, though, he was unexpectedly critical. Never before had it annoyed him when the tarts resorted to artifice or immodesty. Now, by contrast to the good woman he'd wed, he felt tainted just by standing there.

He was so stunned by that revelation that he could not concentrate on the words being spoken. Finally, Perry nudged him. "Ready to go to Mrs. Dankworth's?"

"Certainly."

To John's astonishment, Loosey Lucy possessively settled her gloved hand on his sleeve. He could not help but feel the brush of her jiggly bits as she sidled up to him. *Dear God, I pray no one sees me with this woman.* Especially Aldridge. Or one of his spies.

$\mathcal{C}$hapter 17

The following day when she arrived back at Finchley House, an ill-dressed man awaited. "Are you sure he's here to see me, not his lordship?" she asked Sanford.

"He specifically said he wanted to speak to the countess."

She invited him into the library and indicated for him to be seated upon a chair.

"I'll stand, my lady. My business is short. I have a proposition to make to you."

Her brow quirked.

"My name's Peter Moore." He said the name as if it should bring recognition.

"You write for the *Morning Chronicle!*" More than any other publication, the Morning Chronicle thrived on printing notices of John's most shocking deeds.

He cracked a smile. "Indeed. I've just come from your husband. He's engaged me to suppress certain of his activities from being printed. He will pay handsomely."

It stung that even though he was now married, John was still planning to engage in activities which needed to be suppressed from print. "I fail to see what this has to do with me."

"If you pay me less than a third of what your husband is paying, I'll allow you to have access to the items being suppressed."

Melancholy slammed into her like an avalanche. Raw emotions threatened to overpower her. Her heart sank. Her pulse pounded. When the odious man first spoke, she'd felt humiliated. Even stronger than her humiliation was her disappointment in her husband. By the time the slimy Mr. Moore had stated his proposition, rage tore through her.

"Leave my house." She glared at the ill-dressed reporter with more malice than she'd ever directed at another living soul.

"But, my lady- -"

"Leave, or I shall call my footmen to forcefully remove you."

He stumbled toward the door, muttering under his breath. "Ain't never had a wife refuse my services before."

Once he was gone and she'd heard the home's entry door slam shut, she collapsed onto the room's sofa. She felt soiled. How could anyone believe she would countenance spying on her husband in so devious a manner? Such an activity was contemptible. Even if her marriage had been based on love and affection, so vile a practice could rip apart the closest bonds.

An even heavier weight on her bruised heart was the knowledge that John was conducting himself in some kind of shameful manner of which her brother would never approve. Was it gambling losses? Excessive consumption of spirits? Oh, she thought, a thud in her heart, was it a loose woman?

Hadn't she been the one to suggest John use a portion of his newly acquired money to buy newspaper men's silence? Hadn't she insisted that their marriage would in no way change his lifestyle? Hadn't she said he could have a ladybird?

Then, words had come easily. She probably would have said anything to have him honor their marriage. Now, she could stand the loss of his fortune. Now, she could stand being married to a sot. Now, though, she did not know how she was going tolerate her husband keeping a ladybird.

Seeing how the widows of Trent Square were growing as close as the most affectionate of families and how dearly they loved their children and their children loved them impressed upon Margaret how lonely this marriage had made her. More often than not, she was rattling about this big, comfortable house with no one except servants. She missed Caro.

Perhaps a visit to her former home to be surrounded by those who loved her would dispel some of her gloom.

* * *

The only thing that made going to Almack's palatable was that Perry was going to be there too. They could suffer together. As John stole a sideways glance at Maggie, sitting beside him in the darkened coach, he realized there was one more thing to make so boring a night acceptable: he was honored to be escorting his lovely wife. What man did not enjoy entering a room with a beauty on his arm?

"A pity Grandmere won't be at Almack's tonight," he said. "I think she'd be pleased to see how lovely the Finchley emeralds look upon the new countess."

"They are lovely."

As are you. "Will I be obliged to stand up with

each of your sisters?"

"Of course." There was levity in her voice.

"I should prefer to waltz only with you."

"You will always be my preferred partner for the waltz."

He was already stirred by her ever-present rose scent, and now the thought of slipping an arm around her nearly overpowered him. "I'm confident you're the only one who will not criticize my incompetence, especially when I trample your feet."

She giggled. "But, you must own, your lack of skill—not that I'm accusing you of lacking dancing skill—is well compensated for by your good looks and agreeable height. You will always be a highly sought-after dancing partner."

Had his wife just flattered him? The very notion sent his pulse racing. He felt as if he'd just grown two feet. "You're much too kind."

"I'd like to think myself kind, but my compliment was sincere."

He took her hand and squeezed it. Then, for reasons not apparent to him, he continued holding her slender hand. It was bloody good that Knowles and Arlington weren't coming tonight. He'd never hear the end of their teasing about being henpecked.

When they arrived at Almack's, he was disappointed that Perry had not yet arrived. As a country set was about to begin, he asked the abrasive Lady Caroline to stand up with him, all in an effort to ingratiate himself with Maggie's favorite sister.

As they moved to the dance floor, she looked up and smiled at him. A first. "Are you certain Mr. Perry is coming tonight?" she asked.

So the smile had been prompted by her thoughts of Perry. "He gave me his word, and in the two decades we've been friends he's never gone back on his word."

"So he's honorable as well as handsome and wealthy."

Good Lord, was Lady Caroline smitten with John's oldest friend? Hadn't everyone said she was holding out for a duke? Surely she was aware Perry was not from a noble family. Perhaps John had misjudged her. Perhaps she did share some of her sweet sister's lack of affectation.

Throughout the dance, John could not dislodge his thoughts from a potential romance between these two. He rather fancied the idea of Perry getting shackled. What was the old saying? Misery loves company. They could suffer matrimony together.

In his wildest imaginings, though, John could not picture Perry in a domestic setting, could not fathom a time when monogamy would appeal to his friend. Perry without a mistress would be like England without a winter.

Midway through the dance, he observed Perry enter the chamber, stroll up to Maggie, and bow. Though John was no judge of men's appearances, he knew enough about fashionable dress to understand that his friend cut a dashing figure. He wore all black, save for the snowy white of his shirt and well-starched cravat that had been tied to perfection. As it should be. Perry paid exorbitantly for the most skilled valet in all of London.

After the dance, Lady Caroline fairly flew toward the newcomer. The face she put to Perry was diametrically opposite to the rigid demeanor she presented to her sister's UNfavored husband. "You did come!"

"Your wish is my command, my lady." Perry swept into an exaggerated bow, then kissed her proffered hand in much the same way as Arlington had practically slobbered over Maggie's the day they had met.

Lady Caroline—a most forward woman, to be sure—possessively linked her arm to Perry's, smiled up at him, then lowered her voice. "You see my sister Clair is standing with Mr. Rothcomb-Smedley. She's wearing an ivory gown."

Perry nodded.

"I am counting on you to charm her."

What the deuce was going on? John's quizzing gaze shifted to Maggie.

"Caro has concocted a scheme to make Mr. Rothcomb-Smedley so jealous that he'll come up to scratch with Clair," Maggie whispered.

"Do you think Perry will do it?"

She shrugged. "He seems—like most of us—to be at Caro's command."

To John's surprise, Perry nodded agreeably. "I will comply with my lady's wishes—provided my lady will allow me to waltz with her this evening."

Lady Caroline's lashes lowered provocatively. "I should love it above all things."

"Will Mr. Perry not have to make Clair's acquaintance first, before being accorded the right to dance with her?" Maggie asked.

"I plan to rectify that right now." Caro led Perry off to where Rothcomb-Smedley was standing.

John was stunned. Stunned by Perry's capitulation to the arrogant sister, and even more stunned by the vast difference between the two sisters.

When the next set started, Perry swept into another exaggerated bow and asked that Lady Clair stand up with him. As Lady Caroline rejoined Maggie and him, Rothcomb-Smedley appeared stunned as he stood alone on the perimeter of the dance floor.

A devilish look in her eyes, Lady Caroline addressed John. "You would have been so proud of your friend."

"Why?"

"Because he was positively exorbitant in his praise of Clair's beauty."

"I did think Mr. Rothcomb-Smedley looked vexed," Maggie said in her meek little voice.

They all turned at once and regarded the distinguished Parliamentarian. Mr. Rothcomb-Smedley, did indeed look lost. When he finally looked in their direction, he began to stumble across the dance floor to join them.

They all exchanged greetings. Maggie had perfectly summed up Rothcomb-Smedley's mental state. He was vexed.

He glared at John. "I don't recall ever seeing you and your friend at Almack's before."

John decided to aid the sisters' scheme to the best of his ability. "We've been remiss all these years, not realizing this is the place where one finds the prettiest ladies." He eyed his wife, then took her hand. "And the type of lady one wishes to settle down with."

To John's astonishment, Maggie took up the gauntlet and continued laying it on thickly for Rothcomb-Smedley's sake. "My husband says that Mr. Perry has always strived to emulate him, and now that my Lord Finchley has married, Mr.

Perry is likely wishing to settle down."

"And," Caroline added wickedly, "He's obviously found much to admire in Clair."

"Now see here," Rothcomb-Smedley boomed. "The man can't just waltz in here and try to claim the woman everyone knows is practically spoken for."

Caroline drilled Clair's suitor with an unflinching stare. "My dear sir, a woman is fair game until such time as she is *actually* spoken for. I am not aware that anyone has offered for my sister."

Rothcomb-Smedley clamped shut his mouth. His face had reddened with anger.

John decided that the evening was proving to be anything but boring. Rothcomb-Smedley was a good enough sort. His commitment to duty was commendable, but the fellow was a bore. It was good to see him squirm like this.

Obviously attempting to soften the man's ill humor, dear Maggie introduced a topic upon which Rothcomb-Smedley enjoyed expostulating. "You must tell us, Mr. Rothcomb-Smedley, how goes the tax bill you and my brother have worked so hard to pass."

His whole demeanor brightened. "As you know, it failed by a mere ten votes last year, and I'm happy to report that six of the those men have been persuaded to join with us and support the tax increase."

"That's good news, indeed," Maggie said.

"Aldridge must be thrilled," Caroline commented.

John nodded. "It's good that we've got dedicated men like yourself and Aldridge seeing to our interests." Even before his marriage to the duke's sister, John had been persuaded to favor the tax increase after hearing Aldridge explain at White's why the monies were needed to defeat the French.

Eying Caroline, John added, "Mr. Rothcomb-Smedley expends all his energies on his duties. Doesn't know how to have a good time like Perry and me."

"Now that you've wed," Rothcomb-Smedley said to John, "Why do you not take your seat in the House of Lords?"

Why would I want to do that? "I'm flattered that you might think I could contribute, but I assure you, it's not for me."

Maggie moved closer to him and set her hand on his arm. "I support my Lord Finchley in every decision he makes, but I do believe his non-participation in Parliament is our loss."

What had she just done? Without asking that he do so, his wife had just—in her own sugary way—told him she thought he should serve in the House of Lords. By Jove! She was more clever than anyone else in this room!

Of course, he still had no intentions in serving. Not even to please Maggie.

Other powerful leaders of the House of Commons were eager to speak and to be seen with Rothcomb-Smedley, and their circle soon ballooned in size.

When the set was finished, Perry escorted Lady Clair back to their group and continued to stand beside her. Even after Rothcomb-Smedley moved to stand at her other side, Perry continued to toss out a plethora of praises on Lady Clare's beauty. "How is it that I am seven and twenty and have failed to cross paths with you before, Lady Clair?"

Before she could answer, a glaring Rothcomb-Smedley did in an icy voice. "You and your circle of friends have never before expressed an interest in *polite* Society. I don't recall ever before seeing you at Almack's."

Perry's sparkling black eyes met John's. "Surely we must have come here before?"

John shrugged. As much as he liked making Rothcomb-Smedley uncomfortable, Rothcomb-Smedley was making John uncomfortable. Two months ago John would happily claim his well-earned reputation as a dissipated rake, but now—in the presence of this able Parliamentarian—John's hedonistic lifestyle embarrassed him.

He was also embarrassed that this man who was younger than he had accomplished so much, and he and his friends had never done anything more than drink excessively, gamble wildly, and copulate prolifically.

Even Maggie and her sisters had done something at Trent Square to which they could point with pride. But John, Perry, Arlington, and Knowles could die tomorrow, and never have left a mark of their existence.

As low as he was feeling, it was about to get worse.

The Duke of Aldridge, his pretty blonde duchess on his arm, strolled into the chamber with the arrogance of a Turkish potentate, all the while glaring at John. As he neared their knot of acquaintances, his gaze switched to Rothcomb-Smedley, and a smile replaced the glare. "Ah, Rothcomb-Smedley, you're just the man I was hoping to see."

The other man's brow lifted. "Indeed, your grace?"

"It's my pleasure to tell you that the Lord Chancellor has finally capitulated to our cause."

Rothcomb-Smedley's face brightened. "He will actually support the tax increase?"

"He will."

"I cannot tell you how indebted I am to you, your grace."

"Not nearly as indebted as I am to you for all you've done for Britain in the House of Commons."

Rothcomb-Smedley turned to Clair, who was smiling as broadly as he. "I feel like dancing an Irish jig with you, my lady!"

"I know exactly how you feel," she said, "for I cannot contain my glee. You and my brother have worked so hard for this. Now that Lord Knolles has thrown his support, the rest will follow. You are to be congratulated." Clair turned to her brother. "You, too, Aldridge. You've been the force behind this success."

The Marquess of Haverstock joined their crowd next. Surrounded by three such successful leaders of the government made John feel even more worthless.

Then, the duke's gaze met his. "A word with you, Finchley."

John's heartbeat drummed.

Chapter 18

The two men were silent as they left the ballroom and descended the stairs. John stayed a step behind the duke as he led the way to an empty chamber at the end of the long corridor on the ground floor. John felt like a convict approaching King's Bench for he knew he had done something which had drawn the duke's wrath.

Because he'd not gambled recklessly since he'd wed, he had a very good idea what he'd done to incite the duke's anger.

And now he understood what it felt like to be falsely accused.

Aldridge shut the door behind them. It was not quite a slam, yet it was not a polite closing, either. As he stood there peering down at John, the wall sconce illuminating the duke's dark face, John could detect the fury in his flickering gaze.

"When you married my sister," Aldridge began, "I warned you that I'd not tolerate any ladybirds—especially so soon after the marriage. You are making a laughing stock of Margaret, and I will not tolerate it." He drew up to John, his fiery anger simmering like hot coals. "I can crush you."

John swallowed. Even as a school boy being reprimanded, he had never spoken back, never defended himself against accusations—mostly because the accusations had always been justified. But this was different. He did not so much want to shield himself from the duke's anger as much as he wanted to protect Maggie against these assumptions.

"I do not doubt that you're capable of crushing me, but may I remind you that doing so will harm your sister. I, your grace, will not tolerate anything that will hurt my wife."

The duke raised a quizzing brow. "You should have thought about that before leaving Drury Lane with a trollop."

"I know it looks bad. I will own that I was seen departing the theatre with a lightskirt on my arm, but once I got to our destination, I could not bring myself to break my marital vows. I give you my word."

The duke snorted.

"Now that I am married," John continued, "I need to strive to be more mature, to not be so subject to the encouragement of my . . . dissipated friends." He couldn't believe he'd just called his dearest friends dissipated, but it was the truth.

"I am relieved to know that you realize how immature your actions have been. I had wanted someone older, someone more mature for Margaret. In fact, I'm sure it will come as no surprise for you to learn that I never wanted her to marry you. Yet, to my disappointment, she fell in love with you. She's by far the most sensitive—and loving—of all my sisters."

John was stunned. *She fell in love with you.* He had never really considered that Maggie could love him. But then he realized she was merely a very good actress. She wanted his title and the respect and freedom it would give her as a married woman. She could not want him. Especially when there were men—noble men like Rothcomb-Smedley—available. "And she's the most virtuous woman I've ever known. Her very goodness has ruined me for the other sort of women."

"I hope to God you're telling me the truth." Aldridge's lips formed a grim line.

"I hope I do not flatter myself by telling you that you can ask anyone who knows me, and they will confirm that I do not lie."

The duke's eyes rounded. "It's the same with Margaret."

"Yes, I know. Unlike me, though, she is possessed only of good qualities."

Their eyes locked. The lone sound to be heard was the muted strains of the orchestra playing far above them.

"I hope to God you're telling me the truth, Finchley." Aldridge stalked away.

As John silently followed him up the stairs and back to the ballroom, he'd never felt more like a recalcitrant lad.

Their group had swollen even more by the time they returned. Morgan and his wife, Lady Lydia, had joined the others. Even though John disliked this type of gathering, he was beginning to fancy the notion of being a member of a large family like the Haverstock-Aldridges. As an only child, he'd always longed to have siblings. Perhaps that is why he was always so subservient to Perry. He'd been desperate for playmates. Especially popular ones like Perry.

It was a pity he and Aldridge didn't rub along better. He'd always liked Morgie, but as John took his place next to Perry, who had Lady Clair on one side of him and Lady Caroline on the other, and smiled and nodded at Morgie, Morgie quickly averted his gaze.

It was as blatant as a cut direct.

What had John ever done to relinquish his standing with the jovial Morgie?

He was soon to get an inkling.

Morgie was watching Maggie as she was standing up with Lord Selby. "Yes, indeed," Morgie said to his wife, "now that I'm a member of your family I think of all your sisters as my sisters—including Lady Margaret because she's now sister to your Elizabeth."

"Remember, dearest," Lydia said, "she's no longer Lady Margaret but is now Lady Finchley."

He mumbled under his breath.

Even though John could not hear the words, he could tell by the movement of Morgie's lips that he had said, "She's too good for the likes of him."

Blazing anger tore through John. His first instinct was to send a fist crashing into Morgie's face even though he would never be so ill mannered to do something like that in so public a place. Then, he simmered down.

For he knew that in his affection for Maggie, Morgie merely voiced what everyone else did—and which John knew to be the truth: Maggie *was* too good for him.

* * *

As soon as it was apparent to Margaret that the orchestra was striking up a waltz, her eyes met John's. Wordlessly, he moved to her. "I beg to stand up with the loveliest lady at the ball."

She smiled up at him and placed her hand in

his. Whenever their hands linked she was always reminded of that first day at St. George's when they'd stood at the altar declaring their vows. She'd been startled, in a most satisfying way, at how pleasurable such physical contact could be.

As was dancing with him. She gloried in the feel of his hand resting at her waist, at the notion of their bodies facing each other so intimately. And, quite naturally, she thought of how it would feel to have him lying beside her. In her bed. She was well aware that John could never think of her as a desirable woman. He would never be able to consider her as anything other than the mousy woman he'd married.

Not only John. Every person in the chamber tonight likely would believe the same. No one would believe that the ever-so-proper former Lady Margaret Ponsby could fantasize about allowing the notorious Lord Finchley to peel off her clothing and sink into her.

But that was indeed the direction of her thoughts whenever she was with the notorious man she'd married.

What a pity that she was too proud and too shy to ever let him know what she truly wanted. *Why can't I be more like Caro?* If Caro hungered after a man, the man would know it. Caro went after what she wanted, and she always got it.

Underlying her happiness at waltzing with her husband, a deep dread reverberated through every cell in her body. Why had Aldridge sought a private word with John? The expression on her brother's face had been just short of thunderous.

Obviously, her brother knew something about her husband—something neither John nor Aldridge wanted her to know. Either her husband was losing large amounts at play, or . . . or he was dallying with a doxie.

That had to be why that odious newspaper man had breezed into her house to negotiate. What woman would ever wish to hear that her husband's affections were elsewhere engaged?

Margaret recalled overhearing Lady Haverstock and the duchess discussing the intimacies of marriage. Lady Haverstock had told Elizabeth that a man whose bedroom needs were taken care of at home need never stray elsewhere.

If only Margaret were in a position to satisfy her husband in that way. If only she could talk plainly to Caro about the origins of her marriage, Caro could likely think of a way for Margaret to seduce the man she'd married.

But Margaret could not tell Caro or anyone else that she'd married a stranger who had no intentions of honoring his wedding vows to her.

Not asking him why her brother wished to speak with him was one of the hardest things Margaret had ever done. Husbands did not like prying wives, and she dare not skate on the thin ice of their marriage.

As her thoughts flitted to Caro, she and Mr. Perry swept past. Margaret could hear her sister outrageously flirting with John's wealthy friend. "I shan't allow you to call upon me until I'm assured you've forced Mr. Rothcomb-Smedley to propose to Clair. And I'm sure he will. He was exceedingly jealous of you—with good reason. You're quite the most handsome man here tonight. Your eye for fashion is impeccable, and your dancing is more than adequate."

Margaret was unable to hear Mr. Perry's reply because they moved away. Margaret had to own that Mr. Perry—while she did not believe him half as handsome as John—was a far better dancer. She would not be surprised to learn that Caro's feet were not trod upon a single time.

Unlike Margaret. Poor, dear John really was a most inferior dancer. Thankfully, his height and handsomeness more than made up for the deficiency.

"Dearest?" she asked.

"Yes?"

"Do you think Mr. Perry could fall in love with Caro?"

"How in the blazes should I know what Perry wants? I would have lost my stable by wagering that he'd never step foot in Almack's." He shrugged.

"I take it Mr. Perry's never been attracted to decent women before."

Her husband did not answer.

"You men always stick together! You're not going to tell me about your friend's baser instincts, are you?"

"Certainly not. You're a lady."

I wish I weren't.

She was pleased to see Clair dancing with Mr. Rothcomb-Smedley. That man had taken Clair for granted for far too long. It was time he realized what a treasure he had in Clair. As Margaret observed them, she was able to detect a softening in Mr. Rothcomb-Smedley's manner. More than that, he could not remove his adoring gaze from her. He was quick to smile, and Margaret was convinced that he was seeing Clair in an altogether new light.

Some of Caro's schemes were not so bad after all.

"I thought tomorrow we could go to Trent Square," John said.

"So you can play with the lads?"

"Of course."

"Since I'm not to instruct on the pianoforte tomorrow, I should love to watch you." *And keep an eye on the beautiful Mrs. Weatherford.*

Her husband sighed. "I wish I could dance every dance with you. You're the best partner I've ever had."

It was comments like that which made her forget the melancholy that had arisen when her powerful brother had stolen John away. "Thank you. You're my favorite partner." *In every way.*

"I say, the longer we've been together, the more I think of what you told me the day you convinced me . . . to pretend as if we were the happily married couple."

"What was that?"

"You said we'd always be loyal to one another. And though we've known each other less than two months, I feel as if we've always been friends. Just like with Perry."

She herself had introduced the analogy of friendship the day she coaxed him into accepting their marriage, but hearing it on his lips felt flat. While she was pleased he regarded her with such tender sentiment, friendship was only one component of the relationship she wished to establish with John. "My dearest Lord, no woman wishes to hear that her husband thinks of her as a male companion!"

Flustered, he stumbled, crushing the baby toe on her left foot. "Did I hurt you?" he asked with concern.

"No." She hoped he was unable to detect her

wince.

"Forgive me. Pray, forgive me, too, if I gave the impression I think of you as a male." His feet stilled, and he looked down at her, his smoldering gaze whisking along her face to settle for a second at the low-cut bodice of her sea mist gown. "I am fully aware of your feminine attributes."

Her pulse accelerated. *I have attributes?* "I do hope that's a good thing."

Shrugging, he continued with the dance. (If the movements of his feet could be called dancing.) "I have tried to think of you as a fellow, but it's too bloody difficult."

"I assure you, I'm happy to know that, and I hope you'll be happy to learn I could never think of you as I think of Caro or one of the girls."

"Indeed I am!"

"You have earned my complete allegiance. You are dear to me, and I will always support you, always be your advocate."

"By Jove! I feel the same about you. In fact, you are not at all annoying—as I'd expected you to be."

"Did you just compliment me?" She burst into laughter.

"I meant it purely as praise. Sincere praise— which you have most heartily earned. I cannot think of a single detriment to you."

She felt as if she had stacked another brick. "Then I shan't enlighten you!"

She was sorry that the orchestra chose this moment to end the waltz. She would have been perfectly happy to glide across the dance floor in his arms all night long. Most reluctantly, they began walking back to where her siblings congregated. She did wish Aldridge would be nicer to John.

Though the notion of what John must have done to merit Aldridge's wrath made her feel beastly, she was bolstered by the confidence that she looked her best tonight. Her dress was perfection. The frothy sea mist green trailed elegantly behind her, and much of her back was exposed. Caro has sworn that no woman at Almack's could possibly rival her. "I have it on excellent authority that men love to see a lady's exposed back, and yours is lovely," Caro had said.

Therefore, Margaret ever so subtly moved in front of him as they made their way to the edge of the ballroom. Then suddenly her progress was impeded. She stumbled forward. But her dress did not move. There was a ripping sound.

Without even turning around, she realized John had stepped on the train of her gown.

She felt a swish of air on her backside. Dear God, were her undergarments under display?

"Oh, Maggie Love," John said remorsefully. "You'll never believe what's happened."

She was too vexed to even realize he'd just referred to her as *Maggie Love*. She would die of mortification if everyone at Almack's was currently perusing her unmentionables. She took a deep breath to keep from chiding him. "I forgot to gather up my skirts. I fear you've trod upon them."

He closed the small gap between them. He was so close she could smell his sandalwood scent and could feel his breath when he spoke huskily into her ear. "Stay close to me. My body will shield your. . . exposure from view."

She had never been so humiliated. Just a moment earlier she had thought herself beautiful.

Now, she was likely a laughing stock. She began to take tiny steps toward the stairway that would lead to an exit from the building. She couldn't be gone soon enough.

"Forgive me," he said solemnly when they finally reached the top of the stairway. "I told you I was useless in a ballroom."

Morgie, two cups of tea in hand, was approaching them. Once again, he ignored John but flashed a hearty smile at her. "Ah, Lady Margaret! That is, I meant to say, Lady Finchley. Lyddie says I'm to ask you to stand up with me. Daresay she'd wish me on a dragon to keep from having to dance with me herself." His face blanched. "Not that I could possibly think of you as a dragon. You're like my very own little sister, and you look most fetching tonight." He scowled at John in much the same way as her brother had. "Will you do me the goodness of standing up with me once I deliver these cups?"

"It's kind of you to offer, Mr. Morgan, but my husband and I are obliged to leave at once." Were she not so shy by nature, she could have explained further, but never would she be able to discuss something like exposed unmentionables. Even if Morgie was practically family.

"A pity," he said with disappointment. "You're quite one of my favorite dancers." He started toward the ballroom, then stopped and turned around. "You will tell Lyddie I asked you?"

Mortified that he'd see her unmentionables, she swung back around. "Yes, of course."

On the ground floor, she backed into a wall of the entry hall whilst her husband went to retrieve her velvet cloak. Once he settled it upon her shoulders, she felt like going limp with relief.

In the coach on the way home, he apologized profusely.

All of a sudden she started to giggle.

"Pray, what's so blasted funny?"

"You. The things you try to do to keep from having to go to Almack's with me!"

Humor flashed in his eyes. "Well, now, does that mean you'll spare me these assemblies in the future?"

"Absolutely not. You're still my preferred dancing partner."

"If you call what I do dancing." Unconsciously, he drew her hand into his, and the interior of the coach grew quiet, the only sound the rhythmic clopping of hooves on the streets.

"Do you know, John, as embarrassed as I was for others to see my . . . well, you know, those under-garments, I wasn't embarrassed for you to see them."

"You may not have been, but I bloody well was!"

So much for her attempt to lower the barriers to their intimacy. If only they served champagne at Almack's. With that effervescent liquid to loosen her inhibitions, she would have eagerly asked him to kiss her again. Throughout the remainder of the ride home, she struggled to summon the courage to ask, but she was far too shy.

* * *

He hated like the devil what he'd done to her beautiful dress. When they arrived at their house, he apologized again. "I say, Maggie, I'm beastly sorry for ruining your gown."

"It's not ruined. My maid will be able to repair it."

He lifted a hopeful brow. "Truly? You're not just saying that so I won't feel so bloody bad?"

She shook her head. "I assure you Annie's a magician with a needle."

The coachman opened the carriage door.

"Allow me to carry you into the house," John said to Maggie. "I shan't want to drag your beautiful skirts along the pavement."

"You're so gallant. The last time you carried me to prevent me from falling upon my face after I imbibed too much champagne."

"I wish you wouldn't bring up that night." He left the coach, then turned back and scooped her into his arms.

"It was an exceedingly happy night for me. Why do you not want me to bring it up?"

How could he tell her how agonizing it was to remember taking her in arms and not want to repeat it? Being this close to her was pure torture. "I fear my behavior that night was anything but gallant."

"*Contraire!* You did a lady's bidding."

True. She had asked him to kiss her. Why in the devil must he keep thinking about that? He was painfully aroused.

He swept through the doorway and carried her upstairs to her bedchamber. For a fraction of a second, he stood frozen in the doorway, his gaze leaping to the big curtained bed. He did not belong here. Not with the sweet likes of Maggie.

He drew a deep breath and strode across the chamber, depositing her on the silken bedcovering. "Good night, my lady. Should you like me to ring for your maid?"

"I can manage."

He went through her dressing room to his,

banging the door shut behind him, then peeled off his clothing.

For a very long time he lay in his bed, drenched in thoughts of making love to Maggie. Not rushing to her bedchamber was the hardest thing he'd ever done.

$\mathcal{C}$hapter 19

The next day he went to Trent Square and played cricket with the lads, giving special attention to Weatherford's boy. The little fellow looked so much like his father. As sad as John was over his friend's death, he recognized that George Weatherford would live on in this child. Their resemblance did not stop with the physical. When Georgie took the bat, his stance was identical to his father's. And there was something in his laugh that reminded John of his dead friend.

When John had heard that Weatherford had married right after he'd left Oxford, he'd felt sorry for him. What a pity, he'd thought, to be tied down when there were so many lovely ladies to be had, so many good times ahead. Perry, Arlington, and Knowles had all concurred. Why would a man wish to get shackled so young?

He no longer asked himself that question. Though Weatherford may not have been wealthy, he had things—priceless things—that John and his closest friends did not. His gaze had flicked to Weatherford's beautiful widow, then to the little piece of George Weatherford whose skinny little arms gripped the cricket bat in the exact same way his father had. John swallowed over the huge lump in his throat. *Good Lord, why am I being so maudlin?*

Could anything on earth be more precious than having one's own son? What man on his death bed would not wish to know that part of him would live on?

Though Maggie had praised him for his attentions to young Georgie, John knew he wasn't coming to Trent Square merely to help the boy. He was coming to Trent Square because he wanted to be there. He wanted to spend time with these lads, wanted to share what had taken him a lifetime to learn, wanted to feel warmed by the sun instead of sitting around White's gambling or sparring at Jackson's studio.

Every day now for the past two weeks, he'd come to Trent Square to impart to the lads some of the things they were missing by not having a father. On one day, he'd given them riding lessons on his own mount. That activity had been wildly popular. He'd followed along at the side of each of the lads as they took turns atop his gelding.

Mostly, they played cricket within the fenced park area in the center of Trent Square. Each day, Mrs. Weatherford had insisted upon coming. She had a little folding chair she'd bring so she could sit and watch her lad laughing and playing. It seemed to John she smiled much more often now.

Sometimes—on days like today when Maggie was not obliged to instruct upon the pianoforte— she would come and watch, too. He didn't think she liked cricket because when she was there observing the game she seldom smiled. When she thought he wasn't looking, a melancholy look would sweep over her. He'd continued to reassure her that her presence was not required, but she pretended she wanted to be there.

On this day, Georgie's hit went farther than he'd ever before managed, and he began to run like the wind. John's delighted gaze connected with Mrs. Weatherford's. "Your boy's showing great progress."

She favored him with a luscious smile. "All owing to you, my Lord. How will I ever repay you?"

"The joy is all mine." He meant the words.

The gate opened, and Lady Caroline came strolling into the park. As was her usual persona with him, she glared. *What in the bloody hell have I done now?* She went straight to her sister and wedged between her and Mrs. Weatherford. It seemed to him she was cold, too, to the widow, but perhaps he was just imagining it. She slowly faced Maggie. "You came in your coach today?"

"I did."

Lady Caroline directed her glare once more at him. "And Lord Finchley?"

"We did not ride together today. He came on his horse."

"Then will you please take me home?"

"Are you ready now?"

"I am."

"I take it you're not interested in a game of cricket played by novices."

"You are correct."

To his astonishment, as his wife started to leave, she came to him and brushed her lips across his cheek.

"Good-bye, love," he said as naturally as if he were commenting on the weather. Now why had he gone and called her *love*? People would think . . . exactly what he and Maggie wanted them to think: that they were a truly married couple.

* * *

She had lived with Caro for enough years to know when something was troubling her sister. After they were in the carriage, she asked, "What's the matter?"

Caro's eyes narrowed. "I know everything about your marriage."

Margaret felt as if she'd just been knocked down by a cannon ball. It took her a moment to even try to articulate a response. She cleared her throat. "By everything, what precisely do you mean?"

"I know about the coincidences, about *Miss* Margaret Ponsby of Windsor."

"I shall be very vexed with Mr. Perry. He told you, did he not?"

"He only told me what I had a right to know! He's Lord Finchley's closest friend, and he knows. I'm yours, and I did not know! My God, Margaret, how could you?"

Margaret's lashes lowered. She couldn't look Caro in the eye. "Because I cannot remember a time when I did not worship him from afar."

"Not once did you ever say a word to me!"

"I knew you thought he was dissipated."

Caro tossed back her head in a haughty manner. "I'd never even met him."

"But you did know about his reputation as a rake."

"That's true."

Both women were silent for a moment. Finally Caro said, "Do you mean to tell me there has never been another man who appealed to you?"

"Never. Only him."

More silence. Finally Caro sighed. "And you still fancy yourself in love with him?"

Margaret nodded.

"And you've . . . not been intimate with him?"

Margaret shook her head.

"Do you *want* to be intimate with him?"

"Oh, yes, more than anything!"

Caroline giggled. "Methinks a vixen lurks beneath my shy sister's meek exterior."

"I could never act like a vixen."

"You're going to have to if you hope to win Finchley's affections."

Margaret eyed her sister skeptically. "What are you saying?"

"We have to form a plan—a scheme to capture your husband's heart." Caro took her sister's hand and squeezed it within her own. "All I've ever wanted is for you to be happy."

"Oh, Caro, I'm so vastly unhappy right now." She burst into tears.

Caro hugged her close and allowed her to weep until she could articulate why she was so utterly unhappy. "I'm afraid John's fallen in love with the beautiful Mrs. Weatherford. He wants to be with her—and her boy—every day. And have you seen the way she gazes so adoringly at him?"

"Forgive me for planting those seeds in your mind. You are probably reading too much into the widow's gratitude. She's, quite naturally, grateful to Finchley for all he's done for her and her lad." Caro pursed her lips. "Of course, you must own, the man you've married *is* exceedingly good looking."

"How could I not own it? I've admired him since long before I ever came out of the school room."

"Now, it's for you to make him aware of your

womanly charms."

"How do you propose I do that?"

"Not shyly. If I wanted the man to whom I was lawfully wed to bed me, I would never deny the attraction. Remember always that men would happily mate with a fence post if it would gratify them. You've got to make him know you're a woman ripe for his lovemaking. Be particularly honest."

"I can't very well say *I'm madly in love with you.*"

Caroline shook her head. "No, don't say that. Say something like, *When I lie in my lonely bed at night, I throb for you.*"

Margaret's cheeks turned hot. "I couldn't say that!"

Caro stared into her sister's eyes. "Tell me true, have you ever lain in your bed and throbbed for him?"

Margaret swallowed and nodded solemnly.

"I promise you, the man has not been created who would not happily comply after a lovely woman makes such a declaration. Men are made for just that sort of thing!"

Now Margaret giggled. "And you know this because?"

Caro shrugged. "Not first hand. Not yet. But I can't deny throbbing in certain unmentionable places whenever I'm with a certain man."

"Christopher Perry?"

Her eyes flashing mischievously, Caro nodded. "I'll have him, too. I mean for him to propose marriage."

"Surely you wouldn't be so forward with him as to speak of throbbing parts."

A sly smile barely lifted Caroline's mouth.

"When I contrived to be alone with him yesterday for a few moments, I said—in a husky, breathless voice—*When you look at me like this, I feel as if you're slowly stripping me of every article of clothing.*"

"You didn't!"

"I most certainly did."

"And what did he say?"

Caroline's eyes flashed with mirth. "It wasn't so much what he said as how a certain part of him reacted."

"He raised a brow?"

Caro laughed out loud. "A much lower part."

"I don't understand."

"You are too, too innocent. Do you not know about how a man's . . . dangling part juts out like a cannon when he's aroused?"

Margaret's eyes rounded. "I've never heard of such a thing! Are you sure you aren't making it up?"

Her sister shook her head. "You need to become adept at peering at the bottom of men's torsos. You'll be able to tell when a man desires you."

Margaret's mouth gaped open. "How do you know these things? Surely you've not . . ."

"I have not, but our rakish brothers, before they went in the army, told me all manner of things."

"And you never told me?"

Caro directed a haughty look at her sister. "So it seems we both held secrets from one another."

"I don't understand why Harold and Compton would have told you and not told me about those matters."

"You goose. Because they know how bashful

you are. But if you want to earn Finchley's undying love, you must forget your shyness. Pretend you're me. Then tell him—preferably in a low, throaty voice—that whenever he's near you have the most provocative thoughts. And when he asks you what they are, you say something like *I think about your hand beneath my skirts*, or tell him you dream of lying perfectly naked with him."

The blush once more stole into Margaret's cheeks. "You know I could never say those things."

"You must coach yourself to be assertive like me. Pretend to be me. Once is all that will be required. Once he's bedded you, I am certain he will realize his good fortune in having you for a wife, and he'll be enslaved by his love for you."

"I cannot imagine John ever being enslaved by love for any woman."

"You're not being fair to him. He has undergone a vast change since you've wed. Mr. Perry's always lamenting that Finch spends less and less time with the fellows. He hasn't even been fencing at Angelo's or sparring at Jackson's in more than a fortnight."

Margaret frowned. "Because he wishes to spend every day with Mrs. Weatherford and her son."

"I believe he's merely exercising his guardianly duties with the boy, and I also believe he's coming to realize there are more important things in life than the perpetual search for dissipation."

"He's never with me at night. He'd much rather be with Mr. Perry and their other friends."

"Then you give him a reason to want to spend his nights with you." She directed a bemused stare at Margaret. "You do know lovers can contrive such things whether it be day or night, do you not?"

"I am not a total moron."

As they rode on, she thought of what Caro had said. She made it sound so simple to engage John's affections.

"Using a portion of the advice I'm administering to you, I will have a proposal of marriage from Mr. Perry."

"You'll actually tell him you throb for him?"

"I most decidedly will! Men love those kinds of intimacies far more than we do. Women are governed by our hearts; men are governed by their . . ."

Margaret raised a flattened palm.

* * *

As they rode to Trent Square the following day, he continued with the custom of sitting at his wife's side. He'd come to associate a light rose scent with her. He was reminded of the way his lovely mother always wore a lavender scent. To this day, lavender evoked happy memories of the gentle press of his beautiful mother's lips onto his cheek, of her sitting beside his bed when he burned with fever. The smell of lavender always infused him with happiness.

Now, the smell of roses, of Maggie's roses, was having a similar effect upon him. He found that he enjoyed being with her. He admired her greatly. He also felt protective of her, as if he wanted to shield this fine woman from knowledge of the evils of the world—and from knowledge of his own offenses. That's why he'd offered to pay Moore to suppress news of his foul deeds. The funny thing was, since he'd married Maggie, there had been a marked difference in his behavior. He had repeatedly insisted to his friends that Maggie had nothing to do with taming him. But he had to own that her brother did.

His gaze flicked to her. How elegant she looked in the blue frock she was wearing. Today her eyes matched the colour of the dress. Since the weather was fine, she wore no pelisse, no cloak. He was powerless not to stare at the promise of her smoothly rounded breasts. At first he felt guilty for even lowering his gaze to that part of her. He still feared Aldridge had spies everywhere. But then he realized Aldridge believed that they shared a bed. John gave an inward bitter laugh. Aldridge even believed Maggie was in love with him!

There was one disadvantage of riding in Maggie's carriage. Every time it was just the two of them inside a coach, he remembered the passion of their shared kiss.

And every time he was in the coach with her, he battled a strong desire to repeat The Kiss. Even though he had vowed to himself he would not kiss her like that again.

"Do you think Georgie's big enough to have a pony?" he asked, principally in an effort to purge his mind of this numbing desire he felt for her.

"Certainly not! He's only three."

"I'm almost certain I had a pony when I was his age, and it's not like I would permit Georgie to trot off without me at his side."

"Shall we ask your grandmother? She'll know at what age you got your first mount, and besides we haven't seen her in more than a week."

"Excellent suggestion." He tapped at the coach roof, then directed the driver to Berkeley Square.

His grandmother's delight at their visit was

mostly directed at Maggie. "You look lovely in blue, my dear, does she not?" Then Grandmere deigned to meet his gaze.

"Indeed she does."

Maggie went and sat beside Grandmere on the sofa, then he sat beside Maggie and drew her hand into his. He could tell by the expression on his grandmother's face that it pleased her to see them showing affection to one another. "Maggie suggested you are the one to answer a question for us."

The old woman lifted a brow. "And what might that be?"

"Do you recall how old I was when I got that pony?"

"I most certainly do. It was the same age as your papa got his first mount—much to my protestations that my son was too young." She shrugged. "When it comes to their cattle, men will have their way."

"I was three, was I not?"

She nodded solemnly. "Much too small, in my opinion, but either your Papa or a groom always ran along beside you."

He eyed his wife, a cocky expression upon his face.

"Why all this interest in young lads?" Grandmere asked, then a stupendous smile broke across her face. "Do not tell me there's to be an addition to our family!" He'd never heard his grandmother sound so gleeful.

His gaze flicked to Maggie. A blush crept up her cheeks as both of them shook their heads in denial.

Grandmere's face fell.

He went on to explain to his grandmother

about his ward.

"I was very sorry to read of George Weatherford's death in the newspapers," she said. "I met him just that once he stayed with us at Tolford Abbey and thought him a very fine young man."

"You would be so proud of how seriously John's taken to his role as the lad's guardian," Maggie said. "He goes every day and plays cricket with all the lads at Trent Square."

"That's the house for the officers' widows that the Duchess of Aldridge established?"

Maggie nodded. "John is now spending more time there than any of us."

Grandmere favored him with a shimmering smile. "I cannot tell you how happy I am to know this. You are demonstrating considerable maturity."

He tossed a grateful glace at Maggie. "That's what my friends keep telling me."

"Then that's the best news I've had since the day of your wedding." His grandmother directed a softened gaze at Maggie.

The old lady had been incapable of concealing her wholehearted approval of Maggie as countess to her grandson. It occurred to him he could have looked the kingdom over and not found a better woman than Maggie. That is, if one wanted to be married. Which he certainly did not. But if he did, he could not do better than Maggie.

He wondered about the men she had turned away, men who *wanted* to be wed to her. Were they prostrate? They would have to be. The knowledge gave him a heady sense of possession. He stood. "We need to push along to Trent Square." He offered Maggie a hand.

"I hope next time the two of you pay me a joint visit is to announce that the countess is breeding."

Poor Maggie turned scarlet.

* * *

As they continued on to Tent Square in the coach, she kept thinking about what Caroline had said. Was it her sister's provocative remarks or the nearness to John that made Margaret tingle in private places? All the while she kept thinking about gathering up the courage to speak as boldly as Caro had suggested.

Though Caro was likely right about how eagerly such words would be accepted by a man, Margaret also knew she was incapable of saying something that was so blatantly erotic.

Once and only once Margaret had been able to suppress her own shy personality and force herself to act as she thought Caro would. She had to own, that ploy had been wildly successful. She had no doubt her success was due solely to her emulation of Caro. If mousy Margaret had attempted to persuade John to allow her to move in with him, she would still be sharing a bedchamber with Caro at Berkeley Square.

Margaret determined that when night came, she would draw on stores of courage summoned from throughout this day. Then she would forget her shy persona and speak to him as Caro suggested.

This time tomorrow she hoped to be married in every way.

When they arrived at Number 7, Margaret was surprised that the duchess's fine carriage was not in front of the house. She and Mrs. Leander were to make their selection of the new cook that morning. As Margaret and John entered the house, Clair rushed to greet them. Margaret's staid, cerebral sister had never before acted so exuberantly. She was flying down the stairs, her hair whipping every which way as she giggled like a ten-year-old girl. "You will not believe all the wondrous things this day has brought!"

Margaret eyed her sister. "It cannot be that the duchess has given birth four months early, or I think it would *not* be wondrous news. What is so blissfully wonderful?"

"Elizabeth is with Lady Haverstock."

"Her lying-in has arrived!"

"Better than that! The babe is here. Lord Haverstock has his heir."

Margaret remembered the last time when poor Lady Haverstock had given birth to a still-born babe. "And the babe's healthy?"

Clair nodded. "Haverstock himself rushed to Aldridge House this morning to tell our brother he is the father of the most perfect little son. A huge son. Lord Haverstock believes Lady Haverstock carried the babe for ten months."

"That is indeed wondrous news, is it not, John?" Margaret peered up at her husband. She had little doubt he must think discussion of babes utterly boring, but he attempted to feign interest in the subject. "I'm very happy for Lord Haverstock. What man doesn't want for a son?"

The mention of *man* and *son* in the same sentence coming from her husband's mouth sent Margaret's heart racing. Was he merely being polite? Or was he hungering for a son? Had being around the beautiful widow and her little boy made John wish to make a home? With them? Would John wish to have his own son with Mrs.

Weatherford? Margaret knew most men of their class kept mistresses, many of whom bore them illegitimate children. Look at the Regent's brother, the Duke of Clarence. He and the actress Mrs. Jordan had ten children—all of whom the duke acknowledged openly.

Movement at the top of the stairs caught Margaret's eye, and she looked up to see Caro gracefully descending. "Has Clair told you her own stupendous news?" Caroline asked as she reached the bottom step.

All eyes moved to Clair.

"Before he went to the House of Commons today," Clair said, "Mr. Rothcomb-Smedley came to me. He'd been unable to sleep." Her gaze lifted to Caroline. "It appears I owe much to your scheme with Mr. Perry. My dear Richard said he would not know a moment's peace until I would consent to be his wife."

Margaret flew to her and nearly crushed her sister with hugs of happiness. "This *is* wondrous! You two were made for each other."

John waited for the all the hugging to cease, then offered his congratulations. "I suppose this means Perry will no longer have to pretend to pay you court."

Clair nodded. "I must express my appreciation to him. I owe my joy to Mr. Perry."

Margaret shrugged. "I suppose Mr. Perry no longer will have a reason to come to Almack's or the like."

Caro glared.

For reasons Margaret could not comprehend, she felt compelled to aggravate her favorite sister—likely because Caro was so thoroughly didactic. "You must know my husband and his friends do not enjoy assemblies and balls—not when there's the camaraderie of other males and the pursuits that bring them so much more pleasure."

Caro stomped her foot. "I refuse to believe that—not when Mr. Perry is possessed of such excellent dancing skills."

John gave the sisters a quizzing expression. "Perry dances divinely?" He started to laugh. "Hidden talents, I daresay. Wait until I tell Arlington and Knowles."

"We shall see," Margaret said to Caro. "Mr. Perry may still call upon you. After all, did you not tell me that men favor such topics as you last discussed with him?" How shocking that Caro had actually told Mr. Perry that she felt as if he'd peeled off every article of her clothing. Had she no sense of shame? The very thought made Margaret's cheeks hot.

Yet she admired her sister's gumption in going after what she wanted. *If only I could be more like Caro.*

Tonight, I will.

"Oh, dear," Clair said, "I hope that if Mr. Perry begins calling upon Caro, Mr. Rothcomb-Smedley does not deduce their scheme that caused him to propose."

Caroline gave a haughty air as her gaze circled them. "If Mr. Perry should prove to be interested in engaging my affections, I shall instruct him to say he transferred his affections from one sister to the other."

John laughed again. "Perry's never been one to be dictated to, but far be it from me to know what goes on in that man's mind. Where Perry's concerned, you, Lady Caroline, proved me wrong once before."

"But, my dear husband, my sister is more than a match for your friend. Caro always gets what she wants."

The sisters' gazes locked.

Caroline tossed back her head and laughed. "La! I could not be so presumptuous that I would attempt to manipulate a strong-willed man like Mr. Perry." She obviously spoke for John's benefit.

And she obviously did not share her sister's reverence for the truth.

By then several of the widows—especially those with sons—gathered around them, all the young boys eager to play cricket with his lordship. Mrs. Weatherford turned to Clair and curtsied. "Allow me to congratulate you, my lady, on your upcoming marriage. I pray you're as happy in matrimony as I was."

The way the widow spoke, it sounded as if she might still be in love with her husband. Had the woman's attraction to John been nothing more than jealous assumption on Margaret's part?

As the boys gathered around John, Margaret met his gaze. "I'm off to teach at the pianoforte, and I'm vexed with you that you've stolen Robbie away from me."

John shrugged. "Can I help it if lads prefer cricket to all else? It was the same with me when I was a boy."

"It still is!" She stood on her tiptoes and brushed a kiss across his cheeks as she went to climb the stairs.

Clair looked at Abraham but spoke as if she were making an announcement of great portent. "I would say I'm going to work with Carter and the household accounts, but methinks the student has surpassed the teacher."

"That's not true, my lady," Abraham Carter said, shaking his head. "But the student most certainly had an excellent teacher."

"I know firsthand what a fine student you make, Carter," Mrs. Hudson said. "There's a matter I'd like to discuss with you. Would you do me the goodness of accompanying me on a stroll around the square?"

"Certainly, madam."

* * *

Whilst his wife and her sister went to see the new Haverstock babe, John went home. Sanford, a troubled look on his face, met him in the entry corridor. "I pray I've done the right thing, your lordship. Your female caller insisted that she wait for your return."

A female caller? He hoped to God it was not Mary Lyle. From his butler's disturbed look, something told John this female wasn't the sort he was accustomed to seeing at a fine home in Mayfair. "What is the female's name?"

"Miss Margaret Ponsby."

$\mathcal{C}$hapter 20

He hadn't thought on the Windsor spinster's name in several weeks. How had she found him? He'd been careful to only use his family name of Beauclerc on the contract. How had she learned that the man she had planned to marry was the Earl of Finchley?

Why had she come today? It suddenly occurred to him that the woman had never received the hundred guineas he'd promised her.

He strode to the library and opened the door. She had not taken a seat but was perusing the books in his library. "Miss Ponsby?"

She turned around. The woman was old enough to be his mother. Possessed of black hair lightly threaded with gray, she was ugly. What a contrast the two Margarets were!

His thoughts flashed to how distraught he'd been after he'd wed Maggie. Now, he realized that a Higher Power must have known what was best for him that day, must have guided the most flawless creature to become his wife. What had John ever done to deserve such blessings?

"Lord Finchley, I believe you're guilty of being in breach of contract with me."

"Pray, be seated."

He sank into a chair by his desk and regarded her. "I beg your forgiveness. I am under an obligation to pay you a hundred pounds. You shall have two hundred. I'm sorry you've had to come all the way from Windsor." Obviously, the woman knew the Beauclercs were the Earls of Finchley.

She glared at him. "I want an annuity."

"I am not a wealthy man. The reason I wished to marry was to get my hands on my grandmother's money. I've not been successful."

"But now you've married an heiress. A duke's daughter. I think you'll pay. I'll tell your grandmother—and the Duke of Aldridge—about your matrimonial scheme."

She was bluffing him. Outside of himself, no one knew about his matrimonial scheme except for Maggie, Perry and his solicitor. All them were completely trustworthy. Anything she thought she knew was pure conjecture. Even if she had hit the nail right on the head. "You're at liberty to do so. But then you'll not get a farthing from me."

Her shoulders sank. She looked pitifully defeated. He did feel beastly that he'd forgotten to send her the hundred quid. She looked as if she could use it. "It was unforgiveable of me not to send you the money." He unlocked the desk drawer where he kept a pouch of sovereigns. At least a hundred of them. "Pray, Miss Ponsby, I beg that you accept this in partial acceptance of the debt I owe you. There are a hundred here. I'll have my solicitor bring you another hundred in Windsor this week." This time he would not forget the unfortunate woman.

He stood and strode to her.

She stood and accepted the pouch, then began to leave the room. When she reached the door, she turned back. "You've fallen in love with Lady

Margaret, have you not?"

His eyes widened. And he nodded.

John Beauclerc, the Earl of Finchley, never lied.

* * *

Margaret and Caroline went to Haverstock House to see the new babe. The marchioness, in white lace, sat propped up in her bed surrounded by those who loved her. The marquess sat on the side of the bed, holding his wife's hand. Was it the sunshine streaming in through the casements illuminating them like deities in Renaissance paintings, or did the two of them actually glow, Margaret wondered.

Their babe slept in a cradle near the bed, with Lady Lydia giving him her full attention.

"You just missed the duchess," Lady Haverstock said. "She's been here all day, but Aldridge insisted she go home to rest."

"My friend," Lord Haverstock explained, "worries about the babe my sister's carrying."

"He's as bad as Morgie was," Lady Lydia said, shaking her head.

"Where *is* Morgie?" Lord Haverstock asked.

Lydia smiled. "He decided he wanted to take his son for a ride through the park. He won't own it, but he's exceedingly proud of little Simon."

Lord Haverstock rolled his eyes. "He may not own it, but he's one proud papa. Everyone at White's knows the little fellow's first word was Papa."

Now Lydia rolled her eyes. "I daresay everyone's grown tired of hearing how Simon is possessed of extraordinary athleticism because he walked at so early an age."

Margaret moved to stand over the cradle and

gaze upon the sleeping babe. Like his parents, he was dark haired, only his little wisps of hair were much finer, like down. He was so small, even though he was big for a newborn. He lacked the reddish complexion of those who've just left the womb. With his smooth, fair skin he did look he was a month old. He was awfully precious. "You two have a beautiful babe."

"Thank you," the marchioness said in a low voice. Then she eyed her sister. "I can stand it no longer. I daresay it's been half an hour since I've held our little lamb. Please bring him to me."

Lydia beamed. "Any excuse to pick him up." She reached down and tucked a thin blanket around the sleeping babe, then lifted him, cooing and planting soft kisses atop his head as she gave him to his mother. "It seems like it was just last week when Simon was that tiny."

Lady Haverstock's cooing and kissing of the slumbering babe were indistinguishable from Lady Lydia's, Margaret thought. What a beautiful mother she was, all in white lace, her dark tresses curling about her beautiful face. The picture she presented as she gazed adoringly at her infant, her loving husband leaning over the pair of them, was worthy of a Rafael.

How Margaret would have liked to hold the babe! But Lady Haverstock had waited so long for this day to come, Margaret hadn't the heart to take him away. Perhaps next time.

"I do hope he has his mother's fine looks," Lord Haverstock murmured.

Lady Haverstock shook her head, laughing. "I wish for him to be the image of his papa."

"It matters not what either of you want," Lydia chastised.

As she stood there in the marchioness's chamber, Margaret was seized with an intense sense of emptiness. She wanted John to love her as Haverstock loved his Anna, as Morgie loved Lydia. She wanted a son, a son borne of their love. Like the Haverstocks and Morgans. As she stood there amidst such happiness and merriment, she had never felt more alone.

When she returned to Finchley House she told herself her veil of melancholy might be lifted if John were there. She was determined to force herself to act as if she were Caro. She would gather her courage and tell him of the desire that strummed through her whenever she was with him. She knew enough of men and their needs to know that it would be difficult for a man to not jump at such bait.

When she arrived home, the house was quiet. She climbed the stairs to her bedchamber, hearing no sounds that would indicate John might be there.

From habit, she went first to her room. Annie had left a candle burning beside the bed, and a fire burned in the grate. Her eye darted to her dressing room—which abutted her husband's dressing room. *I must act as Caro would.* She drew a fortifying breath.

Emboldened, she strolled through her dressing room, through his, and came to his bedchamber, where his valet was scooping her husband's boots from the floor.

"Oh, my lady, you've just missed his lordship."

"Has . . . has he gone for the night?"

"Yes. He told me not to wait up for him."

Now she felt even lonelier, were that possible. Her secret hopes of consummating this marriage tonight were crushed.

* * *

White's was thin that night. "Where in the bloody hell is everyone?" John asked Arlington.

Knowles responded. "The House of Commons is voting tonight on the tax bill."

Though heretofore he had little interest in the political arena, John realized his wife's sister would soon be married to the powerful Mr. Rothcomb-Smedley, and John didn't want to be the family fool. "What do you say we go sit in the gallery there tonight?"

Perry's brows lowered. "Have you not known me for two decades?"

"I have," John responded.

"And in those two decades have I ever demonstrated the slightest interest in the affairs of government?"

"You've demonstrated interest only in drinking, gaming, and whor- - -"

Knowles cut off Arlington. "Certainly you never demonstrated an interest in your studies."

Perry took a long look at the faro box on the next table, then glared at Knowles. "Pray, enlighten me as to why it's necessary in life that I speak in Latin. Or Greek. I've been gone from university for almost seven years and cannot remember a single instance when I needed such knowledge."

Knowles shrugged. "It's one of a gentleman's necessary accomplishments."

Perry laughed. "I'd rather be a rake." He turned to meet John's gaze. "In that vein, I have a most decided treat in store for you, old boy."

"What would that be?"

"We're all going to Brighton tomorrow to see

the steeplechase from Brighton to Hove. I've let a house there for us—and we shall have all the feminine comforts a man could desire. Do you know, Finch, Mary Lyle says she wants you back. I've arranged for her to come."

"And," Arlington added, "I doubt Aldridge has spies down on the coast. You can cavort to your heart's content."

If he wanted to cavort.

As John stood there facing his longtime friends he began to feel an outsider. He did not want to go to Brighton. He never again wanted to see Mary Lyle or other women of her ilk. He would rather be watching the action in the House of Commons tonight than standing there at White's with his dissolute friends, drinking brandy and playing faro.

Since he'd been a boy of eight or nine he'd been dictated to by the popular Christopher Perry. But no more.

He drew in a deep breath. "If no one means to go to watch the parliamentary proceedings with me, I shall go by myself."

Perry raised a single brow. "We leave early tomorrow for Brighton."

John eyed Perry. "I'm not going."

"It's not as if Aldridge will have spies inside Perry's lodgings," Arlington said. "We'll see that the women stay indoors, if that's what you're worried about,"

John's gaze fanned over his three friends. "My decision has nothing to do with Duke of Aldridge."

Perry started to chuckle. "I see. You've finally bedded Lady Finchley."

"And why shouldn't a man bed his own wife?" John challenged. It was no different than telling a lie. He never, ever lied to Perry. Yet tonight he wanted Perry to believe he and Maggie were married in that most vital way. "Has it never occurred to you that a man can tire of dissipation?"

He thought of Georgie Weatherford, of being a father. He thought of Rothcomb-Smedley and his duties in Parliament. He thought of the serious-minded Haverstock and Aldridge, whom no one could deny were honorable men.

He felt less a man and more a boy.

"I wish to bring pride to my grandmother and to my wife. I've been thinking even of taking my seat in the House of Lords."

"Put your hand on his forehead, Knowles," Perry commanded. "Finch must be mad with fever."

"I've never felt better. I choose to act like a man." He turned and walked away.

He was almost ashamed to admit that he was six-and-twenty years of age and had never once taken enough interest in the proceedings of the House of Commons to actually take in a session at St. Stephen's Chapel in the Palace of Westminster. He took a couple of false starts before he managed to find St. Stephen's and climb the stairs to the gallery where he squeezed into one of the last remaining seats. Members below—some raucously—discussed the merits of the tax bill.

He found himself admiring Rothcomb-Smedley. The man could not be more than five and twenty and already he held one of the most important posts in government. All because of dedication and nobility of character.

Fleetingly, John wondered if this time next year

Rothcomb-Smedley and Lady Clair would have a son. How rich their lives would be.

Especially when compared to John's.

During a lull in the proceedings below, his gaze wandered, then connected with the Duke of Aldridge's. His brother-in-law was not more than twenty feet away from him. Their eyes linked. The duke nodded, then spoke to the man beside him, who scooted down. Aldridge indicated for John to come sit beside him.

He excused himself and a moment later was lowering himself onto the bench by Aldridge.

"I did not know you were interested in things like tax bills," the duke said.

"My interests seem to be changing. In fact, I'm thinking seriously about taking my seat with you in the House of Lords."

A smile slowly spread across the duke's face. "I will help you in any way I can."

"As I will help you."

Aldridge regarded him for a long moment. "Then you approve of the tax increase?"

"How could I not when it's so necessary?"

The smile Aldridge bestowed upon him made John feel as if he knew what it felt like to be coronated.

After the votes were tallied, and the measure was proclaimed to pass, all the men surrounding them began shaking the duke's hand, their faces lifted with pleasure. "You must be very proud," one man said to Aldridge, "since you're the moving force behind this bill."

"Wellington will likely bow at your feet," another said.

"It's been a momentous day, to be sure," the duke said.

John thought of Rothcomb-Smedley's proposal of marriage and of the Haverstocks' new babe. And now successful passage of the tax bill. It was indeed a momentous day.

He would like to have rushed home to share the good news with Maggie. She would be so proud of her brother's success. But by the time they left St. Stephen's, it was after three in the morning. Maggie would be asleep in her bed.

$\mathcal{C}$hapter 21

When she awakened the following morning, her maid presented her with a note from her husband. Even though they'd been married for nearly two months, she had never seen his handwriting. A smile curved her lips as her gaze swept over the page. His hand conveyed the same breezy, carefree, youthful traits that imbued John. It was indistinguishable from that of a youth of sixteen.

Dearest Maggie,

I am obliged to miss going to Trent Square today as there are other matters of import that demand my attention. I expect to be away all day, but I beg that you join me for dinner at my grandmother's house. I have sent a similar letter to her, notifying her of my intentions of spending the evening with the two most important women in my life. If all goes well I will be at liberty at that time to make an announcement that I hope will please you both.

Affectionately,
John

That she was the only person to call him John and he was the only one to call her Maggie still had the power to gladden her. How pathetic she was that she must take pleasure in such little things.

The pleasure she derived from her husband's note, though, was no small thing. He had said she was one of the two most important women in his life! He wanted to spend the whole evening with her. More bricks were being laid in the foundation of their marriage.

How ominous his letter was. What kind of announcement could he possibly make that would please both women? Had he acquiesced to a firm resolve to stay away from high-stakes play? Had he—remembering his unfortunate father's demise—determined to become a teetotaler? Though she could wish for a promise from him to stay away from lightskirts, she knew her husband well enough to understand he would never discuss such a subject in the presence of his grandmother.

It was really awfully mysterious how she had come to understand him so well. She'd never before been a particularly intuitive person, but with him she was. It was as if there was some magical connection between them. She could not remember a single instance when her intuitions about him had been wrong.

From the first she had understood his great aversion to marriage. She knew that he embraced his freedom to pursue pleasure with a great heartiness. She realized he would rather be with his friends than to mingle in polite society.

She also understood that though he deserved his reputation as a rake, his intrinsic good was at odds with the actions that had defined him the past decade. His grandmother saw beneath the reckless behavior to the fine man he truly was.

There had always been—on Margaret's part—

an exclusive bond to him. The attraction had been there for as long as she could remember. No one, no obstacle, or no thing had ever been able to diminish its fierceness.

She wished his grandmother could see him with Georgie and the other lads. Something inside her melted. How she longed for him to have his own son. What a wonderful father he would be. His grandmother knew that.

Now Margaret did too. As much as she wanted her own son, she wanted John to become a father even more passionately.

I must mimic Caro.

In her hands was the ability to see that dream come to fruition. If only she could seduce him. All the subterfuge would be worth it if she could get him to get her with child for he would adore a son. She would adore a son. And Grandmere would adore a great grandson.

After she dressed, she scurried downstairs and found Mrs. Primm. "Do you know if we have any champagne here at Finchley House?"

"I believe there's a case laid away in the wine cellar."

"Please have it sent to the dowager's house on Berkeley Square with a note that says Lady Finchley has sent it for tonight's celebration."

As determined as Margaret was, she knew she could use all the help she could get.

* * *

This was the first time in weeks she'd gone to Trent Square and not found her husband there. All the lads were vastly disappointed.

As was Mrs. Weatherford, judging by the disappointed look on her pretty face. "I believe," Mrs. Weatherford said, "I've learned enough about cricket to take them out today."

"It is a lovely day," Margaret said.

"Will you come with us, or is this your day for the pianoforte?"

"It's pianoforte day," Margaret said, feigning disappointment.

Mikey came running up to her, his little arms held up. Even though he was excessively fond of Margaret, she knew his first interest was being swung into the air. She hugged him close for a moment, smacking his cheek with kisses, then swept him through the air as he squealed.

His mother stood watching, a smile on her face.

Margaret set him down and eyed his mother. "How's the new cook?"

"She's most satisfactory."

Margaret helped Mrs. Weatherford gather up the cricket equipment John had left there and assisted in corralling all the lads out to the park area.

When she returned to the house, Mrs. Hudson was descending the stairs, a dreamy expression on her face.

For some unaccountable reason, Margaret's gaze leapt to the widow's left hand. Every day since the two women had met a year earlier, Mrs. Hudson had worn her deceased husband's plain gold wedding band.

But not today.

Margaret smiled up at her.

"May I have a word with you, my lady?"

"Would you like to walk along the pavement?" Margaret asked. "It's a lovely day."

"Indeed I would." Her gaze swept to Carter. "Will you watch out for Louisa?"

He bestowed an equally dreamy expression at her. "You need never ask."

"I am so blessed to have Carter in Louisa's life. No birth father could be more loving."

The women left Number 7 and began to walk along in front the houses on the square.

"I wanted you to be the first to know," Mrs. Hudson said.

"That I was right about Abraham Carter being in love with you?"

Mrs. Hudson nodded shyly. "After you spoke to me that day, I realized the feelings I felt for him were very tender."

"But both of you were too shy to disclose the feelings."

The other woman nodded solemnly."He's possessed of such a noble countenance, I knew he would never make the first step."

"So what did you do?"

"I prayed for the Lord to give me the courage to declare my feelings for him. I practiced what I was going to say for days. And finally I told myself that I held the keys to my happiness in my hands. Failing to act upon it could punish all three of us, could deprive us of all those things I had once shared with dear Harry."

"So you had finally realized that you were meant to be married again?"

Mrs. Hudson nodded. "I can think of no finer man to unite with than Abraham."

"Indeed he is." Margaret's step slowed. "So I take it the Lord gave you the courage? Pray how did you bring this about?" Perhaps Margaret could learn from this woman.

"First I contrived to be alone with him." She swallowed. "Since you're a married woman, I can tell you that because I've been wed before, I know a bit about physical intimacy. I know how to gauge a man's reaction to it."

This was exactly the kind of information Margaret needed to hear. "With a true gentleman, the woman often has to make the first move." Margaret thought of The Kiss. As much as John had enjoyed it—and she had no doubts of that—he had not initiated it. Nor would he. He respected her far too much. More's the pity. "So what did you do?"

"First I asked him to walk with me as you and I doing right now. I told him I needed to discuss something about the household accounts. Then I managed to link my arm through his. It was the first time we had ever touched in the soon-to-be-a-year since we'd met. Still, that was somewhat stiff and formal." The widow blushed. "Then, it embarrasses me to tell you, but I made sure the sides of my breasts rubbed against him."

Margaret wondered if Mrs. Hudson then eyed the lowest part of Abraham's torso to see if it did that cannon thing Caro had told her about.

"I. . . I believed he was not unaffected by my intimacy."

So she had looked at his private part! Really, Margaret should not be thinking of her former footman's private part.

"After I finished discussing the deliveries that were to be paid for that day, we started back to Number 7. When we reached the steps to the front door, I stopped. I stepped on my tiptoes and brushed a kiss across his cheek."

"Did you say anything?"

"I thanked him for being the most important man in my life."

"And he just let you walk into the house?"

A smile broke across Mrs. Hudson's face. "Actually, no. He told me I was the most wonderful woman he'd ever met and that if I weren't still in mourning for my husband, he should like to always take care of me."

"So you're to be married?"

The widow nodded happily. "We wanted to wait to tell the others once I'd had the opportunity to speak to you." Mrs. Hudson clasped Margaret's hand. "We owe our happiness to you."

Margaret held both of the other woman's hands. "True love like yours would have found a way, but I am happy I helped to speed it along. I cannot tell you how much this pleases me. I know you two will be very happy together."

* * *

Later that day Margaret had her coachman stop at St. George's Hanover Square. She kept thinking of Mrs. Hudson's words about the key to her happiness lay in her hands. Just as it did with Margaret. Like Mrs. Hudson, she must pray for the courage to make John see how good a marriage between them could be.

It was much warmer in the church now than it had been that day, the day of her marriage to John. Then it had been cold.

Like that day, she had the church to herself, and like that fortuitous day, she ambled to the candles at the side of the church and lighted one, then knelt to pray.

Dear Lord, You once gave me the courage to emulate my sister, and it resulted in fulfillment of my fondest hope. Now I beg that once more you enable me to speak to my husband as a true wife should. I pray for the blessed consummation of this marriage I've wanted all of my life—and which I know can be good for him too. I ask all of this in Your name.

* * *

Leaving nothing to chance, Margaret selected her gown for the evening's mysterious celebration. She wore what she had called her bridal dress. It was the one she'd had made for the dowager's ball. It was what she had worn the only time she and John had ever exchanged a passionate kiss.

Their only one.

She still remembered how approvingly he had looked at her that night, still remembered the thrill of his earnest compliments. It had been the most romantic night of her life.

Tonight would be even more romantic.

After she dressed, her maid clasped the diamonds around her neck and stood back to peer at her mistress. "Oh, my lady, you look beautiful!"

Margaret knew she could not look better.

She stood and took one long glance in her looking glass.

Every single weapon in this war of love would be used.

Including champagne.

Chapter 22

"How lovely you look, my dear," the dowager exclaimed when Margaret swept into the drawing room. "Please come sit by me." She patted the silken sofa where she sat.

"I wanted to wear my finest dress for the occasion."

"It's the one you wore on the night of your ball, is it not?"

Margaret nodded.

"John Edward could not remove his eyes from you all night. Even when he danced with your sisters, it was always the vision of your loveliness that drew his attention throughout the evening."

"I wish I'd known." She had never felt more lovely than she had that night. She had known that John thought her pretty, had known that he found her desirable. Tonight she wished to recapture all that magic.

And soar to the next level.

"I take it John Edward will be along soon?"

"I know no more than you."

The old woman's eyes widened. "Then you don't know what his surprise is, either?"

Margaret shook her head. "I'm completely in the dark."

"Yet you're anticipating a happy announcement?"

"I am. I know not what it is, but I know many changes have come over him these past two months. I believe he *will* make you proud of him."

"I don't suppose *you* have an announcement to make?"

Margaret sadly shook her head. "Nothing could make me happier." Well, there was something. . .

"Will you have champagne?"

"Indeed I will."

"So thoughtful of you to send it over for our celebration. Whatever it may be."

As Margaret finished that first glass of champagne, she heard the heavy steps of a man on the corridor. John's steps. She had learned to distinguish his footfall from that of all other men. Her pulse roared as she eyed the doorway.

Though he had not changed into dinner clothes he still looked devilishly handsome in his dove breeches and navy blue coat. An ever-so-slight line of dark stubble on the lean planes of his face indicated a manliness that sent her heart racing even faster.

He stood framed by the doorway as his gaze swept over the chamber, then lingered on her. His expression went from casual to intense. His dark eyes simmered as they perused her. Then he looked up. Their eyes met, and he smiled. "You look beautiful."

"Thank you," she murmured.

"You are just in time for dinner," the dowager said. "Pray, help an old lady up."

He rushed to his grandmother and assisted her. "It will be my honor to escort you two lovely ladies into the dinner room."

As they strode toward that chamber, the dowager said, "Are you not going to ask what we're having to eat?"

"I assumed my grandmother would serve her favorite grandson's favorite dinner."

Margaret was briefly taken aback. Finally something she did not intrinsically know about her husband.

The old woman sighed. "I never seem able to surprise you. You read me like a Minerva novel."

The dowager had arranged the chairs so the three of them could take an intimate dinner and not have to shout down the table. Margaret was to John's left, his grandmother to his right.

"Did you know your wife sent over a case of champagne for us tonight?"

John's flashing eyes met Margaret's. "Thank you for thinking of that."

A footman began to pour each of them a glass of champagne as another brought out a tureen of clear turtle soup.

Once their bowls had been filled, the dowager turned to her grandson. "Well, John Edward, I can wait no longer. What is this delightful news you have to share with us?"

* * *

He drew in a long breath. "I hope it pleases both of you." His gaze went to his grandmother. "You've beseeched me for some time to demonstrate maturity."

"I don't want you to come to an early demise like your reckless father."

He nodded, then turned to Maggie. Her sweet face was illuminated by the soft glow of candles from the chandelier suspended above them. "And you said something some time back that planted an idea which has taken root."

Her brows raised in query.

He patted her hand. "You're far too perfect a wife to try to dictate to me. You merely said- -"

"I thought you would make a fine Parliamentarian?"

A smile broke across his face. This woman who had come to know him so thoroughly could finish his sentences. "Yes."

"Does that mean . . .?" His grandmother eyed him, her fair eyes shimmering with happiness.

He nodded sheepishly. "I have spent the day educating myself on how to go about being a meaningful member of the House of Lords." He looked back at Maggie. "I started the morning with your brother. He was immensely helpful. Then I met with Lord Haverstock."

"Two of the finest men in the kingdom," the dowager said.

"Since I married you," he said to Maggie, "I've come to realize there are more important things in life than the constant pursuit of pleasure. If I could be half as conscientious as your brother and Lord Haverstock, I would count myself successful."

"I know you will be, my boy. I've always said you're possessed of honor."

Maggie sipped her champagne. "Your grandmother's right."

A footman entered the chamber with a salver-covered tray.

"What is your favorite meal, dearest?" Maggie asked.

He had finally grown accustomed to being Maggie's dearest—so accustomed, in fact, that were she to fail to address him thusly, he would be disappointed. "And I thought you knew everything about me."

"You must own, you've never shown much inclination to dine with your wife."

"You're an angel to put up with me."

She set down her champagne. "I love being married to you."

Maggie did not lie. Could she really mean that she loved being married? His heartbeat drummed. Could she possibly mean she might could love him?

For too long he had denied his attraction to this woman he'd wed. There was not another woman in the world he would prefer over her. When he said she was the perfect wife, he had spoken the truth.

He thought, too, of her with Mikey. God, but he wanted her to have her own son. His son. God, but he wanted her to be his wife in every way.

She inhaled deeply. "Allow me to guess. Lobster."

He chuckled, then eyed his grandmother. "This woman I've married knows me even better than you do. Sometimes I believe she reads my mind."

"That, my boy, is how it is in good marriages. You'll come to read her mind, too."

It was a talent he *did* seem to be acquiring.

He lifted the salver and began to pass around the plate of lobster.

"A man who's going to be an important member of Parliament needs to have a fortune at his disposal," Grandmere said.

What the deuce was she trying to say? Did she *not* want him to serve in the House of Lords? He regarded her from beneath lowered brows.

"I shall summon my solicitor tomorrow so I can make a generous settlement upon my favorite grandson."

The air that had stilled in his lungs swished out. "I should be very grateful to you, and I vow not to squander a farthing."

Grandmere's little pink mouth lifted into a smile, and her blue eyes glittered with satisfaction. "Aw, my boy, this is a first."

"What?"

"You actually made a vow. With your propensity to honesty, this is as good as a signed contract."

Throughout the dinner, he kept refilling his wife's champagne glass, all the while remembering the last time she had imbibed great amounts of champagne. She'd asked him to kiss her. He wanted to kiss her again.

No kiss had ever affected him as profoundly as The Kiss. By the time the dinner was finished, all he could think of was being alone with Maggie in the carriage. Kissing her. Loving her.

* * *

Maggie was not as foxed as she'd been the previous time she'd imbibed great amounts of champagne, but he still felt compelled to steady her as they made their way to the coach. Inside, she scooted as close as possible to him.

At last. They were alone in the coach. As he sat there contemplating how he would make the first move, his wife stunned him. Her hand splayed over the interior muscles high in his thigh and began to trace sultry circles.

His breath grew short. He was instantly aroused.

Her lashes lifted and she spoke in a low voice. "Do you like my dress?"

"It's beautiful. You're beautiful."

"Such a dress allows exploration. I should like

to feel your lips feathering along my neck, my chest . . . even lower," she said, her voice a seductive whisper.

He groaned and hauled her into his arms for the most passionate kiss of his life. Her mouth opened willingly, eagerly, and he was lost in swirling sensations of almost unbearable pleasure.

His lips trailed along her elegant neck, her smooth shoulders, then lower. He pushed down the bodice of her dress, freeing a breast. Her breath hitched when his mouth closed over a taut nipple.

He could go mad with desire.

When the coach pulled up in front of their home moments later, he restored her clothing, then she flung both arms around him. "Lady Finchley invites Lord Finchley to her bed."

He couldn't believe this was his Maggie. His shy wife. He vowed that he'd never run out of champagne again. He had never wanted anything more, but . . . "I shouldn't like to take advantage of a woman who'd had too much champagne."

Her hand cupped his bulge, and she spoke throatily. "I drank the champagne to ensure that such activities would occur."

He seized her hand. "You truly are the perfect wife."

* * *

The moment her bedchamber door closed behind them, she flung herself into his arms. As he planted his feet there and embraced her, he knew this was the place where he wanted most to be, the woman he wanted most to love. "We mustn't muss so beautiful a dress. Allow me to help you out of it."

He would have preferred a slow disrobing, revealing each delectable part of her in lazy increments, but he feared he might explode from want. He eased off her dress until it pooled at their feet, then he began to loosen her stays. When her breasts sprang free, he gasped, scooped her up into his arms, and strode to the bed.

"Should you like me to blow out the candle?" he asked softly, his heated gaze fanning over the smooth curves of her silken body. She was the loveliest, most desirable woman he'd ever seen.

"As soon as I see your cannon."

Cannon? What the bloody hell was she talking about? "My cannon?"

Her eyes simmering, she slowly nodded. "Caro says—not from personal experience, mind you—that when a man desires a woman, his thing juts out like a cannon."

In spite of the tenderness of the moment, he burst into hearty laughter.

He moved even closer, reverently cupping her pretty face in his hands as he spoke softly. "I love it when my wife drinks champagne. I love it when my wife casts off her shyness and speaks truthfully. And I love it when my wife is bashful. I believe I've come to love everything about you."

The idea of a maiden gawking at his engorged need, though, troubled him. He must go slow with an innocent like her. Even if she was the most desirable woman he'd ever known. "I suggest we blow out the candle. I disrobe. Then my lady has permission to *feel* my cannon."

Her eyelids heavy with desire, she nodded.

Soon, his naked body stretched out beside hers while he drew her into his arms and greedily kissed her. He savored the feel of his precious wife's slender body pressed against him.

He gently eased her to her back and nudged her thighs apart, then he mounted her. Taking her hand in his, he guided her to take a hold of his staff, and her fingers instinctively coiled around it.

His innocent wife understood how to find that most special spot, where each of them soared to a place a thousand times more pleasurable than winning the sweepstakes.

For a long time afterward he held her in his arms, wishing like the devil this night would never end. "Thank you, my love, for being the perfect wife."

* * *

His words had finally broken her from her stupor of unimaginable bliss. She gently laid her face on his chest, kissing the dark hairs that sprinkled there. Then she murmured, "When you call me your love, what do you mean by it?"

"I suppose I mean that you're my love."

"Is that the same as being in love?"

"Until you, I've never been in love, but I suppose that does describe how I feel about you."

"And my honorable husband would never tell a lie. Would you?"

"Once. Recently. I wanted Perry to believe I bedded you."

"Does that mean you've been wanting to bed me before tonight?"

"It does."

"I have a confession to make. I lied to you."

"When?"

"When I persuaded you to accept our marriage. I lied when I said I didn't want a real marriage."

"You actually wanted to be married to me?"

"Always. Only you."

He held her tightly. "Then I must be the luckiest man in the kingdom."

She kissed his cheek. "And I'm the luckiest woman."

$\mathcal{C}$hapter 23

He loved the feel of her sitting in the carriage as close to him as skin. He took possession of her slender gloved hand and brought it to his lips. "You're quiet this afternoon."

She nodded thoughtfully. "Sadly, it's my nature. I have another confession . . ."

"You've told another falsehood?"

"Not exactly. But twice now I schooled myself to pretend I was Caro so that I could aggressively secure that which I wanted most."

The very idea that *he* was what she wanted most nearly debilitated him with pride. He drew her into his arms and held her tightly. *Twice?* The first, the day she came to him to solidify this marriage. The second . . . he drew in a breath at the memory, last night. "Then I am indebted to your sister, and I'll never again ill-judge her authoritarian ways."

"Now that I'm the most fortunate woman in the kingdom, I will no longer have to resort to such a performance."

He lowered his brows in mock outrage. "Surely my lady was not performing last night."

Her lashes lifted, and she bestowed a glorious smile upon him. "When I'm in your arms, I am not Caro, not even mousy Margaret. Then I am Lord Finchley's lady."

He kissed her hand and spoke from his heart. "Who's made Lord Finchley the happiest man in the kingdom."

Their coach turned off busy Piccadilly and began to wind its way through quieter neighborhoods toward Bloomsbury. "What were you doing that day at St. George's?" he asked.

"I prayed that I could be married. I prayed that I could emulate Caro."

"Did you pray to marry me?"

"I asked the Lord to guide me to a decent man."

"And at the time you believed I was a profligate?" Which he supposed he was.

"I thought perhaps you were. But Our Heavenly Father knew you were honorable, and he sent you to me." Her lids lifted. "I returned there, to St. George's, yesterday to ask for help in my Caro imitation last night, for help in seducing you."

He groaned. "Pray, no more talk of seduction. You've disturbed my sleeping cannon."

She giggled.

"As many times as we made love last night, there's a chance that . . ." He thought of her holding a babe of her own. His babe.

"I could be breeding?"

He nodded. "I owe so much to George Weatherford. He always knew what was best for me, and now I believe he knew that by asking me to see to his son's needs I would come to learn what things in life were truly most important."

"Like a son of our own?"

He nodded. "You will be the most wonderful mother a child ever had."

She giggled again. "I'm so happy."

"It's a pity my friends cannot understand that making love to one's own wife is a million times more satisfying than tupping a trollop."

To his astonishment, when their coach arrived at Number 7 Trent Square, Perry's luxurious coach was already there. John lifted a brow and regarded his wife. "My friend must be truly smitten with your sister."

Maggie shrugged.

As he and his wife were approaching the home's entry, the door opened, and out marched Perry, Arlington, and Knowles, all of them carrying cricket gear and followed by a flock of excited lads.

Perry eyed him. "Keeping all the fun for yourself, haven't you, old boy?"

"I didn't think you'd be interested."

"Who wants to be cooped up in a musty fencing studio when one can be playing cricket?"

Knowles came abreast of the other two. "Why did you not tell us you were guardian to Weatherford's lad?"

Before he could respond, Arlington closed in on him. "Why did you not tell me how stunning Weatherford's widow is? You know how enamored I am of copper-haired beauties."

"You could not do better than to get shackled," John said. "I've come to recommend it highly." He turned to Perry. "Is Lady Caroline trying to slip the noose around you?"

"I will own, there is a strong desire in that quarter, but Lady Caroline's a woman who would demand fidelity."

"I've come to recommend fidelity most heartily." John turned back, his eyes glittering with love, and met Maggie's gentle gaze as she stood watching him, Mikey in her arms.

How long would it be before she would be

holding their son?

Epilogue

One Year Later. . .

The Haverstock and Aldridge families were all gathered at the duke's Glenmont Hall for the baptism of Ann Clair Rothcomb-Smedley because Clair wanted her first child to take the sacrament at Glenmont's medieval chapel, as had she and her prodigious number of siblings.

John had never been at a family gathering that included so many babies, though he supposed little Simon Morgan was no longer considered a babe. The Duke of Aldridge's son—the Marquess of Ramsbury, who was called Ram—had just started walking, and he flitted from following about his slightly elder cousin Charles Upton, the future Marquess of Haverstock, to hovering over his only female cousin, whose little whimpers fascinated him.

Just a month earlier the family had gathered here for the baptism of John's own son, named Frederick in honor of the family's first earl. Little Charles Upton had little opportunity to hover around baby Frederick because Frederick's own parents practically fought over the privilege of holding their son.

Christopher Perry, the guest of Lady Caroline, ambled up to stand beside John, his eye going to the sleeping babe in his friend's arms. "I fail to see what's so blasted fascinating about having a babe. It's not as if they can even play cricket yet."

"One year ago I would have wholeheartedly agreed with you." John's tender gaze whisked to his Maggie, who was striding toward them, no doubt to steal Frederick from his arms. He'd known she would be a wonderful mother, but the capacity of her heart was even more boundless than he'd thought possible. He now knew what it was to be loved with an unquenchable passion, knew what it was to love her in the same way. He peered down at their son, and his chest expanded. No man could ever be happier.

He eyed Perry. "Loving a good woman and having a son of one's own trumps having a horse win the Derby, breaking the faro bank at White's, or any other pleasure-seeking activity I can think of."

Perry shook his head, a sour expression on his face. "I have fallen in love."

"With Caro?" John asked.

"Yes. But as much as my family would like the connection with a duke, I'm terrified of Aldridge. How do you cope?"

John's voice gentled. "We've become brothers. We want the same things." John's affection for Aldridge was every bit as great as it was for Perry. By marrying Maggie, he *had* acquired a brother.

"Next you'll want me to stand for Parliament," Perry said, narrowing his eyes.

"I will never presume to tell you what to do— not when Lady Caroline is so adept at that."

Lady Caroline and Maggie approached them, and Perry and Caro walked off toward the folly on the distant hill. John wondered if this was the day

Perry might ask for Caro's hand.

Maggie did steal her sleeping infant from him and proceeded to press soft kisses over the top of his dark, downy hair. "I wish I could always keep him so small."

John settled an arm around her. "I promise once he's old enough for cricket, I'll keep you supplied with babes in arms for the next twenty years. I always wanted to have a large family."

He pressed a kiss at her temple. "Another bonus from marrying my Maggie. I love your family."

"It's *our* family now, my dearest."

"I am so happy I want to spread the joy. I've been thinking of how much I owe to Miss Margaret Ponsby for answering my newspaper advert. Had it not been for her, the coincidence of the names, finding you at St. George's would never have occurred." He paused. "Would you object if I settle a small annuity on her?"

"I think that's a wonderful idea."

"Have I told you the luckiest day of my life was the day I found my heart's delight at St. George's?"

"It's time you realize what I've always known."

The End

Author's Biography

A former journalist and English teacher, Cheryl Bolen sold her first book to Harlequin Historical in 1997. That book, *A Duke Deceived*, was a finalist for the Holt Medallion for Best First Book, and it netted her the title Notable New Author. Since then she has published more than 20 books with Kensington/Zebra, Love Inspired Historical and was Montlake launch author for Kindle Serials. As an independent author, she has broken into the top 5 on the *New York Times* and top 20 on the *USA Today* best-seller lists.

Her 2005 book *One Golden Ring* won the Holt Medallion for Best Historical, and her 2011 gothic historical *My Lord Wicked* was awarded Best Historical in the International Digital Awards, the same year one of her Christmas novellas was chosen as Best Historical Novella by Hearts Through History. Her books have been finalists for other awards, including the Daphne du Maurier, and have been translated into eight languages.

She invites readers to www.CherylBolen.com, or her blog, www.cherylsregencyramblings.wordpress.co or Facebook at https://www.facebook.com/pages/Cheryl-Bolen-Books/146842652076424.

Made in the USA
San Bernardino, CA
11 September 2016